Books by Mark Cheverton

The Gameknight999 Series
Invasion of the Overworld
Battle for the Nether
Confronting the Dragon

The Mystery of Herobrine Series: A Gameknight999 Adventure
Trouble in Zombie-town
The Jungle Temple Oracle
Last Stand on the Ocean Shore

Herobrine Reborn Series: A Gameknight999 Adventure
Saving Crafter
The Destruction of the Overworld
Gameknight999 vs. Herobrine

Herobrine's Revenge Series: A Gameknight999 Adventure
The Phantom Virus
Overworld in Flames
System Overload

The Birth of Herobrine: A Gameknight999 Adventure
The Great Zombie Invasion
Attack of the Shadow-Crafters
Herobrine's War

The Mystery of Entity303: A Gameknight999 Adventure
Terrors of the Forest
Monsters in the Mist
Mission to the Moon (Coming Soon!)

The Gameknight999 Box Set
The Gameknight999 vs. Herobrine Box Set
The Gameknight999 Adventures Through Time Box Set (Coming Soon!)

The Rise of the Warlords: An Unofficial Interactive Minecrafter's Adventure
Zombies Attack!
The Bones of Doom (Coming Soon)
Into the Spiders' Lair (Coming Soon!)

The Algae Voices of Azule Series
Algae Voices of Azule
Finding Home
Finding the Lost

ZOMBIES ATTACK!

THE RISE OF THE WARLORDS BOOK ONE

AN UNOFFICIAL INTERACTIVE MINECRAFTER'S ADVENTURE

MARK CHEVERTON

SKY PONY PRESS
NEW YORK

Copyright © 2017 by Mark Cheverton

Minecraft® is a registered trademark of Notch Development AB

The Minecraft game is copyright © Mojang AB

Sky Pony Press books may be purchased in bulk at special discounts for sales promotion, corporate gifts, fund-raising, or educational purposes. Special editions can also be created to specifications. For details, contact the Special Sales Department, Sky Pony Press, 307 West 36th Street, 11th Floor, New York, NY 10018 or info@skyhorsepublishing.com.

Sky Pony® is a registered trademark of Skyhorse Publishing, Inc.®, a Delaware corporation.

Visit our website at www.skyponypress.com.

10 9 8 7 6 5 4 3 2

Library of Congress Cataloging-in-Publication Data is available on file.

Cover design by Brian Peterson
Cover artwork by Vilandas Sukutis (www.veloscraft.com)
Technical consultant: *Gameknight999*

Print Paperback ISBN: 978-1-51072-737-3
Print Hardcover ISBN: 978-1-51072-831-8
E-book ISBN: 978-1-51072-741-0

Printed in Canada

ACKNOWLEDGEMENTS

As always, I want to thank my family for their continued support of my obsessive writing practices. Their understanding of my insanity about writing is a constant source of encouragement for me, though I know the only cure is to continue to write.

To my readers, thank you for setting Gameknight999 aside and meeting my new friends, Watcher, Planter, Blaster, Cutter, Mapper, and Er-Lan. I think you're going to love them as much as I already do.

ZOMBIES ATTACK!: AN INTERACTIVE READING EXPERIENCE

Zombies Attack! is a very important book to me for a few reasons. First, it's the start of a completely new series set in the world of Minecraft, with never-before-seen characters and a new location: the mysterious Far Lands! Writing the Gameknight999 novels has been a blast, but after eighteen books, I knew it was time to challenge myself and come up with new stories and characters for readers to enjoy (and you never know, there may still be more adventures starring the User-who-is-not-a-user down the road . . .).

Second, *Zombies Attack!* is the first ever truly interactive novel set in the world of Minecraft. Have you ever read a great Minecraft story and thought, "Wow! I'd love to actually play like this in the game, battling the same monsters and exploring the same buildings and worlds"? I definitely have, and was inspired enough to make my dream a reality. With the help of some very talented friends, I've created a custom *Zombies Attack!* Minecraft map that matches the storyline of this book. That means that as you're reading, you'll be able to follow along in the actual Minecraft game itself, visiting the same buildings and biomes, fighting the same monsters, and even more, all the same as the book.

After you've met Watcher, the main character of *Zombies Attack!* and hero of the Rise of the Warlords series, you'll be able to live out his adventures yourself in the Far Lands, facing monsters, uncovering treasure, and trying to defeat dangerous bosses like the zombie general, Ro-Zar, and the zombie warlord, Tu-Kar.

Pulling this off required a lot of planning, and I had to carefully craft the story as my team was helping to build this custom map. There are many Easter eggs in these pages that will point you towards special treasure while you're playing the *Zombies Attack!* map, so read carefully.

Before we get into the fun stuff (like "How does it all work?"), I want to stress that although these bonus features for *Zombies Attack* are lots of fun, and I fully encourage all readers to try them out, they are not required to read the book and enjoy it. Just like my Gameknight999 series, the Rise of the Warlords trilogy is a fun and exciting story set in the world of Minecraft, filled with interesting characters I've grown to love. If you just want to read along, you'll enjoy *Zombies Attack!*

and the upcoming sequels just as much as my previous books. However, what makes these books different is that they've been written with some very cool bonus features in mind, and I hope you take the opportunity to check them out; they are awesome to play and explore!

How do I play the *Zombies Attack!* map?

The *Zombies Attack!* custom map is available on my Gameknight999 Minecraft Network server **(server IP: mc.gameknight999.com)**, which many of you have visited and play on already. Detailed instructions for how to access the map for *Zombies Attack!* can be found by visiting my website, www.markcheverton.com, where there are video tutorials and more to get you set up and having fun in no time. Or, you can scan the QR code (more information on how to do that in a moment) on page xi to take you straight to the right webpage (be sure to have your parents' permission to use third-party Minecraft servers).

When you first enter the *Zombies Attack!* map, you'll find yourself in a special room where you can join up with other players around the world to play the map with. The more people you have in your party, the more difficult you'll find the game, but playing with other users is lots of fun! Each time you play, you'll get a score related to how many monsters you destroyed and how quickly you made it through the game. Be sure to check for hidden loot; there will be hints throughout the book, telling you where you might find better armor and cool weapons.

Good luck, and watch out for zombies—there will be *a lot* of them waiting to meet you!

What if I can't play on a server?

Never fear, we've thought of that! Even if you don't have access or permission to play on third-party Minecraft servers, you'll still be able to download the *Zombies Attack!* map and go through the adventure on your own. Unfortunately, the custom software that was written to create all the epic boss battles will only work if you play on my server, and will not work for you at home. So monsters might not pop up exactly like they do in the book this way, but the maps themselves are still really fun to explore, and there are still many, many random monster spawners around that will keep you busy.

You can download the game (again, after getting your parents' permission), by visiting my website or scanning the QR code on the next page and scrolling down to the download link at the bottom of the page. If you need help loading the world into Minecraft, I've included links to several YouTube videos that I've found extremely helpful. These videos will show you how to download the map file as well as well as how to load and run the file on your computer.

Will the *Zombies Attack!* map work with my computer?

Unfortunately, you can only log into the Gameknight999 Minecraft Network with the vanilla PC version 1.11 or 1.12 of Minecraft. The Windows 10 version, as well as the Xbox, Pocket Edition, or other console versions of Minecraft, will *not* work on the Gameknight999 Minecraft Network. So, if you use those versions of Minecraft, you won't be able to join the online game server and play the custom *Zombies Attack!* map. In addition, the downloadable version will not work with any of these versions either. I wish this wasn't the case, but I don't have any control over what these other versions can run.

What are QR codes and how do I use them?

Even if you can't join the server or download the single-player game to see first-hand what the fabulous structures created by our expert builders look like, that's okay; there are still fun things to look at! Throughout the book, you will find square, black and white checkerboard patterns called QR codes. These QR codes are linked to pages on my website that show images of the buildings constructed by our building team, and give you more information about the structures and history of the Far Lands. You might find even some screenshots of different Minecrafters playing through the game . . . maybe you! Be sure to send me your screenshots from inside the game, and I'll do my best to post them online.

 To scan the QR code, you'll need a QR reader on your smart phone. There are many free QR readers available for all phones. I recommend you go to your phone's app store to find one (with your parents' permission, of course). I downloaded one for my iPhone and it works great, even though there are some ads across the bottom. Simply enter your QR reader app, then point the phone's camera toward the QR code. The software should detect the code very quickly, then redirect your phone to the website. The QR code here, for example, will take you to the webpage for *Zombies Attack!* custom map lobby.

If for some reason you aren't able to use a QR reader on your smart phone, feel free to visit my website, where I'll have the same links up for readers to explore.

Putting together this interactive experience was something I've been thinking about for a long time, and it was only possible through the incredibly hard work and patience from a group of people who deserve lots of recognition and applause. *Zombies Attack!* was programmed by Luca Panjer (devLuca) and tested by Joseph Bamber (Quadbamber). We also had an incredible building team from the Gameknight999 Minecraft Network putting together all of the epic constructions for the game: Project Director Joseph Bamber (Quadbamber), Head Builder Will Shepherd (Mr_man12), Builder Adam Pugh (Arp97), and Builder Ben Archer (Benma98).

They've created some amazing structures and buildings that I've done my best to describe throughout this book, but walking through them is even better.

From the beginning, my goal has been to merge the experience of playing Minecraft and reading Minecraft-inspired books into a one-of-a-kind experience. I hope you enjoy the game and playing along while you read! Don't get discouraged if you don't beat the *Zombies Attack!* custom map on the first try, or if you get squashed by the zombies lying in wait for you; this game will take some clever thought and strategy to make it through unscathed. If you are not successful, keep trying. I guarantee it's possible.

Hope to see you in the Far Lands!

—Monkeypants_271

You should never feel as if you must prove you're good enough to others to be accepted. Be the best version of yourself, and accept who you are, and don't be concerned about what other people think.

CHAPTER 1

Watcher stood atop the tall watchtower, gazing down upon the village, disconnected from the community that bustled with activity below. The morning sun, painting the village with bright reds and warm oranges, rose above the eastern horizon, signaling the start of a new day. The NPCs (non-playable characters) were eager to get up and begin a new day's work; nighttime and its ever-present collection of zombies, spiders, endermen, and creepers was always a welcome thing to put into the past.

Watcher gazed toward the rising sun, trying to look past the haze that always obscured Minecraft's features in the distance. Out there, somewhere, was the line between the Far Lands, where he lived, and the Overworld. Rumor had it, someone had once visited the Far Lands from the distant Overworld, but it had only happened once in Minecraft's entire history. Even though Watcher had never been there, he knew that the Overworld was the central part of the Minecraft universe, where strangers with silver threads of light reaching up high into the air walked the land. But that was in the Overworld and none of those creatures, known as users, had stepped foot in the Far Lands for centuries; they were a thing of myth and legend.

The Overworld was the center of Minecraft, a place where users interacted with NPCs and monsters and animals. Some of those interactions were not very positive, and Watcher had heard stories of griefers doing unbelievable harm to those that lived in the electronic world.

But out in the Far Lands, Watcher was millions and millions of blocks away from all that. The Far Lands wrapped around the Overworld like a gigantic donut, only one with no sprinkles. Watcher had once heard that as strange as the Overworld seemed to him, the Far Lands had once been home to things even stranger than users: powerful beings such as gigantic monsters and mythical sorcerers who had long ago clashed over control of the land. The young boy had never seen anything like that in his time, though; the Far Lands *he* knew were a more peaceful part of Minecraft, even if dangers still existed.

Turning his attention back to the task at hand, Watcher performed his job, which was watching out for monsters. He scanned the thick oak forest that hugged close to the village, looking for creatures lurking in the shadows of the boxy trees. Out here, in the Far Lands, zombies and skeletons did not burst into flames if they were exposed to the sunlight, like they would in the rest of the Overworld, but they still preferred the darkness of shadows or night. Watcher knew if any monsters were skulking about, they'd be found in the shade cast by the trees.

Suddenly, he saw something move from behind the square trunk of a tall oak. And then something else. It was difficult to see what they were, for the shapes were still far away, but there was definitely something there. Watcher imagined it could be a group of zombies, or maybe skeletons out on the hunt. Images of a million different possibilities played through his head as the daydreaming he was famous for began to dominate his mind.

Should I ring the alarm? Watcher thought.

"No, I'll wait until I can see them better," he mumbled softly to himself.

Leaning forward, he peered into the forest, holding his rectangular hand next to his face to shield his eyes from the light of the square sun.

One of the creatures stepped into the clearing. There was a flash of brilliant light that momentarily blinded the young boy.

"What was that?" Watcher extending his body farther over the edge of the tower. "Maybe it was a wizard, like the ones described in our history books."

His imagination instantly went to the NPC wizards that existed hundreds of years ago in these Far Lands. In school, they'd been learning about the history of the Far Lands and the strange things that existed long ago; not only NPC wizards, but also monster warlocks and terrifying creatures. A great war had ravaged the land long ago, wiping these monsters, warlocks and wizards from the face of Minecraft, and now they only existed in those historical tomes. All that remained of those ancient times were the elaborate structures sprinkled across the deserts and forests, and occasionally enchanted relics found in dark caves or hidden chests. That was where Watcher's imagination went; anything that pulled him from his miserable, mundane life was a welcome relief.

But it can't be a wizard, he thought. *That's ridiculous.*

And then he saw the figure clearly; it was one of the village warriors returning from the evening patrol.

More of the warriors emerged from behind trees and bushes, their iron armor reflecting the sun's rays like highly polished mirrors; the NPCs looked as if they were made of light. As the soldiers neared the village, many of them sheathed their heavy broadswords and tucked their shields back into their inventories.

"Anything to report?" a voice asked from behind.

Watcher turned and found Tiller climbing up through the trapdoor that was set into the roof of the tower.

"No, nothing," Watcher replied, glad he didn't signal a false alarm.

He would have been embarrassed if he'd said they were wizards in the forest. The last time he'd imagined something and reported it, Watcher had been bitterly teased by the older kids in the village, calling him Dreamer instead of Watcher for weeks. They had picked on him relentlessly, making the young boy feel unwelcome everywhere . . . which was nothing new. The only person that had stood by his side was his best friend, Planter.

The thought of her made him turn toward the fields. And there she was . . .

Watcher smiled.

Planter was heading into the fields with a hoe over her shoulders, her beautiful blond hair shining bright against the dark green smock, a yellow stripe running down the center. The long flowing strands swished back and forth as she walked, a cheerful spring always present in her gait.

Tiller said something, but Watcher didn't hear . . . he was lost, gazing at Planter in peaceful delight.

"What?" Watcher asked.

He turned and faced Tiller.

"I said your shift is done, I'll take over," Tiller said. "You've been up all night, and maybe you should get a little sleep before classes start."

"I'm not going to school today." Watcher stepped to the trap door and stood on the first rung of the ladder. "Tryouts for the army cadets are today."

"Oh no, you aren't trying out again, are you?"

Watcher nodded.

"Don't you remember what happened last time?" Tiller asked, a look of sympathy in his dark eyes.

He could never forget; it had been the most humiliating day in his life. Watcher wasn't the biggest, or strongest kid in the village. In fact, he was the opposite; he was the smallest and weakest, but what he lacked in physical prowess, he made up for with a fast mind and a clever wit. And this time, Watcher had a new idea, a clever strategy that would allow him to pass the tests and become a cadet in the army.

"I have a plan this time." Watcher's eyes grew bright with confidence. "I've been analyzing the way all the soldiers fight. They each have a pattern that's predictable. I can take advantage of that pattern to score some hits before I get annihilated." He took a huge breath and stuck out his scrawny chest. "It'll be different this time."

"I hope so for your sake," Tiller said. "I guess if you're gonna do this to yourself again . . . umm . . . good luck."

"Thanks." Watcher grinned, then slid down the ladder.

When he reached the ground floor, he shot out of the cobblestone structure, excited about the upcoming test. The young boy thought about going to see Planter and telling her what he was doing, but she was on the other side of the village; he couldn't see her and get back in time. Just thinking about his friend put a smile on Watcher's face.

"Oh well," he said in a low voice. "I guess it's time to do this."

Turning away from the fields, he headed for the practice yard. Running between wooden buildings, he passed his own home. Through the window, Cleric, his father, was visible in his white smock, always perfectly clean and wrinkle free.

"Go get 'em son." Cleric waved.

Watcher waved, then sprinted past.

I wish Mom were still alive to see this, he thought. *She'd be so proud when I become a cadet.*

The thought of his mother caused confidence to blossom within Watcher's soul.

"I can do this." His voice was barely a whisper, meant only for him . . . and her.

When he reached the practice yard, Watcher found the other boys and girls already in a neat line. He fell in right next to a tall black-haired girl. She towered over him even though they were the same age . . . for the most part, everyone towered over him, even kids younger than him. He didn't care. It wasn't important how big or strong someone was . . . what mattered was how they'd react in a tense situation. A person who could come up with creative solutions in battle was more valuable than just a block head who could only swing a sword . . . at least, that was his theory.

"If you're not here for the Cadet Corp, then you better scurry along," a hulking soldier said.

Watcher noticed he was staring right at him. The soldier raised an eyebrow toward him.

"You in the right place?" he asked again.

Watcher smiled and nodded.

"You remember what happened last time, son?"

"I'm here to try out for the cadets." Watcher's voice was loud and clear.

"OK, it's your funeral," the warrior replied.

The other kids laughed.

"Quiet down!"

Everyone instantly became silent.

"That's better." The soldier walked up and down the line of kids, glaring at each, trying to intimidate them. "Here's how it's going to work. Each of you will use a stick and face one of the soldiers in mock combat. If you show any potential, then we *might* ask you to stay for a second round of tests." He turned and faced Watcher. "Anyone dropping their stick, then tripping over it and hitting their head so hard they go unconscious will be disqualified and will not be allowed to test ever again. Is that understood?"

All the other kids turned and looked at Watcher, a few of them giggling loud enough for him to hear. He knew the question was directed at him, and was meant to embarrass. But Watcher wasn't going to react; he just nodded, a look of grim determination on his square face.

"Okay, then," the hulking villager continued. "Do we have a volunteer to go first?"

Watcher stepped forward. He could feel what little courage he had starting to falter as uncertainty crept into his mind like a venomous spider.

"I'll go . . . first." Watcher's voice cracking a bit.

Some of the other kids giggled.

"Quiet!" the soldier barked.

An uneasy silence wrapped around the practice yard. Watcher took a deep breath, then moved to the rack of weapons and grabbed a stick. He stepped to the middle of the practice yard, waiting for his opponent, his heart pounding in his chest.

"My, you're eager for this, aren't you, boy," the soldier said in a low voice.

Watcher remained silent and gripped the pretend-sword tightly. He'd studied all the soldiers and knew what to expect. They each had their tell, that small indication that told what they were going to do, and Watcher knew them all. He had no doubt, he could land a few hits on any of the soldiers, with the exception of one. Fencer was the fastest and strongest of the warriors. He had no tells, no weaknesses; he was the best swordsman in the village. As long as his opponent was anyone else, he was all right.

"Let's get a warrior out here," the training leader shouted. "We have an eager trainee who wants to test his courage."

Beads of sweat trickled down Watcher's head, some of them tumbling through his curly reddish-brown hair and finding their way into his ear. It wasn't very hot out today and the sun wasn't very high, but he was sweating profusely.

"I can do it . . . this time," Watcher whispered. "I am brave, and I'm clever."

He thought about something his father, Cleric, had

told him the day before: "Strength and muscles are devoured by time, the strongest soldier always ending up as frail old men. But intelligence and creativity: those muscles never stop growing."

"I can do this . . . I can do this . . . I can . . . oh no . . ."

And then Fencer stepped out of the barracks, a long wooden stick in his huge hands. The warrior glanced at Watcher, and a look of sympathy came across the big NPC's face. He shook his head slightly, telling Watcher to abandon this course of action. In response, Watcher nodded, then took a step closer, his heart now thundering in his chest, his breaths dry and raspy.

"I'm not gonna take it easy on you," Fencer said.

"I know," was all Watcher could say as his dream of being in the army slowly slipped from his fingers.

I'm lost, he thought. *But I must go through with this. I'm not gonna quit.*

Fencer raised his stick, getting ready to advance, while Watcher dropped into a defensive stance. Suddenly, someone banged a tool against an iron chest plate . . . it was the alarm!

"ZOMBIES AT THE FRONT OF THE VILLAGE!" Tiller shouted from atop the watchtower.

"Zombies?" Watcher said, confused.

"Zombies?!" Fencer said.

That was when the war began.

CHAPTER 2

The sorrowful wails of zombies filled the air. Watcher couldn't tell how many there were, but from the smell coming from the disgusting creatures, it seemed like a lot. The perpetual east-to-west breeze dragged their stench across the village like a diseased fog.

Soldiers in their iron armor ran for the front of the village, each with a sword and shield in their hands. There was part of Watcher that wanted to go with them, but another part, the smarter part, told him to just stay out of the way . . . and so he did.

Running for his home, he found Cleric outside, his older sister, Winger, was approaching from the direction of the blacksmith's shop. She was holding up a pair of the newest Elytra wings she'd constructed, and had likely been getting ready to do a test when the alarm rang.

"Watcher, stay by the house," Cleric said. "Any wounded will be sent this way. You need to help them." He turned to his daughter. "Winger, go to the supply shed and get ready to help any wounded on that side of the village. Both of you know your jobs . . . now get to work."

Without waiting for an answer, Cleric headed to the front of the village. Winger gave her younger brother a wink, then headed for the supply shed. Around him, NPCs were in a panic. Many looked for their assigned battle station, but there hadn't been an attack by monsters for a long time, and many didn't even know what to do.

A cheer rang out from the front of the village.

"What happened? Does anyone know what happened?" Watcher shouted.

Someone with a pickaxe in his hands ran to the back of the village. "They're retreating," he said. "The zombies are running away. Our warriors are chasing them away."

"But that's not right." Watcher could still smell the zombies' stench. "If they're running away, then why is their odor so strong?"

"Odor . . . what odor?" The NPC sounded confused, but kept running; few in the village had Watcher's sensitivity when it came to the five senses.

 He turned and glanced at the large windmill with its white vanes turning slowly. It stood on the edge of the village, the breeze helping the huge machine to grind wheat into flour. But the large structure was not moving correctly. The large blades jerked a bit as if something was gumming up the mechanism. Suddenly, something crashed within the structure, causing one of the blades to break off and fall to the ground, embedding itself into the soil.

The smell of zombies was getting stronger.

A sound from behind drew his attention. Turning, Watcher peered into the oak forest that surrounded the village. He thought he saw something moving. With the sun still rising from its evening nap, the long shadows in the woods made it difficult to see. But he was sure he'd seen something there . . . or did he?

"I probably just imagined it," Watcher whispered.

He recalled his daydreaming moment atop the watchtower; was that what was happening now? Fatigue nagged at Watcher's body, making him question what he was seeing. He'd been up all night on guard duty in the tower, and was stressed by the Cadet Corp tryouts . . . which didn't happen. Causing an unwarranted panic by claiming there were monsters in the forest, right after the zombie attack, would not be good.

It's likely just my overactive imagination, he thought.

The zombie smell was getting stronger and stronger, though.

The faint sound of muffled moans trickled through background noises of the village. NPCs were still running about in a panic, unsure what was happening or where to go. Many were shouting, giving orders to the confused while others were just asking for help, afraid they were doing something wrong. It was pandemonium in the community; everything was chaotic.

Suddenly, the terrible odor of rotting flesh wafted across the village as if driven by a hurricane. The stench was accompanied by sorrowful moans and angry growls.

"Zombies invading from the back of the village!" someone shouted.

"More coming from the sides!" another exclaimed.

From around the windmill, zombies flowed like a terrifying green wave of razor-sharp claws and pointed teeth. They shuffled out of the forest, emerging from the shadows like specters in a nightmare.

"Where are the soldiers?" a voice shouted from the front of the village. "We need our warriors!"

But Watcher knew where they were; the zombies had lured them out of the village, chasing the first wave of monsters, leaving the village undefended.

"I must do something," Watcher said to no one, but he was too scared to think.

Villagers ran back and forth, some of them pulling out stone swords to face the monsters, while others just ran to the homes and hid. Fear was painted on every square face as individuals tried to figure out some way to protect their loved ones.

"*Grrrr . . .*"

A growl sounded from right behind him. Watcher turned and found himself face-to-face with a zombie clad in chain mail and holding a bright, iron sword.

A zombie in armor and *wielding a sword . . . impossible!* Watcher thought, stunned.

"This villager is too small." The scarred monster glared at the young boy. "It should be destroyed."

"Just hit it on the head," a larger zombie in full iron armor replied. "The warlord can deal with this villager later."

"As you command, General Ro-Zar."

Watcher glanced at the zombie commander then back to the soldier. Terror ruled the villager's mind. His feet felt leaden. His arms felt numb. He was paralyzed with fear.

The monster raised his sword high in the air. He gave Watcher a toothy grin, then brought it down. Pain exploded in his head as dizziness overwhelmed his senses. He struggled to stand, but another strike with the flat side of the sword came down, causing him to tumble to the ground. The terrified shouts of his friends and neighbors filled the air as Watcher tried to remain conscious . . . and then he was engulfed in darkness.

CHAPTER 3

Pain surged through his skull like liquid fire, erupting into new pinpoints of agony with every heartbeat. Watcher's head felt as if it had been crushed, put back together again, then crushed a second time. Carefully, he opened his eyes but didn't move. He'd been conscious for a while, but remained motionless, hoping to go unnoticed. It had worked.

To his horror, the young villager had watched as the zombies moved from house to house, rounding up NPCs and forcing them to the front of the village while other zombies went through every house, taking weapons, armor, and anything made of gold. The monsters seemed excited when they found the occasional gold shovel or helmet; it didn't make any sense. Gold was a weak metal . . . it made for poor tools or weapons or armor. Why would the zombies want it?

Focusing on the sounds around him, Watcher listened for monsters. It had been quiet for a while; maybe it was safe to move again. Slowly, he sat up, his head throbbing with pain.

He glanced around at what remained of his village. Flames still licked up the walls of many of the structures, and more than one home was completely burned to the ground. Smoke billowed up into the air, creating columns of ash that looked like thick, sooty fingers reaching up into the sky. The gentle east-to-west wind that always flowed through Minecraft dragged the smoke across the sky until it spread out into a sickly gray haze that tried to blot out the sun.

Just then, Watcher realized the shouts and screams of friends and neighbors at the front of the village had ceased. While he had been lying on the ground, pretending to be unconscious, Watcher had heard the screams of his fellow villagers, but now everything was eerily quiet. That made him nervous.

Carefully getting to his feet, the young boy looked around, then dashed into the nearest building; his family's home. One wall was blasted apart; likely the work of the creepers that had accompanied the zombies on this attack. Stepping through the rubble, he stood in disbelief at the destruction. The inside of their home had been torn apart. It looked as if an army of zombies had marched through it, overturning everything in sight.

He ran to the back of the house and went into his room. Clothes and items were thrown everywhere, haphazardly discarded all over the ground and furniture. His father, Cleric, had been bugging him recently to clean up his room. Now he was right, it *did* look like a horde of monsters had stormed through.

Is my father even alive? A shiver of dread slithered down his spine.

"He'll probably never have another chance to make me clean it up again." Watcher choked back a tear.

He couldn't hear anyone in the village. If his father and sister were still around, they'd be looking for him. *Am I all alone?*

"Winger, I hope you're all right. The last thing I said to you last night was you were the worst big sister, ever. Now I wish I could take it back."

Guilt and sadness spread through his soul. He was a terrible brother and an even worse son; he'd let his father and sister get captured or killed . . . and now he was all alone.

The warriors had never returned from the forest, at least as far as Watcher could tell while he'd been lying on the ground. Some of the NPCs had tried to defend their families in their homes. They'd fought back, but had been quickly overwhelmed by huge numbers of zombies. Once everyone had been rounded up, the real horror show had begun. Watcher had laid on the ground and listened as the zombies destroyed the sick and the very old. It had been as if they only wanted those strong enough for some mysterious task.

One of the zombies had just stood by and watched the carnage. Watcher had only seen the monstrous commander once. He was a big monster, larger than the rest, his arms and chest rippling with muscles. A long scar ran down one side of the zombie's face, the eye under the scar a menacing, milky white. The creature wore sparkling chain mail, and had laughed as the villagers were destroyed. It was clear this monster was the commander by the way all the other zombies had seemed afraid and did whatever he'd said; none of them questioning his orders or the terrible atrocity they'd carried out.

Watcher would never forget the sound of that monster's laugh. It was a hacking kind of laugh, as if the zombie were trying to cough up a chicken bone that was stuck in his throat. The zombie commander had cackled with delight as the elderly had begged for mercy, giving them none. They had all been destroyed in the blink of an eye. The image of that monster laughing as his friends were slain was forever burned into Watcher's mind.

Terrified, he had just stayed on the ground, pretending to be wounded and insignificant—both of which were true—and hoping the terrible warlord would just go away. Once they'd culled the weak and useless from the rest of the villagers, the zombies had surrounded the NPCs and drove them out of town as if they were nothing but a herd of cattle. Meanwhile, Watcher just stayed behind in the shadows, completely forgotten . . . as usual.

Images of his friends' and neighbors' faces popped into his mind. They showed terror, panic, sadness, despair . . . every one of them knowing it was the end.

And I did nothing. The sour taste of cowardice was heavy on his tongue.

Wiping a stray tear with a stained green sleeve, Watcher searched his room, to see if the monsters had left anything behind that might help. Moving to a mound of dirty clothes, he carefully uncovered the wooden chest that hid beneath. The lid creaked as it opened. He paused, listening for the growl or moan of a monster. Silence, like that of a graveyard, filled the village.

Reaching into the chest, Watcher found his brown leather armor and a bow and quiver full of arrows. Quickly, he stuffed the items into his inventory, then grabbed the loaves of bread from the wooden box and many pieces of fruit and cooked meat. It was more food than he needed, but it never hurt to have extra. There was an iron sword in the chest as well. Watcher picked up the blade for a moment, the heavy weapon drooping in his grasp. He thought about the moment, just before facing off against Fencer, when he'd held up his pretend sword at the ready. If he ever had to fight, for real, with a heavy blade like this, he wouldn't stand a chance.

What was I thinking? . . . I'm not a soldier.

Watcher knew he was too weak to wield a blade . . . ever. If he ever tried to fight with a sword, he'd likely just get himself killed. He was good with a bow, but none of the other soldiers thought a bow and arrow was a *real* weapon.

With a sigh, he dropped the sword back into the chest, then closed the lid. It squeaked again.

"This zombie heard a sound," a voice grumbled from outside the shattered home.

The putrid stench of rotting meat drifted through the air, followed by a sorrowful moan. Footsteps scrapped past an open window as a group of zombies shuffled nearby. Fear exploded through Watcher's nerves. It felt as if he had been hit by a bolt of lightning.

What do I do . . . they'll catch me.

Something fell to the floor in the outer room, followed the crunching of something, probably a chair being kicked across the room by a zombie foot.

They're in the house!

"Careful, that could have hit someone," a zombie said.

Watcher's nerves felt as if they were aflame as panic ruled his mind.

The offending zombie grumbled something that was unintelligible.

Glancing around the room, Watcher looked for a way to escape, but the only door led back into the main house.

A zombie growled, saying something Watcher couldn't understand as it trampled more of their belongings with its clawed feet.

Watcher was trapped and there was no escape!

"Check all the rooms just in case there's something useful here that was missed," the squad leader commanded.

Watcher slunk down next to the chest, and pulled some of his clothes over his head, covering himself. Just then, the door flew off its hinges as it was kicked into the room. Feet stomped inside, the rancid smell of decaying fleshing filling the air. Watcher wanted to gag and cough, but knew he couldn't make a sound or he'd be caught. Waves of fear crashed down up on him, making him want to just curl up in a ball and shake, but the young boy knew any movement would mean capture . . . or worse.

"This house was searched," one of the zombies growled. "The whole village was searched. Hardly any gold was found."

Why would the zombies want gold? The thought echoed in the back of Watcher's mind.

"Tu-Kar, the zombie warlord, commanded that it be searched again," another monster said in a deep voice. "This zombie, Ka-Vir, was put in charge of the search. If any zombie refuses a command, Ka-Vir will report them to Tu-Kar. Death will certainly be the punishment."

Two other zombies moaned, then continued to shove things about in Watcher's room. The wooden floorboard creaked as a zombie stood right next to his pile of clothes. The monster pushed some aside.

"Fe-Mar has found a chest," a zombie said.

More feet pounded across the floor as the monsters approached, their clawed toes scratching into the wood.

"Get out of the way, fool. Ka-Vir will inspect this chest."

Watcher heard bodies falling to the ground; likely the commander was shoving the other zombies out of the way. The clothes over his head shifted about as the lid to the chest was slowly opened. A space between an old pair of pants and green shirt opened, allowing light to stream into his hiding place. Watcher peered through the gap. A large zombie wearing an iron chest plate gazed down into the chest. He pulled out books and wooden tools and threw them across the room, growling all the while. But then he grew silent as his dark eyes widened in surprise. Slowly, he lifted the iron sword from the chest and held it over his head in triumph.

"See, Ka-Vir has found an iron sword," the squad leader moaned.

"That should belong to Fe-Mar," a zombie growled that was out of sight.

Ka-Vir slammed the lid of the chest. The clothes settled across Watcher's head, sealing the opening and plunging him into darkness again.

"Is Fe-Mar challenging Ka-Vir?" the squad leader asked.

A tense silence filled the room. Watcher could imagine the monsters glaring at each other, sizing up their opponent. But the longer the silence, the less likely the challenger would attack.

"Ka-Vir thought so," the squad leader said. "It is time to leave. All zombies, head for the next village. The zombie warlord, Tu-Kar, will be attacking it soon. Any gold in that village will be taken, as well as the able-bodied villagers. Everyone out!"

The other zombies grumbled complaints, but walked out of the room. Their footsteps shuffled through the home, then out into the courtyard, but the stench of the creatures still lingered.

Was there still a zombie in the room? Watcher thought.

His sense of smell, as well as his sharp eyesight, was legendary, but sometimes it worked to his *dis*advantage. Like right then, Watcher couldn't tell if the odor in his nostrils was just left over from those terrible creatures handling items, or if a monster was waiting for him to move?

The silence in the room was terrifying. Watcher strained his ears, trying to gather every sound . . . listening for a raspy breath, or claw scraping against the floor, or . . . Fear kept Watcher motionless for what felt like ten minutes, his heart pounding in his chest. Taking a nervous breath, he felt confident the terrible, decaying stink of the zombies had finally dissipated . . . they were gone. With fear still surging through his veins, he carefully and slowly parted the clothes and peeked into the room. It was empty. Quietly, he emerged from beneath the pile of clothes and surveyed his room. Everything was destroyed. Models he'd carved out of wood were shattered, pots he'd made for his mother long before her death lay crushed on the ground, stories he'd written for school ripped to shreds. The zombies had done more than just search his room; they'd viciously destroyed everything and anything he'd ever created.

Now he had nothing.

Watcher moved out of his room and back into the shattered remains of their home. Memories of his once-happy childhood seemed to evaporate as he glanced about at the devastation.

"What are these zombies doing? Why did they attack us and why are they looking for gold?" Questions tumbled around in Watcher's head as he tried to wrap his brain around what had happened.

Stepping through the crumbled wall, he moved through the village, looking for survivors. Suddenly, he heard a cough near the village well. Sprinting past burned out homes and destroyed shops, he reached the well and found one of the village elders leaning up against it.

"Carver, are you okay?" Watcher reached into his inventory and pulled out one of the loaves of bread and handed it to the old man, but the villager refused the offer.

Carver shook his gray-haired head. "It is too late for bread to help me."

The old villager was suddenly raked with dry, hacking coughs. He flashed red as his HP (health points) dropped, then looked up at Watcher.

"All this was the doing of the zombie warlord, Tu-Kar." Carver took a strained breath. He was getting weaker. "They captured the strong and healthy villagers, and left the old and infirm."

"I think the zombies took many of the elders behind the stables and . . ." Watcher didn't want to finish the statement. "All I did was lay on the ground and listen as the zombies destroyed every last one of them. I was so afraid they'd find me."

Carver nodded his head sympathetically. "There was nothing you could have done. You've never been a warrior. You aren't big and strong. If you'd tried to stop them, you'd be dead, too."

"At least I could have tried." Guilt filled every part of Watcher's soul. He stared down at his feet, afraid to look Carver in the eyes. "I heard one of the monsters say they were looking for gold. Why would zombies want that?"

Carver coughed again, then reached out and grabbed the boy's leg. Watcher looked up and met the old man's eyes.

"Listen to me. This isn't your fault." Carver sucked in a wheezing breath. "We can only do what we are capable of doing, and your gift is not one of strength or fighting skill."

"Then what is my strength?" Watcher asked. "I've asked myself that question my whole life and haven't been able to answer it. What am I good for?"

"Watcher, you are the cleverest child I've ever known. It is the task of every person, through their life, to answer that question: 'What is my role in life?'" He coughed again; his HP was nearly depleted. "Many never find that answer, and they go through life feeling incomplete. I hope you are able to answer that question before the end of your days. Remember, true strength doesn't come from muscles or a blade, it comes from . . ."

Carver coughed violently, then looked up at Watcher, an expression of fear on his wrinkled face. He flashed red one more time, then disappeared, leaving behind three glowing balls of XP (experience points). The multi-colored balls rolled across the ground and flowed into Watcher, adding to his own XP.

Watcher was stunned. Carver had just died, and he'd been able to do nothing to help him, just like the rest of his friends and neighbors.

"Dad, Winger . . . are you still alive?" Watcher's thoughts went to his father and sister. They were probably terrified, if they were still alive. All he had done to help them—to help *anyone*—was to lay on the ground and pretend to be dead.

The bitter taste of cowardice burned in the back of his throat as anger began to bubble up from within his soul. The anger slowly morphed into rage . . . an unquenchable rage.

"I'm not gonna just stand here and let everyone I know be captured or destroyed," Watcher said to the patch of soil where Carver had been moments before. "The next village is in danger, and someone must go warn them." He looked around, hoping some hero would emerge from the smoke and rubble to lead this quest, but he was alone . . . all alone. "I have to help those people, and maybe free my friends and family in the process. I'm sure it sounds ridiculous . . . Watcher, the weakest and most cowardly of villagers trying to stop the zombie warlord. But if I hide from this like a scared silverfish again, then my cowardice will continue to consume me."

Watcher drew his bow and held it in his left hand.

"I'll try to make your death meaningful, Carver."

He raised his right hand with fingers spread wide in the salute for the dead. Clenching his fist, he lowered his hand, then pulled an arrow from his inventory and notched it to his bowstring.

"Dad, Winger, I'm coming for you. I won't abandon my family, even though I'm terrified."

With a false look of determination on his square face, Watcher walked out of his village, pursuing his friends and family, likely never to return again.

CHAPTER 4

Tu-Kar, the zombie warlord, glared down at his prisoners in disgust. His enchanted chain mail sparkled in the shade of the large oak tree, casting pinpoints of iridescent light on the surroundings, the spots of purple light shining down upon the terrified prisoners. The warlord laughed a hacking sort of laugh, making many of the NPCs look away in fear.

"Is this the best that village had to offer?" Tu-Kar glanced up into the clear blue sky and shuddered. He knew zombies in the Overworld would burst into flames under the hateful glare of the sun, but here, in the Far Lands, monsters were immune from its harmful rays. No one really knew why, but many suspected it had something to do with the monster warlocks from the ancient times.

"Many of the warriors that were drawn into the forest did not survive the combat." One of the warlord's subordinates stood before Tu-Kar, his iron armor scratched and gouged from numerous battles.

"Tu-Kar's orders were to spare the warriors and capture them," the warlord growled, his good eye narrowing in anger, while the scarred, milky-white eye remained unresponsive.

"This zombie, Mi-Lar, personally led the battle," the armored creature replied. "The villagers were given the chance to surrender. Even though they were outnumbered, the idiotic NPCs chose to fight, rather than give up. Only three surrendered after they were wounded. The rest of the warriors were destroyed." Mi-Lar stood a little taller. "Only five zombies were lost in the battle."

"Mi-Lar did well." Tu-Kar nodded, showing his approval. "A promotion is earned. From this day forward, Mi-Lar will be known as Os-Lar."

"Many thanks, Warlord," the newly promoted Os-Lar replied.

"Assign guards to the prisoners." Tu-Kar's armor flashed, giving off a burst of purple light. "If any cannot keep up with our march to the next village, then take all their food and leave them to starve."

"It will be a pleasure." Os-Lar gave his commander a toothy grin.

"Zombies!" Tu-Kar stepped up onto a leafy bush. His deep voice boomed through the forest, aided by the enchantments in his sparkling chain mail. "Another village filled with NPCs stands in this army's path. More prisoners will be taken, and their hidden supplies of gold must be found and taken."

The zombies began to growl and grumble as they drew near, magically drawn to their commander.

"The last village offered too little gold," the warlord continued. "Kaza will not be pleased. And if Kaza is not pleased, then Tu-Kar is not pleased." A frightened expression flashed across his scarred face. Putting aside thoughts of the terrible monster Kaza, he continued. "The zombie race has made a bargain with Kaza, the Wither King, and it will be upheld. Gold will be delivered to the Capitol in exchange for more iron tools of war. When the zombies have enough swords and armor, then it will be time to turn the tables on Kaza and show that monster who is really in charge!"

The zombies growled their excitement, some of them

banging swords against chest plates. Those without weapons pounded their clawed fists against their green, rotting chests.

"For now, the zombies will do Kaza's bidding. But soon, this army will rise up and take what is due to us . . . everything!"

The monsters moaned excitedly, some of them scratching their long claws against the trunks of the trees, thirsty for violence.

"The army must hurry to the next village while they are still unprepared." Tu-Kar looked down at Os-Lar. "Remove one of the prisoners and have them destroyed in front of the others. That will motivate the villagers' obedience. Once that doomed villager is gone, then a small group of zombies will escort these prisoners to the rendezvous point. Tu-Kar's group will bring those captured in the next village, as well as whatever gold is found."

"Yes, Warlord." Os-Lar bowed his head, then turned and glared at the prisoners. Many of the villagers began to weep.

"Be warned, Os-Lar," the zombie commander said.

Os-Lar turned and looked up at his commander.

"It is likely that Kaza will also be at the rendezvous point." Tu-Kar glared at the zombie. "Say nothing of our plans, under pain of death."

"Of course, Warlord," Os-Lar replied.

"Then go." Tu-Kar stepped off the bush and held his iron sword high in the air. "Zombies assigned to the next village, follow Tu-Kar to victory!"

His enchanted chain mail glowed bright for just a moment, sending out a rippling wave of magical energy, then grew dim again. The rest of the zombie army, mesmerized by his command, followed him without question or fear, unable to refuse the order.

Tu-Kar walked along the grass and brick path, strutting as if he owned the entire forest. A wounded zombie limped along in front of him, partially blocking the path. The zombie warlord reached out and shoved the monster aside, causing him to fall to the ground with a thud. The creature cringed as if he expected to be hit again, but the commander ignored the wounded monster and continued his arrogant gait.

"Foolish zombie," Tu-Kar growled. "If any monster cannot keep up, they are to be destroyed."

His enchanted chain mail grew bright for just an instant, then faded, just as two other monsters fell on the wounded zombie, tearing into the creature's HP until he was eliminated. The zombie warlord laughed as he continued down the path, the screams of other wounded monsters filling the air.

"Soon, enough gold and prisoners will be supplied to Kaza," the warlord growled. "When all the weapons and armor are given to Tu-Kar's army, we will turn on Kaza and destroy him. Then, the zombies will take over all of the Far Lands."

The monster laughed a maniacal laugh as he strode toward the next village and the victims that would soon be his.

CHAPTER 5

Watcher followed the ancient path that led deeper into the Far Lands. He glanced nervously at the thick oak forest that hugged the trail with its leafy embrace. At any instant, the young boy expected monsters to come charging out of the woods and attack; his ability to daydream and imagine things that weren't actually there was legendary in his village.

Thoughts of his village friends flittered through the back of his mind. Watcher wondered how many of them were still alive and how many had been . . . no, he didn't want to consider *that* possibility.

Snap . . . Watcher thought he heard a twig break, as if a boot had crushed it.

He froze and stared into the shadows.

"Was that just my imagination?" The young boy's voice was barely a whisper.

Pulling his bow out of his inventory, he notched an arrow and scanned the forest. In this section of the Far Lands, the forest was incredible dense, with only the smallest amount of light able to penetrate the leafy canopy and reach the forest floor. Watcher knew strange things happened in the Far Lands, everyone knew that, and it made him that much more nervous.

Out of the corner of his eye, Watcher saw something move through the shadows. His heart beat faster, thudding in his chest like drum.

Strange monsters were rumored to exist in the dense forest, though no one had actually seen them. Ancient ruins from castles and watchtowers and fortresses dotted the landscape, built from some long-deceased civilization hundreds of years ago. Magical relics from that forgotten age appeared now and then, some with powerful enchantments that could harm the strongest monster or destroy the bravest villager. Everyone, including monsters and NPCs, knew to be cautious in the Far Lands, because you never knew what could happen or what kind of magical and dangerous beast you might disturb.

Leaves crackled as if they were crushed underfoot. Watcher spun around and drew back his arrow. His keen eyes scanned the shadows for movement. This was no daydream . . . there was something in the forest, and it was getting closer.

"I have an . . . an arrow pointed right at you." Watcher's voice cracked with fear.

No sound came from the forest. In fact, it seemed all the animals—the sheep, the cows, the chickens—all of them had become completely silent, and that silence was deafening. It was as if the forest itself was waiting to see what would happen . . . and who would survive.

Watcher shook as waves of panic slithered down his spine. He wanted to run, he wanted to hide, he wanted to just curl up in a ball and hope it all just went away; the young boy was paralyzed with fear.

Just then, a voice whispered into his ear.

"You really need to be careful with that little bow and arrow of yours; it might poke someone."

Watcher screamed, then spun around. Before he could fire his weapon, the bow was torn from his grip and tossed to the ground. Gritting his teeth, Watcher prepared himself for the killing blow. But instead of being struck, he was greeted with laughter.

"Watcher, you're as white as a skeleton," the voice said. "Calm down, it's just me, Blaster."

Panic faded from his mind, allowing Watcher to see who stood before him. It was one of the boys from his village—his cousin.

"Blaster?" he whispered. "BLASTER!"

Watcher enveloped his long arms around him and hugged with all his strength.

"I thought I was the only person that survived from our village and was still free."

"Nope," Blaster replied. "We survived as well."

"*We?*"

Blaster just smiled, then put his fingers to his mouth and whistled. Up the trail, a girl dressed in a green shirt and brown pants, a yellow stripe running down the center, emerged from behind the trunk of an oak tree.

Watcher's heart nearly leapt out of his chest. "I can't believe it."

She walked toward him, her long blond hair swinging back and forth like waves of liquid gold. Her bright green eyes locked onto Watcher's blues, and for a moment, all the horror and sorrow of recent events seemed to evaporate away as she smiled.

"Planter . . . you're alive," Watcher breathed, his heart pounding in his chest.

He ran along the path and enveloped her in a massive hug that threatened to crack some ribs. Her hair smelled of apples and sunshine. Watcher took in the scent, her presence filling him with relief and joy.

"I can't believe you're alive." Watcher wiped away tears from his cheeks. "I figured everyone was either dead or captured by the zombies. But here you are . . ."

"I won't be alive for long if you don't let go, so I can breathe," Planter replied.

Her voice was like the most beautiful music he'd ever heard. Watcher released the hug and held her at arm's length, a gigantic grin on his square face.

"Sorry, I thought I was all alone out here."

"You didn't hug *me* like that," Blaster said with a grin.

Instantly, Watcher felt his cheeks blush. "Well . . . I . . ."

He turned to scowl at his cousin, but Blaster had disappeared. Watcher saw movement in the shadows, a dark shape behind a tree. Stepping out of the shadows, Blaster emerged right next to him. For the first time, he noticed his friend was wearing leather armor, dyed black, allowing him to blend in with the darkness.

"You keep disappearing," Watcher said.

Blaster smiled. "It's the armor. My dad—you know, your uncle Tracker—always said it was important to dress for the occasion. And right now, merging with the shadows seems like a good idea."

"You're right about that, cousin," Watcher replied.

"Have you seen anyone else?" Planter asked.

"No, I've been all alone . . . until now. I know the zombies followed the road this way, but I haven't seen them yet." He glanced to where the rocky trail curved behind a small hill in the distance, looking for the monstrous army. Watcher wasn't sure if he wanted to see them or not. He swallowed nervously. "I heard the zombies say something about going to the next village on this path."

"We need to follow them and try to help," Blaster said.

"With what? All I have is my bow and some leather armor." Watcher tapped his knuckles to the brown leather tunic.

"I have these." Blaster drew two long curved knives from his inventory, holding one in each hand. "My dad trained me to prepare for the unexpected. I've trained with these knives since I could walk. I can handle myself if we come across some zombies. But we need better weapons for you and Planter."

"I don't need a weapon," Planter objected. "I'm not a fighter."

"Hate to break it to you, but *everyone's* a fighter now." Blaster put away one of his knives. "We need better weapons and armor, and then we need to catch those monsters."

"And do what?" Planter asked.

Watcher glanced at his two friends, an expression of uncertainty on his face. "We free our families . . . I guess."

The two villagers stared at him, surprised.

"Look, I know everyone thinks I'm not very strong or very brave, but the zombies got my dad and sister." Watcher took a nervous swallow. "If I don't try to free them, I'll hate myself for the rest of my life."

"I don't know if the zombies have my mom or not," Blaster said. "She sent me out into the forest when the first attack started. My dad went with the other warriors to chase the zombies; it was a trap. I saw the monsters bring the surviving warriors back and my dad wasn't with them." Blaster paused for a moment as the painful memory played through his mind. A tear trickled from one eye. The boy quickly wiped it away. "I'm sure he's dead, but I don't know what happened to my mom. I have to save her and anyone else I can find."

"Planter, what about you?" Watcher asked. "Were your parents captured?"

The girl glanced at the ground, her long blond hair falling across her shoulders and shielding her face from view. Watcher could hear her weep softly. He wanted to comfort her, but knew she needed a little privacy for her grief. After a few moments, she spoke.

"They were at the door, pounding on it, demanding we come out." Planter spoke softly as the memory played through her mind. "My dad knew if we opened the door, we'd be killed . . . or worse. So he broke out a window in the attic. It was a small window, just a single block wide. I was able to squeeze through and climbed up onto the roof." She raised her eyes and brought them to Watcher. "I heard the zombies crash through the door, then there was some fighting. You both know my dad wasn't very good with a sword, but I knew he wouldn't let them take Mom. He tried to fight them off, but there were just too many of them." She wiped her cheek, leaving a moist stain on her sleeve. "I knew when the fighting stopped and everything grew quiet in our home, my parents were gone."

"How did you get away?" Blaster asked.

"Our house was in a part of the village where all the homes are close together. I was able to jump from one roof to the next, and then I finally jumped to the ground and ran into the woods."

She hung her head and stared at the ground, gritting her teeth. Watcher could tell she was fighting the storm of emotions raging within her. A few tears trickled from her eyes, but she wiped them away quickly.

"I wanted to help my dad fight, but there was nothing I could do." Planter looked up and held out her hands, showing they were empty. Her eyes were filled with sorrow and grief. "I had no weapon . . . nothing. All I could do was listen."

"Planter, I'm so sorry," Watcher said.

"My mom and dad died in our home for no reason. Zombies are evil." She glanced at Blaster's knife, then looked up at the boy in his dark, leather armor. "Maybe I'm not a fighter . . . right now, but I think it's time I learned. Blaster, can you teach me?"

"Absolutely."

"But we don't have any weapons other than your knives." Planter looked up at Blaster, then to Watcher. "How do we get more?"

"I have my bow," Watcher added, but Planter ignored him.

"My dad told me something once," Blaster said. "He said, 'Always hope for the best, but prepare for the worst.' So my dad, Tracker, did exactly that."

"You mean he always hoped for the best?" Planter asked.

Blaster nodded. "But he also prepared for the worst. We have a hidden cache of weapons and armor, tucked away somewhere secret."

"Where?" Watcher asked.

"It's in the old deserted watchtower."

"You mean the one they say fell into a sink hole and is mostly buried?" Watcher asked. "You know where it's located, don't you?"

Blaster nodded, then removed his black leather cap. His hair was just as dark as his helmet, the curly locks disheveled and going in all directions at once.

"But that's off the trail!" Watcher said.

"Yeah, it's deep in the woods."

"If we go there, we'll be completely on our own, with nobody to help us." Watcher's voice sounded worried.

"Look around, genius, there's nobody around to help us now," Blaster said. "We're on our own, whether you realize it or not. We need food and water, and better weapons."

"It's time we taught the zombies a lesson," Planter said, an angry tone to her normally lyrical voice.

Watcher looked at her closely. The sadness that had just filled her eyes was now completely replaced with hate and a thirst for revenge. The thoughtful, kind, and understanding girl he knew in his village was disappearing right before him and being replaced with someone that was angry and hungry for violence. It pained his heart, but he knew they were both right. They needed weapons and supplies if they were going to help their families and friends. But something about this path they were about to follow worried him.

Am I gonna lose myself to violence and revenge, like Blaster and Planter? Watcher thought. *Or can I still stay true to myself?*

The question echoed in his head, causing fingers of dread to knead his soul. But then the images of what *might* have happened to his father and sister percolated through his mind, pushed aside his concerns. Terrible images of what *might* be played through his mind like a terrifying nightmare. He had to save them, somehow, though he knew he wasn't a good fighter, or very brave or strong. But Watcher knew he had no choice.

"Okay, let's go get us some weapons," Watcher said.

"All right." Blaster slapped him on the back. "Follow me."

The boy, still in his black armor, walked down the path, then shifted to running, Watcher and Planter fast on his heels.

CHAPTER 6

Blaster led them down the path, the boy now wearing forest green leather armor to blend in with the grass covering the trail. He carried his two curved knives as if ready for an imminent attack. The sight of those knives gave Watcher a feeling of security, for he knew Blaster was a skilled fighter; everyone in his family was good at fighting.

Watcher's uncle Tracker, Blaster's father, was the warrior of their family, and Watcher's dad, Cleric, was the scholar. There had never been any animosity between the two; Tracker had never thought himself better than Cleric because of his muscles. In fact, everyone in the village looked up to Cleric, even though his skill with a sword was nonexistent. Watcher never understood why Cleric commanded so much respect, yet Watcher seemed to receive such disdain and ridicule from his peers for being weak. He always wanted to ask Blaster about it, but never had the courage; he was afraid to hear the answer or learn what Blaster really thought of him.

Lost in thought, he bumped into Blaster, having not noticed the boy had stopped.

"What is it?" Watcher drew an arrow and notched it to his bow quickly.

"Why are we stopping?" Planter asked.

"From here, we leave the trail." Blaster stuck a square finger under the edge of his leather cap and scratched his ear. "If we go north, eventually we'll run right into the old watchtower."

"How can you tell where we are?" Watcher cast nervous glances at the surroundings. "All the forest looks the same to me. You're sure this is the right spot?"

Oak trees stood majestically throughout the woods, their branches stretching out, sometimes brushing against their neighbor. The jagged limbs cast strange, monstrous shadows across the forest floor, creating a spooky environment that chilled Watcher's blood. He was never much of a woodsman; he preferred staying in the village whenever possible, or at least staying on a well-known path. When he was younger, he'd gotten lost in the woods, and his uncle had to go out after him to find him. Watcher had been terrified at the time, and remembering that experience still made him nervous whenever he was far from home.

"You see that tree there?" Blaster pointed to a tall spruce.

"Yeah." Watcher nodded.

"Anything look unusual about it?"

Watcher moved to it. He ran his hand up and down the trunk, feeling the rough bark under his fingers. The blocky leaves were a dark green, sticking out all along the length of its trunk, waving gently in the breeze. He inhaled, taking in the smells of wood and sap and rich leaves and life.

The moo of a cow floated out of the forest, mixed with the oinks of multiple pigs.

"It looks like a normal tree to me."

"No, it's not supposed to be here." Planter grinned. "I can see that now."

Blaster nodded.

"I don't understand," Watcher said, puzzled.

"This is an oak forest, and that's a spruce tree." She moved next to Watcher and ran her hand over the bark. "What's a spruce doing here?"

"Exactly." Blaster nodded. "My father planted that tree long ago, as a marker. It leads us to the supplies he hid so long ago. Come on."

Blaster glanced up at the sky and watched the clouds; they always moved from east to west, even in the Far Lands. Getting his bearings, he turned to the left and headed north, his two companions following.

The thick canopy of branches and leaves overhead blotted out the square face of the sun approaching the western horizon. The shadows were long across the forest floor, making it difficult to see very far. Watcher's imagination created monsters in the distance, lurking behind tree trunks or crouching behind bushes. He shook unconsciously. Suddenly, someone bumped into him, rescuing him from the imaginary monsters.

"You look pretty serious," Planter said. She ran through a small patch of light, the yellow rays of the sun making her blond hair appear to glow like the finest spun gold. Turning, she smiled, causing Watcher's heart to skip a beat.

"Ahh . . . what?" He felt like an idiot.

"I said, you were looking pretty serious," Planter said.

"Umm . . . I was just thinking about my sister."

"Winger?"

He nodded.

"Did you know that your sister gave me the first pair of Elytra wings she ever made?" Planter said.

"Really?" Watcher ducked under a low-hanging branch, narrowly avoiding a face full of leaves. "Did they work well?"

Planter laughed. "I jumped off the roof to test them, but I didn't know how to make them open."

"Ouch," Watcher said.

She nodded. "I was probably too young for them, but I wanted to fly really bad."

"Did you ever get a chance to use a pair of Elytra?"

"Well, I—"

Blaster's voice floated out of the darkening forest, interrupting them. It was hushed and cautious, silencing Planter's comment. "We're getting close."

The boy had become invisible again, his black armor merging with the shadows. And then Watcher spotted him, the razor-sharp edge of his knives reflecting the last few rays of sunlight that penetrated the leafy covering overhead.

"Blaster, what do you know about this watchtower?" Planter asked, her voice hushed.

The fading light from the setting sun made them all a bit nervous. Watcher cast anxious glances around at the darkening forest. A chicken clucked nearby, startling the boy. He turned and scanned the surroundings for the offending fowl, but couldn't find it.

"My dad told me it was built in the ancient days, when the Far Lands were first formed." Blaster came closer and walked at her side. Pulling off his leather cap, he scratched his head. "He said it was once a wizard's tower and was the center of magic in those days. But there was some kind of great battle that made it sink into the ground, and it was finally abandoned."

"You think there are still magical items hidden there?" Watcher asked.

"My dad and I searched all of its rooms and halls and found everything we could. But who knows . . . maybe there are still items hidden away."

Suddenly, the rattling of bones filled the air. Blaster skidded to a stop and held a hand up, calling for silence.

"Get to the shadows." Blaster donned his black leather cap and disappeared into the darkness.

Watcher and Planter both moved into a dark shadowy patch and crouched. Drawing his bow and an arrow from his inventory, he notched the shaft to the string, then peered into the darkness.

"The sound came from over there," Planter whispered into his ear, pointing off to the left.

Watcher could feel her breath against his neck.

Turning, he peered into the forest. His keen eyes searched the shadows, using the edges of his vision to look for movement. Everything seemed still; Blaster had disappeared, the skeleton had stopped moving, and the animals in the forest became gravely silent.

The quiet was unnerving.

Turning his head slowly, Watcher scanned the shadows, look for any kind of . . . and then he saw it, the glint of light bouncing off a polished stone. A bow creaked in the distance, likely belonging to the bony monster. Turning, he drew his arrow back and then fired. The arrow streaked through the forest, then struck a tree right next to the skeleton.

"Did you hit it?" Planter whispered.

Watcher didn't reply. Instead, he pushed his friend to the ground just as an arrow zipped by over their heads. Quickly standing to his feet, Watcher drew another arrow and aimed, but now the sound of startled screams filled the woods. The skeleton was shouting out in pain as it tried to escape, the clattering bones filling the air.

"The skeleton is trying to run away," Watcher whispered. He tracked the sound with his bow, estimating the speed and distance. "Blaster must be chasing him."

Watcher aimed ahead of the monster, far enough to put an arrow in a tree right in front of him, then released the shaft. He could hear it whistle through the air, then *thunked* into the trunk of a tree. The clattering of the bones stopped when the monster skidded to a stop. Suddenly, the sound of blades scraping against bones filled the air. The skeleton yelled out in pain and fear, then grew silent.

Scanning for movement, Watcher peered into the shadows, looking for more threats. He thought he heard the crack of sticks and the crunching of leaves, but saw nothing in the shadows. And then suddenly, Blaster was at his side.

"Don't worry, I got him," the boy said as he removed his leather cap and ran his fingers through his tangled hair. "He tried to get away, and was moving pretty fast, but then he stopped for some reason. After that, it was all over for him."

"Good," Planter said. "I hate skeletons. I'm glad you were there, Blaster."

Watcher wanted to mention it was his first shot that had directed Blaster to the monster. He also wanted to brag that it was his second arrow that had stopped the skeleton from fleeing. But Blaster was already on the move, heading for the ancient watchtower, Planter following close behind. Sighing, he followed the pair, his eyes still scanning the darkness for monsters.

They moved in silence through the woods, passing from an oak forest to one filled with tall spruces. The dark green leaves were not as closely packed together, allowing the sky overhead to peek down on the travelers. As they marched, the sun kissed the western horizon, casting out orange rays of light that pierced through the gaps in the foliage. It splashed warm orange and red light on the surroundings, creating a magical scene. To the east, the sparkling faces of the stars emerged from behind the blue curtain of daytime, slowly advancing across the sky as the tiny pinpoints of light pursued the square face of the sun. Watcher was about to comment on the serene beauty of the scene when Blaster stopped right in his tracks.

"We're here."

Before them stood the top of a tower made of mossy brick and stone. The structure was capped with alternating rings of quartz and obsidian, the black and white circles making a bull's-eye that pointed up into the dark sky. Beacons hung on the side of the circular tower, casting light upon the colored windows. Around the tower, huge craters scarred the forest floor, as if a storm of meteors had pummeled the land.

"What's with all the big holes in the ground?" Planter asked.

Blaster smiled. "My dad asked me to unearth more of the structure. So I did the thing I enjoy the most."

"You used TNT?" Watcher asked.

"Exactly." Blaster nodded. "I detonated explosives around the tower, then kept going down until I found the bottom of the structure. Once I reached the base, I found a huge part of the building that was completely buried. This wasn't just a tower; it was a gigantic structure with buildings stretching out in all directions."

"Did you search it all?" Planter asked.

The boy nodded. "We searched what we could, but it's really dark down there, and there were lots of traps built into the floors and walls. In some places, sand and gravel had fallen in to block the passages. I still have no idea if we disarmed all the traps down there." He glanced at Watcher, then Planter. "That means you need to be careful down there and stay close to me."

They both nodded.

"OK, come on." Blaster led them down a series of steps that had been carved into the edge of the excavation. "I marked the path to the bottom with redstone torches. Just stay on the path and you'll be okay."

It was slow moving down into the hole, the drop from the edge at times sheer and fatal. They carefully followed Blaster, the young boy traversing the trail with practiced ease.

As he descended, Watcher examined the tower. It was built out of stone bricks, some of them cracked while some had the green luster of moss-covered blocks. At places along the side of the tower, colored windows of yellow and purple and white sparkled in the light of the moon that was just clearing the eastern horizon. Glowing beacons hugged the side of the tower, casting light across the structure. A grid of iron bars ran along the corners of the blocks that made the cylindrical tower, giving it a rugged look, as if it could endure for centuries . . . which it had.

Jumping down the path, Watcher moved from redstone torch to redstone torch, the path likely impossible to follow without the glowing sticks. They took a switchback, following the rough-hewn steps in the opposite direction. This brought the main building into view.

"I can't believe the size of that building." Watcher was stunned.

"Yeah . . . it took a lot of TNT to excavate it all." Blaster smiled. "It was fun."

Connected to the huge tower was a gigantic structure topped with an ornate roof, the pattern across the top of the building made of complicated designs and multiple colors. It was magnificent.

"What do you think the ancient wizards used this for?" Planter asked.

Blaster shrugged as he leapt from block to block.

"I heard my dad say it was once the tower for one of the strongest wizards." Beads of sweat trickled down Watcher's brow, the salty moisture clinging to his reddish-brown hair. "He thought the tower itself somehow magnified the wizard's power, but I don't understand how that could be possible."

"I don't think anyone knows much about the wizards from the ancient times," Planter said.

"I wouldn't mind having one of those wizards here, right now," Watcher said. "I bet they could just teleport us right to the tower entrance."

Blaster chuckled. "Careful what you wish for. Those wizards are gone for a reason. Maybe they caused more trouble than they were worth. Besides, we're almost there."

After three more leaps, Blaster reached a set of brick steps that led to the floor of the structure. They sprinted down the steps and stopped at the entrance of the huge cylindrical tower.

Watcher gasped as he gazed up into the building in wonder. Colored light streamed in through the stained-glass panes that decorated the walls, the beacons on the outside of the building driving the vibrant display.

"I've never seen anything like this in my life." Watcher glanced at Planter. She had a stunned expression on her soft face. "It's—"

"Breathtaking." Planter sighed after completing his sentence.

"Come on, let's get the stuff." Blaster moved into the room, ignoring the colorful windows set in the walls. Instead, he stared down at the ground.

"What are you looking for?" Watcher asked.

"We hid the cache, in case bandits found this place," Blaster explained. "It's buried under one of these blocks." He walked slowly across the floor, then stopped. "I think it's right here."

The boy removed his leather cap, then pulled a pick axe from his inventory and started to dig. Two adjacent blocks shattered under his tool, revealing a wooden chest in the floor. He reached down and flipped open a chest.

"Let's see what we have in here."

Blaster pulled out some chain mail, a stack of arrows, swords, food, some potions, and a full set of iron armor. Blaster took an iron broadsword for himself, then handed all the arrows to Watcher. Planter took the chain mail and draped it over her shoulders, Watcher did the same with a second set of the armor. After he distributed the food and healing potions, Blaster closed the lid and put new blocks over the opening.

Watcher glanced around the room as he adjusted his new armor. Glancing up at the windows, he saw that the pattern of colored panes looked strange.

"Anyone else notice that the colored windows sorta look like a person?" Watcher pointed to the pattern of purple and white panes.

"If that's a person, then what's that above them?" Planter pointed to the yellow and black windows on top.

"Maybe some kind of gold and black hat," Blaster said. "That's kinda weird. You think it means anything?"

Watcher shrugged, then turned and glanced at the wall opposite the entrance. The white and purple windows no longer formed the image of a man. Instead, the purple made the vague shape of an arrow pointing down.

"Blaster, *these* windows look like an arrow, pointing down." Watcher moved closer to the wall. "See it?"

Blaster shook his head, his dark curls bouncing about. "I just figured the ancient wizards messed up on the pattern."

"Not likely. This can't be a mistake . . . it's a message." Watcher moved closer to the wall and stared down to where the colorful arrows pointed. "I bet there's something under here." He tapped his foot on a moss-covered block. "Can you dig it up?"

"Well . . . I guess." Blaster hefted his pick and stood at Watcher's side. "I doubt there's anything there. My dad and I searched all these rooms and passages a hundred times."

"Humor me."

Blaster shrugged, then swung his pick at the block in question. After four hits, the cube shattered, revealing a dark glowing block underneath. After three firm strikes, that block shattered as well.

"Well, I'll be creeper . . . look at that," Blaster said.

"What is it?" Planter asked. "What's there?"

"Another chest, but this one is an ender chest," Blaster said.

"An ender chest?!" Watcher was stunned. "I've never seen an ender chest before."

"Then I guess today's your lucky day." Blaster put away his pick and moved back.

Watcher peered into the hole. The ender chest was black in color, but had green stripes along its sides, and a golden latch holding it closed. He reached down and flipped the lid open, then jumped back, unsure what was going to happen . . . nothing did. Moving cautiously forward, Watcher peered into the dark box. Inside were two items, both glowing with an iridescent purple hue.

"What's in it?" Planter asked.

Watcher reached down and removed the objects. One was an enchanted sword like none he'd ever seen. The other was an enchanted shield.

The blade was made of a shining, mirror-like metal, but had an iron handguard and iron handle. A small, perfectly-shaped diamond was imbedded in the guard on both sides. The blade was not wide, like a normal sword—rather, it was narrow and lightweight. It cast a wide lavender hue on the three companions, its magical enchantment pushing back against the darkness.

The shield sparkled with some kind of magical energy. The front was colored a deep, forest green, with stripes of white radiating out from the center. A ruby-red gem was mounted at the center, the precious stone appearing ominous and powerful.

"You should use these." Watcher handed the blade and shield to Planter.

With the shield held up high, Planter swung the sword through the air, a huge smile on her square face. The blade seemed to whistle, leaving behind a glowing trail of white spots in the air, as if it actually split the air molecules in half.

"I *love* this," she said.

"Then you should keep it." Watcher smiled, seeing her joy.

"Agreed," Blaster added. "You needed a weapon, and now you have one."

"But I didn't find it, Watcher did . . . It should be his."

"No," Watcher said, shaking his head. "You need a weapon, and this longsword will be perfect for you. It's lightweight, maybe because of its enchantment, and seems to fit perfectly in your hand. I want you to have it. Besides, you know I'm no good with a sword, and what am I going to do with a shield? I need both hands to fire my bow . . . that's enough for me."

She looked at him and smiled. His heart felt as if it leapt up to the stars.

"Okay, but it needs a name." Planter paced back and forth. "I've heard that every great sword needs a name, and I'm gonna name this one Needle, because it's so thin and sharp."

"Needle it is," Blaster said. "I think we have what we came for, now it's time to leave. We need to get to the next village and try to warn the villagers."

"Agreed," Planter said.

Blaster closed the ender chest and replaced the block of stone, hiding its presence, then moved to the tower entrance. Planter was right behind him, Needle held firmly in her right hand. As Watcher followed, he thought about how this tower could have been buried so deep in the ground. He got the feeling that a terrible battle had happened here a hundred years ago, and the ghosts of the battle were still lurking in the dark halls and rooms of this structure. Moving out of the tower, he followed Blaster and Planter up the steps that led back to the surface, the redstone torches casting wide crimson circles of light. He stopped for a moment and looked back down upon the building. Watcher was glad to be leaving the ancient watchtower, but he knew their next destination had creatures far more dangerous than his imaginary ghosts, and the trio was heading straight for that monstrous horde.

Swallowing nervously, he notched an arrow to his bow, and continued up the steps, toward the zombie army that had kidnapped his father and sister.

"I'm coming Cleric, I'm coming Winger," he whispered to himself. "I don't know what I'm gonna do when I find you, but I'll think of something."

CHAPTER 7

The sound of weeping villagers filled the air. Some begged for mercy, some sobbed uncontrollably, and others just remained silent, accepting the helplessness of their situation.

"Be quiet!" a zombie guard growled, a look of hatred on his scarred green face. "It seems all villagers do is moan and complain."

"Moaning . . . I thought that was a zombie's talent," one of the prisoners replied.

The guard moved toward the outspoken NPC and struck him hard across the face. The blow knocked the villager to the ground.

"Be wise and be quiet." The monster glared at the fallen NPC, then stomped away.

Two men reached down and helped the injured villager to his feet. They brushed off the dirt and leaves from his smock and continued to follow their captors, the razor-sharp tip of their swords always poking the slowest in the back. A few of the villagers fell to the ground, exhausted from the forced march and lack of food, but the others quickly lifted their fallen comrades to their feet. Any prisoner that could not keep up was pulled aside and never seen again.

"Watch these filthy villagers," the monstrous squad leader said to the other guards. "This zombie must speak with the warlord."

The other monsters grumbled complaints, but the squad leader ignored them and moved quickly to the front of the army.

The zombie cautiously approached Tu-Kar. "Warlord, the prisoners tire."

Tu-Kar turned and looked at the monster. "What is this zombie called?"

"This zombie is named Fo-Lon." The squad leader stood tall and proud.

"And Fo-Lon is concerned about the villagers?"

"Well . . . umm . . . Fo-Lon does not want too many to die before they are delivered to Kaza."

"Hmm . . . that is a wise response."

"So far, three villagers have been executed since being taken from their village." Fo-Lon glanced up at the zombie warlord, his own diminutive size amplified by the hulking commander. He held his head high in spite of being so much smaller. "The pathetic NPCs could not keep up, and their punishment was swift and complete. But many more of the prisoners are weakening. Perhaps resting for the night will allow more of the villagers to survive. If the army does not stop, then zombies will need to carry the weaker ones to keep them alive."

"Zombies . . . carrying villagers . . . never!" Tu-Kar snapped.

"Yes, Warlord."

Tu-Kar turned and glanced at the prisoners. They were huddled together into a circle, zombies on all sides, their booted feet dragging across the grassy trail with fatigue. Many of the monsters poked at the terrified NPCs with swords or with their razor-sharp claws, keeping them moving. Some of the villagers had their arms draped over the shoulders of comrades, their feet barely moving.

The zombie commander looked down at the smaller monster. "Fo-Lon is correct. The villagers must rest or they might all be lost."

Tu-Kar reached into his inventory and pulled out his enchanted chain mail. He draped the sparkling metal over his shoulders, the enchanted links glowing a soft purple. The zombie warlord felt the magical garment bond itself to him, stabbing at his HP and causing a wave of pain to crash through his body.

"Zombies, the army will halt and camp here for the night."

The chain mail pulsed for just a moment, giving off a bright, iridescent lavender glow. Tu-Kar saw a similar sparkle of purple light glowing briefly in the eyes of his zombies, then that too receded. The zombies in the army instantly stopped marching, even if they were not within sound of his voice. A group of monsters directed the prisoners to sit on the ground. Some took out bowls of mushroom stew and distributed it amongst the NPCs.

"Wait." The warlord pointed at some of the zombies with a clawed finger. "Only give food to those that are sure to survive this march and make it to the church. Waste no stew on any that are too weak or sick."

His armor pulsed again.

The monsters handed out the bowls of stew and loaves of bread carefully, skipping those that seemed too frail to survive the entire trek. Some of the villagers tried to take food out of the monsters' hands. They were beaten back with clawed fists or the flat side of a sword.

Tu-Kar smiled.

Some of the villagers glanced toward him, but quickly looked away when the zombie commander glared back. One NPC, an adolescent girl with long brown hair and bright blue eyes, stared at the warlord with fierce hatred in her eyes. When Tu-Kar gazed back at her, the villager refused to look away, her anger stronger than her fear. An old man dressed in white with a gray stripe running down his smock pulled at the girl, trying to get her to avert her gaze, but she persisted, scowling at Tu-Kar.

It made the zombie warlord laugh.

This girl thought she could intimidate him with her stare . . . it was ridiculous. He considered destroying her as an example to the other NPCs, but her anger would likely make her a good slave for Kaza; she was a fighter and would live long, though her suffering would also last long as well. It mattered not to Tu-Kar if one villager suffered or a thousand did. All that mattered was his plan, and delivering these slaves to Kaza was a big part of it. If this NPC girl got in the way, then she would be eliminated without a second thought.

Reaching up, he removed the enchanted chain mail and put it back into his inventory. It was a relief to have it off, but the pain from the magical garment still lingered; its power had a cost to the wearer. One thing zombies could do well was endure pain. The only thing they were better at than enduring pain was *causing* pain, and soon, Tu-Kar, the zombie warlord, would be causing pain to all the inhabitants of the Far Lands.

He laughed a maniacal sort of laugh as the villagers sobbed and moaned. Moving to the front of the formation, he found a pile of leaves and lay down, staring up at the stars and listening to his prisoners' despair.

"Soon, these pathetic villagers will be Kaza's problem and Tu-Kar will be paid what has been promised. That fool Kaza will never expect the zombie revolt until it is too late." The warlord chuckled a hacking laugh. "When Tu-Kar's army is powerful enough, then the zombie people will be safe. Too many times throughout history, the villagers of the Far Lands have attacked the zombie towns and destroyed countless monsters." He scowled as he recalled the stories he was told as a child. "Tu-Kar will make the Far Lands safe for zombies by exterminating the villagers. And even if it means dealing with a creature as vile as Kaza, it will be worth it." An image of his brother popped into the warlord's mind.

The young zombie had been killed in an NPC raid long ago. The thought made him growl with anger. "Soon, the villagers of the Far Lands will learn what it truly means to be afraid."

Closing his eyes, the zombie listened to the sobs and wails of his prisoners, as if it were beautiful music, and laughed again.

CHAPTER 8

Watcher heard the commotion before they reached the village. Shouts of pain and fear from villagers were mixed with the growls and moans of zombies. Swords clashed against armor and bowstrings hummed; the attack had already begun.

It was just after dawn, and the sun had already cleared the horizon. Long shadows stretched out from the base of the oak trees, giving the land a stripped appearance. Watcher stared down the curving pathway, looking for movement ahead, but the conflict was around the next bend.

Blaster, in an effort to remain unseen, took off his black leather armor and donned a forest green set. The color of the leather matched the grass that covered the forest and path they followed. Drawing his two knives, he continued moving toward the sound of battle, a grim look of determination on his square face.

Watcher pulled out the chain mail from the deserted watchtower after seeing Planter do the same. He hoped putting on the jingling armor would still his fears . . . but it did not. Drawing his bow from his inventory, Watcher notched an arrow and pointed it in the direction of the battle. Glancing to his side, he found Planter holding Needle in her right hand, the glowing green and white shield in her left. She looked terrified as well.

"I'm so scared," Planter said. "You look so confident, Watcher. Have you been in lots of battles before?"

The archer shook his head.

"I'm not that confident." Watcher wiped the sweat from his right hand, then gripped his bow firmly. "It's just that I'm used to being scared all the time. You know . . . with the bullies picking on me and the warriors always playing tricks, some of them very painful; I had lots of time to learn how to deal with being afraid. The benefit of always being scared is that you get used to looking brave, even when you're terrified, and that's how I feel right now. I've never been in a battle before. In fact, one of my goals in life was to never be in a battle."

"Well, it looks like you're gonna miss that goal," Blaster said. "I just wish I had some TNT to use on these monsters. A little TNT can really even the playing field." He flashed them both a smile, then, with a firm grip on his knives, sprinted off into the forest. The green leather armor made him slowly merge with the background as he wove his way around trees and shrubs.

"Do you think we should follow him?" Planter asked.

"I don't think so. Blaster likes to sneak up on his opponents, like he did with me on the trail yesterday. He's a lone fighter and we'd just be in the way."

"Well, I'd feel better if we had a warrior here to protect us," Planter said.

Watcher sighed. *I'm here, at least,* he wanted to say, but remained silent.

He wanted to be that person, a great warrior to protect her, but he knew his gift in Minecraft was not strength of arm, but rather ingenuity of mind. He was a thinker, not a fighter, and that was great . . . when you were in a library. But here, on the battlefield, Watcher feared his gift might get them both killed.

Suddenly, a scream pierced the forest. Footsteps pounded the path up ahead.

"Someone's trying to escape," Planter said. "We need to go help them."

Before Watcher could respond, she sprinted toward the sound.

"Planter . . . wait!"

Watcher gripped his bow tight and followed. His heart pumped in his chest like a beating drum. Every shadow in the forest resembled a monster . . . every tree branch a skeleton arm. Imaginary opponents emerged from his mind and filled in the spaces where bravery might have resided. The environment and everything around him enveloped Watcher in a fearful embrace that ignited every nerve in his body.

"I can hear them," Planter said. "They're right around the bend up ahead."

Watcher tried to catch her, but Planter was too fast. She shot around the corner, then skidded to a halt and screamed. Two steps later, he caught up to her and also came to a sudden halt. Before them was a pile of NPC items, stone and iron tools, some food, and a crafting table. They were floating off the ground, rising up and down as if riding on the gentle swells of an unseen ocean. Next to the pile stood two zombies, one wearing leather armor, the other clad in iron. Both creatures held wide iron swords, the razor-sharp edges gleaming in the light of the morning sun.

The monsters were easily a head taller than either Planter or Watcher. Their bodies rippled with muscles, and by the appearance of the scratches and nicks in their armor, these two were not new to fighting. The stench coming off the creatures was terrible. It was the smell of rotten meat and sick, decaying flesh. Watcher could taste the air as he breathed and it made him want to gag.

"What's this . . . two more villagers?" one of the zombies growled.

"We'll take them to the warlord. Tu-Kar will be pleased with more prisoners." The zombies took a step closer.

"You aren't taking . . . us to your warlord," Watcher shouted, his voice cracking with fear.

The zombies laughed.

"Perhaps the skinny one with the bow is right," the taller zombie said. He adjusted his iron armor. "That villager looks too small and weak to be of any use. Kill the boy. The girl will be taken to Tu-Kar."

The leather-clad zombie moved toward Watcher while the taller one approached Planter. Pulling his arrow back, Watcher wasn't sure which monster to shoot. His hands started to shake. A growl came from the monster in front of him as the decaying creature held his sword up high, a toothy grin spreading across his hideous face.

Just then, Planter screamed. She swung Needle at the zombie, but it was easily blocked. She slammed her shield into the beast, causing him to take a step back, as if injured slightly. The zombie growled and knocked the shield from her hand, then grabbed Planter by the arm. He pulled her in close.

"No!" Watcher yelled.

He turned and fired his bow at the creature without thought, instinct taking over his body. The arrow zipped through the air like a bolt of pointed lightning, slipping between two iron plates to find soft flesh. The monster screamed in pain, causing his comrade to turn and look.

Just then, something silver and bright burst out of the forest . . . an NPC warrior. A violent, animalistic scream came from the shining villager as it smashed into the monster approaching Watcher. The zombie's sword swung wildly, heading for Watcher's neck, but he ducked, the blade whizzing past an ear. The silvery warrior battled with the leather-clad zombie, the two combatants locked in a deadly dance. The new villager's diamond blade clashed with the zombie's iron weapon.

In the distance, Watcher could hear more fighting; it was coming from the village. Monsters were growling and moaning in pain as they battled some assailant. He guessed it was Blaster causing havoc amongst the zombies.

"I hope you're okay, cousin," he said softly.

Moving to the side, Watcher drew another arrow and fired it at Planter's assailant while backing away from his own. The shaft bounced off the monster's chest plate, making a pinging sound. Turning, the zombie growled, then charged right at him. Reaching into his inventory again, Watcher pulled out another arrow, but it dropped to the ground. He fumbled for it as the zombie closed the distance. Finally fitting it to his bow, he aimed with his hands shaking, and fired. The arrow flew wide, missing the zombie and embedding itself into a nearby oak. With a laugh, the iron clad zombie shoved Planter roughly to the ground, then pointed his sword at Watcher and growled.

Just then, the monster's comrade was tossed through the air, landing in a heap. The prone zombie struggled to stand, but the newcomer didn't give the monster a chance. The warrior charged at the creature, diamond sword held high.

For the first time, Watcher saw it was a villager, a big NPC in ornately designed iron armor. He brandished a diamond broadsword with the expertise of a seasoned warrior, striking the monster on the ground twice, taking the last of its HP and causing the creature to disappear with a pop. The second zombie turned and charged at the warrior, a savage moan filling the air. The big villager blocked the monster's attack, then advanced, his diamond sword flashing through the air, almost too fast to be seen.

Notching an arrow, Watcher tried to take another shot at the zombie. But it was difficult to aim as the creature battled with the villager. Their bodies crashed into each other as their swords banged together, each of the combatants trying to find an advantage. The monster lunged, poking at the warrior with the sharp tip of his sword. The villager easily blocked the attack, then brought his sword down upon the zombie's shoulder. A bellow of pain filled the forest as the creature flashed red. Staggering backward, the monster stared at his attacker, fear and dread filling the zombie's dark eyes. The warrior raised his huge diamond broadsword, preparing for the final stroke, but before he could swing, Planter attacked the monster from behind. Swinging Needle with unbridled rage, she slashed and slashed at the monster until it finally disappeared, leaving behind three glowing balls of XP.

Watcher breathed a sigh of relief and released the tension on his bowstring. He glanced at Planter and smiled as she stared down at the monster's inventory that now floated on the ground.

"Good job, Planter," Watcher said. "You finished that monster off."

"No time for congratulations, there's still a battle raging." The warrior glanced at Watcher's bow and smirked. "Come on."

He ran toward the village with Watcher and Planter following close behind.

"What's your name?" Planter asked.

"I'm Cutter," the warrior replied.

"Hi Cutter, I'm Watcher and this is—" Watcher said but was interrupted.

"Shhh," Cutter said.

The big villager slowed and tried to walk quietly, but the metal plates that made up his armor clanked together, making stealth impossible.

"What is it, Cutter?" Planter asked.

"The sounds of battle . . . they've stopped."

They moved slowly down the path. In the distance, the village was emerging from the morning fog that frequently blanked the forest. Buildings were burning, sending smoke high into the air, but no one was trying to put them out. No buckets of water were being thrown on the flames; they were just left to burn themselves out.

Watcher peered through the smoke and fog. "I don't see any motion in the village."

"You can't see anything from this far." A look of disbelief came across Cutter's square face.

"I can."

Watcher glanced at Planter, but she was looking at Cutter, admiring his fancy armor.

"Follow me," Cutter said.

 They sprinted down the road and into the village. The smoke bit the backs of their throats, making Planter and Watcher cough, but Cutter seemed unaffected. He strode past the burning homes with a look of wild rage in his steely gray eyes. On the ground, they found a pile of iron armor and weapons. A smell of rotten meat wafted off some of the discarded items.

"It seems someone took care of a few zombies for us." Cutter glanced at Planter and smiled.

"It was probably our friend, Blaster," she replied.

"Where is this *friend?*"

She shrugged.

"I hear something." Watcher turned his head to listen again. "It sounds like a villager moaning."

"That doesn't sound like a villager," Planter said.

"But I hear villagers moaning too," Watcher replied. "I think they need help." He pointed into the smoke. "That way."

Planter took off, sprinted toward the sound, the purple glow of her enchanted sword and enchanted shield casting a lavender bubble in the hazy air. As they ran, the moaning grew louder. Watcher could now hear the voices of villagers, but they sounded weak.

Streaking past the devastation that had been wrought upon this community, they ran around burned out homes and shattered buildings until they came to the front of the village. NPCs both wounded and elderly lay on the ground, struggling to stay alive. Some flashed red as their injuries continued to carve away at their HP, while others sat motionless, a look of despair and defeat on their faces. Across the path leading out of the village stood a line of six zombies, each armored and heavily armed.

"Tu-Kar, the zombie warlord, commands that no one follow the great zombie army." The zombie leader, a tall monster wearing an iron chest plate, glared at the newcomers.

"But you took all the food," an older villager moaned. "We have nothing and will starve."

"Tu-Kar is not concerned about the fates of these villagers," the monster said. "Only those that can work will be spared. Any others are just a drain on resources."

Cutter moved to the villagers and glanced down at them, then focused his angry gaze on the zombies.

"You're in my way." Cutter drew his diamond sword and pointed it at the monster. "Move and I will spare you and your zombie comrades."

"One warrior challenges us," the zombie growled. The scarred monster glanced at his comrades and laughed. "These zombies are the best fighters. A lone warrior doesn't stand a chance."

"He isn't alone." Planter stepped forward with Needle and her shield in hand.

"A girl!" The zombie laughed even harder.

Planter turned and glanced at Watcher, expecting him to move forward. But he knew his place wasn't at her side. He could do more damage from up above. Flashing her a grin, he turned and ran around one of the buildings. Using blocks that lay scattered on the ground, he built a set of stairs, and climbed up onto the roof of a building that was still untouched by the ravages of war.

"Ha ha ha . . ." the zombie commander laughed. "That little archer ran away before the fight even began. Tu-Kar has said before that villagers are all cowards. Here is the proof."

"Watcher's not a coward," Planter protested, but her voice sounded weak and uncertain.

With an arrow notched, Watcher was about to yell down at Planter and Cutter, letting them know he was on the roof, but suddenly, something green shot out of the forest and fell upon the monsters.

It was Blaster.

He sprinted out of the tree line and fell on the nearest zombie. The monster screamed out in pain and surprise as the young boy carved away at the zombie's HP. Blaster was like a green streak of lightning, moving this way and that as he used his curved knives with surgical precision. In the confusion, Cutter charged forward, yelling his guttural, animal-like battle cry. The smallest of the zombies screamed in fright, then turned and fled down the trail, away from the combat, leaving the other five monsters to face the battle. Planter hesitated for just a moment, then charged forward as well, heading for the left side of the zombie formation.

Watcher knew she was no match for the zombies. Without stopping to think, he drew his arrow back and fired. While it was still in flight, he fired again, then turned and shot at a zombie trying to attack Blaster from behind. He fired two more quick shots, then turned back to Planter's opponent. His first two arrows hit the zombie in the gap where the chest plate connected to the leggings. The creature screamed in pain. He glared up at Watcher, then raised his sword as Planter drew near. Without thought, Watcher fired two more arrows at the monster. They hit the creature just as Planter attacked. The monster shrieked in pain, then disappeared when Needle fell upon the creature.

Choosing other targets, Watcher shifted his aim, firing a trio of arrows at another zombie trying to sneak up on Cutter. The three shafts penetrated the monster's leather armor, destroying its HP. The creature disappeared, a frightened moan on its lips. Now, only one of the monsters remained. It was surrounded, with Cutter in front and Blaster behind. Watcher ran off the roof and streaked toward the lone zombie.

"Wait . . . don't hurt that monster," Watcher shouted as he approached. "We need information!"

But he was too late. The monster feigned an attack to the left, then reached out with its razor-sharp claws, trying to tear into Cutter as it blocked the big NPC's sword. Blaster moved forward, his knives a silvery blur. He shredded the last of the creature's HP, causing the zombie to disappear with a look of despair on his scarred, decaying face.

Watcher moved to Planter's side.

"Planter, are you okay?" Watcher asked.

"Did you see him battle the zombies?" she said. "Cutter just went through them like they were made of paper. He was so fast, I didn't even see him destroy them all. Those zombies didn't stand a chance."

"Yeah . . . but did you see my arrows?" Watcher asked meekly.

Planter didn't seem to hear. She was moving toward some of the elderly and wounded, checking to see who she could help. Watcher liked that about her; she was always trying to help others.

"Cutter, Blaster, come over here," she shouted as she knelt next to an old man.

Watcher followed the other two, and stood next to the elderly villager.

Planter held a bottle of water up to the old man's lips, giving him a drink. "Tell them what you told me."

"Well . . . I heard the zombie leader, I don't remember his name . . ."

"Tu-Kar, the zombie warlord," Cutter said.

"Yes, yes, that's it, Tu-Kar."

He struggled to stand. Planter helped him up, then gave him an apple from her inventory.

"Thank you, child." The old man took a bite out of the apple, then continued. "Now where was I?"

"Tu-Kar," Blaster said with a scowl. "You were saying something about Tu-Kar."

"Yes, yes, I remember now," the old man continued. "I heard the zombie warlord . . . what was his name . . . oh yes, Tu-Kar, that's it. I heard Tu-Kar talking about gold. They took every bit of gold from the village, saying it would be used to make the zombie warlord the most feared monster in all of the Far Lands."

"Why would they want gold?" Cutter put away his sword and paced back and forth, lost in thought.

"I heard the zombies saying something about gold when my village was destroyed," Watcher added.

"You look pretty much unharmed from that battle." Cutter's steel-gray eyes glared at Watcher. There was an accusatory tone to his voice.

"Well . . . I . . ." he stammered.

"It doesn't matter right now," the warrior said. "We need to find out where they're taking all those villagers and figure out a way to rescue them."

"I agree," Blaster added.

"Maybe we need to think this through first," Watcher suggested.

"No," Cutter snapped. "It's time for action. We're going after those villagers. This discussion is over."

Before Watcher could object, the warrior turned and headed out of the village, along the path taken by the zombie army. Blaster turned and followed the warrior without pause. Planter looked at Watcher, her stare feeling judgmental for some reason, then turned and also followed Cutter.

"Well, I guess we're going after the villagers now," Watcher said in a low voice. "We don't know where they're going or why, but I guess following them is the right thing to do."

Watcher reached into his inventory and handed the old man what food he could spare. The villager smiled, then tossed apples and loaves of bread to the other NPCs, bowing in gratitude. Turning away from the old man, he followed his comrades, uncertainty filling every aspect of his being. They were chasing the massive zombie army with no idea what was really happening. A hundred unanswered questions bounced around in his head. Watcher remembered something his father, Cleric, told him a long time ago: *"Action without thought is like using blocks of TNT to kill a monster in a crowded room. The TNT gets the job done, but can do more harm than the monster itself."*

"I hope there's no monster in the room when Cutter reaches his goal," Watcher mumbled to himself, then gripped his bow tightly and sprinted after his friends.

CHAPTER 9

Watcher breathed heavily, the heat of the day feeling like a warm blanket lying across his body. The sun was now high in the sky, at its apex and shining bright as rectangular clouds moved smoothly across the blue tapestry overhead.

"I feel bad for the villagers we left in that village," Watcher said. "I left them some food, but I'm not sure how long that's going to last."

"We can't stay and help every charity case," Cutter said.

"They weren't a charity case, they were villagers just like you and me!" Watcher snapped.

"You're wrong." The big warrior glanced over his shoulder and sneered.

"What do you mean?"

"Those people back there decided to play the victim instead of standing up and doing something about their situation." Cutter wiped sweat from his brown, then pulled out a bottle of water from his inventory and look a long drink.

"They were elderly and wounded villagers," Watcher said. "They didn't choose that."

"It doesn't matter," Cutter said. "We need to keep chasing those zombies and free all their prisoners."

Watcher was exasperated. He'd tried to get Cutter to slow down and agree to a plan, but all the NPC wanted to do was chase the zombie army with no plan and nothing prepared.

Watch out, there's a monster in the room, a voice said in the back of Watcher's mind . . . it sounded like something Cleric would say.

"Cutter, tell us how you came to this village right when we needed you." Planter stared at him, admiring his bright armor and shining sword.

"A zombie army hit my village a few days ago," Cutter said. "I've been hunting them for a while, and now I've finally found their trail."

"What happened?" Blaster moved up next to the warrior. "They take out your village like they did the last one?"

Cutter cringed at the question.

"Blaster, try to be a little sensitive," Planter said.

Blaster shrugged.

"It's okay, I can take it." Cutter gave Blaster a nod. "Yeah, they took out my village alright. It was dusk and everyone was getting ready for the night. The first force hit us from the front. We actually smelled them before we saw them; you put a lot of zombies together and they really stink. Anyway, they attacked us and didn't even try to hide their presence."

He took another drink from the water bottle, then put it away and continued walking along the grassy path.

"Our warriors all stormed out when the alarm was sounded. But as soon as the zombies saw us, they turned and ran. The commander suggested we let them go, but . . ." He paused for a moment and looked off at the distant clouds, likely reliving the event. "But I insisted we give chase. I convinced everyone it was better to destroy an enemy rather than letting them get away and come back again."

Cutter sighed.

"So you went after them?" Planter asked.

He nodded.

"The same thing happened in our village," Watcher said. "When they came—"

"I get it . . . Your warriors made the same stupid mistake as ours did." Cutter's voice was monotone, almost emotionless, but they could all see the pained expression on his square face. "We followed those zombies into the forest until we caught them in a wide clearing."

"Did you destroy them all?" Blaster asked.

Cutter shook his head. "They weren't alone. Those zombies had friends waiting for us; it was a trap. As soon as we entered the clearing, monsters came at us from all sides. They outnumbered us by at least three to one. Our commander, Fisher, put us in a circle, and we tried to defend all sides, but there were just too many of them."

He looked at the diamond sword in his hand, and Watcher saw what looked like an expression of regret, or maybe it was guilt, flow across the warrior's face.

"I always wanted this sword, but not like this," Cutter said, his voice almost a whisper. He looked up from the blade. "You see, I always wanted to be in command of our troops. The diamond sword was the symbol of that command. It's been passed down from commander to commander for hundreds of years. No one even knew where it came from; it was just always there. Some say there's something special about this blade, but it just seems like a sword to me." He sighed. "When the village elders chose Fisher over me, I was furious. I yelled and screamed and called them all traitors. I was so foolish back then."

"Why did they give it to Fisher instead of you?" Planter asked.

"They said I was too rash. They all knew I was the best fighter in the village; no one could beat me. But the elders said it took more than strength and skill with a blade to command. They said it took character and thoughtful caution, and maybe in time, I would earn the diamond sword. The elders said I wasn't ready for the responsibility of command."

"That must have hurt so much." Planter's sympathetic voice eased Cutter's tension a bit.

"It did." Cutter nodded. "But a good soldier keeps going, even when it's difficult. So I accepted my orders, and bowed to my new commander, and followed his instructions every time. But when the zombies were at our doorstep, I told Fisher his plan to let the zombies escape was wrong, and insisted we give chase. The soldiers were hungry for a fight, and followed me into the woods instead of staying behind like their commander instructed."

He gritted his teeth as the memories of that moment hammered at his soul. Blaster put a reassuring hand on his shoulder; it was an unspoken acknowledgement of his pain.

"When the zombies fell on us in that clearing, all the soldiers were with me, including Fisher. We fought hard, making the zombies pay. For every villager that fell, two or three zombies were destroyed, but it wasn't enough. At the end, it was just me and Fisher surrounded by seven zombies. I charged at them rather than try to think up a plan with Fisher. I destroyed five of them when my friend and commander fell. The remaining two zombies fled. I'll never forget the one that landed the last blow on Fisher. He was a big zombie, with a line of hair going down the center of his bald head. He wore elaborate iron armor and wielded an enchanted iron sword. The coward had screamed with a deep, guttural battle cry that was scratchy and ragged, then mortally wounded my friend. When I turned to face that monster, he growled something at me, then fled into the woods as Fisher fell to the ground." He paused for a moment as the painful memory replayed itself within his mind. "But just before he died, Fisher said one last thing . . ."

Cutter glanced to the ground and put a hand to his face. Watcher figured he was wiping away tears, but didn't want anyone to know. The three of them looked away as they continued down the trail, giving the warrior a little privacy.

"What did he say?" Blaster asked softly.

"What?" Cutter raised his head.

"Blaster!" Planter chided.

After running his fingers through his tangled and disheveled hair, Blaster just shrugged and asked again. "What did Fisher say?"

"Oh," Cutter took a nervous breath. "Well . . . he said, 'Have faith in yourself to know when to act and when to let another step forward and do what is needed. Trust in others and their strengths will be yours.' And then all that was left of him was his armor and this diamond sword."

Cutter stopped speaking and lowered his gaze to the ground again. He didn't seem to notice the small fern ahead of him on the trail. Without slowing or swerving, the big warrior crushed the delicate plant under his boots, unaware of its presence as if he were in some kind of trance. A tear trickled down his cheek but he quickly wiped it away. With gritted teeth, he looked up. It seemed as if Cutter was refusing to yield to the grief trying to overwhelm him. With a soft growl, he raised his head, all emotion driven from his square face.

"This sword . . . it was what I wanted more than anything. And now I wish I could give it back to Fisher and beg his forgiveness. All those soldiers were destroyed because of me and my hasty decision to attack those zombies. There were no soldiers in our village when the rest of the zombies arrived. They were overrun. Countless NPCs, the elderly, the sick . . . they were all destroyed because of me. All my friends and neighbors were taken prisoner and are now with the zombie army or worse. I'm to blame for it all."

"Cutter, you can't punish yourself for a single mistake," Planter said. "We make the best decisions we can, and that's what you did. But you can't let your guilt devour you."

"You don't get it, Planter." The warrior's voice grew in volume. "I'm not punishing myself . . . I'm gonna punish *them*." He gripped the hilt of the diamond blade tightly in his hand. "Those monsters made a mistake by leaving me alive, and now it's time for revenge. We're gonna chase down the zombies, and find their warlord, then end his miserable life. Nothing will stop me from using this sword to avenge Fisher and all the villagers that have suffered under the tyranny of the zombies. This is a war and there is only one outcome . . . victory."

"Yeah!" Blaster exclaimed. "We're gonna make those zombies pay."

"I'm with you, Cutter," Planter said. "They've hurt my friends and family, too. Now it's time to bring the hurt to the zombies."

They all glanced at Watcher, expecting him to support their violent plans. But instead of blurting out some kind of joyous statement about going to war, Watcher thought about everything he just heard. It seemed like they were rushing forward, following Cutter's impulsive lead without giving it any thought. But he knew that if he suggested anything else, it would cause his friends to lose confidence in him, or even worse, abandon him. Watcher glanced at Planter's excited face. She stared at Cutter as if he were some kind of mythical hero, the adoration clear in her bright green eyes.

"Yeah . . . we're gonna get 'em!" Watcher shouted, trying to seem excited and believable . . . but it just came out sounding ridiculous and sarcastic.

Planter sighed, disappointed, and looked away.

Watcher balled his hands into fists, frustrated.

Everyone was silent for a while as they focused on their march. The group shifted from sprinting, to running, to walking, trying to close the distance on their prey. But it felt like they never drew any closer. Watcher inspected the grass and tried to estimate their distance from the zombie army ahead of them . . . the blades of grass took time to bend back upright after being trampled. It was clear the zombie army was marching fast and hard. That was unusual for zombies.

"How are these zombies moving so quickly?" Watcher asked. "We all know zombies in the Far Lands don't like working together, don't like staying in a large group, and really hate running. All those things want to do is shuffle around with their arms outstretched, moaning day and night."

"Who cares," Cutter replied, "as long as we catch them and destroy all of them. Why a zombie does anything isn't important; destroying them is all that matters."

"But there's something going on here that we don't understand," Watcher said. "Knowledge can be a powerful weapon."

"Did your knowledge help you back there with those zombies on the trail?" Cutter glared at the boy.

"Well, I did shoot—"

"Is your knowledge gonna help us catch up to the zombies?"

"Well, I don't know if—"

"I thought so." Cutter said it with a finality that suggested Watcher's objections were done. "Let me give you some knowledge and then this discussion is done. We're gonna chase the zombie army. When we catch them, we're gonna set the prisoners free, then all of the villagers, led by me, are gonna destroy that zombie army once and for all. You got it?"

Watcher lowered his gaze and stayed silent. He'd heard that tone from different bullies in his life before; what it meant was: *If you speak another word, you'll be sorry.* And so Watcher stayed silent. But still, he felt something important was happening with the zombie army and their warlord.

Why are the zombies working together? It goes against their very nature.

Why are they looking for gold, and where are they getting the weapons and armor?

Questions echoed within his mind, each pointing to something larger than just one zombie warlord with his own private army, going around terrorizing the countryside. There was something going on and he suspected there was a bigger threat lurking in the shadows. If they didn't uncover that hidden threat before it was too late, then they all might be in trouble.

He glanced at Planter and sighed. She was now walking right next to the big warrior, talking quietly with him. It made something bubble up within his soul. At first, he thought it was anger, but it felt different and focused inward on himself. And then he realized what it was he was feeling; it was jealously and distrust. Something about Cutter was dangerous, not just to the zombies, but to Watcher and his friends as well. But right now, there was nothing he could do about it except wait. He just hoped when it was time to act, he'd be brave enough . . . and it wouldn't be too late.

CHAPTER 10

The zombie ran along the path, fleeing from the NPC warriors that had attacked his comrades. Er-Lan was still terrified by the ferocity of the small group of villagers. It had been only a single warrior and three children, but they fought as if they were twice their number. The memory replayed itself in the zombie's mind: the smaller villager with the two knives had moved so quickly, it had been impossible to predict where he would go next; the girl with the enchanted sword seemed timid, but attacked with complete savageness; the large warrior with his diamond sword had overpowered many of his comrade; and lastly, the archer on the rooftop had shot at the zombies with pinpoint accuracy.

These were a lethal combination of martial skills; likely they'd trained together for years. Er-Lan knew instantly that the zombies didn't stand a chance. Reporting the presence of these warriors to the zombie warlord was more important than standing his ground and being destroyed. Besides, Er-Lan was not a fighter. He knew the other zombies joked about him behind his back, but he had no illusions about his skill as a warrior. Er-Lan was smaller and weaker than nearly every other zombie. Even some of the children were better warriors than him . . . it was a fact he'd come to accept.

This time, he would do something that was important to the zombie people: he'd report the presence of these great NPC warriors and finally receive the recognition he deserved.

"I must tell the warlord . . . I must tell Tu-Kar," the zombie grumbled to himself.

Running as fast as he could, Er-Lan left the stone path and headed through the woods. He knew the grassy trail that cut through the forest would take a wide, sweeping turn. Heading straight through the forest would shorten his trek by hours. As he ran, the zombie felt the tug of something in the distance. It was like a soft voice, whispering sweet thoughts into his mind, thoughts he could not ignore: set up camp, make sure the church is secure, feed the prisoners . . . Er-Lan felt compelled to carry out the commands, though he was still far from the army.

"This zombie must hurry, must get to the church and help," Er-Lan mumbled to himself as the magical enchantments spurred him to run faster.

Finally, the zombie reached the old, dilapidated church as the square face of the sun was nearing the western horizon. He emerged from the forest, surprising a group of zombie guards.

"Who is that?" asked one of the sentries.

"It is Er-Lan with important news for the zombie warlord." He was out of breath. Stopping for a moment, the zombie leaned over and puffed heavily.

"The zombie warlord is in the church tower," one of the guards said. "Go quickly before all the doorways are sealed."

"Sealed?" Er-Lan was confused.

"The zombie warlord wants to make sure no other monsters get in or out through the night," the sentry replied.

Er-Lan sighed. He wanted to rest, but knew reporting to the zombie warlord was more important. With a moan, he shuffled toward the entrance of the church. As he approached it, he stared up at its soaring heights. Two huge stone towers stood on either side of the entrance, the steeples reaching up almost to the clouds. A gigantic clock face stood over the main entrance, but no one could really remember when it actually had worked. The back of the structure was covered by a wooden roof, the sides of the church by large, stained-glass windows. Along one side, small slabs of stone stuck out from the sides of the structure; many believed they were used to make repairs on the building long ago. Now they were just covered with moss and vines.

Er-Lan headed for the main entrance. It was a large opening with an arched roof, like an upside-down "V" that made anyone entering the building feel insignificant. Torches decorated the walls, some hidden behind panes of red glass, splashing perpetual hues of dusk on the ground, shading everything with a warm crimson glow. The sun, now kissing the horizon, was adding subtle oranges to the display, creating a magnificent banquet of colors that went unnoticed by the zombies, except for Er-Lan; he thought it all looked fantastic.

Moving through the opening, the zombie entered the church. Rooms sat on the left and right side of the structures, filled with zombie generals and their squad commanders. In the main hall, sitting on a throne made of obsidian and quartz, was Tu-Kar, the zombie warlord.

Er-Lan shuffled toward his commander, head lowered and properly cowed.

"What is this?" the warlord asked, his scratchy voice echoing off the cold stone walls. "Wasn't this zombie part of the rear guard?"

"Yes, sire," Er-Lan voice was timid, barely audible.

"Where are the others?" Tu-Kar voice boomed off the huge glass windows.

The generals, hearing their commander's voice, stepped out of their tiny rooms, and entered the main audience chamber, many of them growling at the tiny zombie standing before their ruler.

"Well . . . the villagers, they . . . umm . . ."

"Out with it!" the zombie warlord demanded. "Tell Tu-Kar what transpired. What happened to the rest of the rear guard?"

"They were destroyed, sire." Er-Lan took a step away from the throne.

Tu-Kar was suddenly on his feet, glaring down at the timid monster.

"Explain!"

"Well . . . the NPCs in the last village attacked the rear guard, and this zombie thought it best to come report to the great Tu-Kar."

"That last village only held gravely wounded villagers and old men," the zombie warlord said. "How is it they were able to defeat Tu-Kar's rear guard?"

"Other NPCs arrived in the village and fought."

He took another step backward, trying to get farther away from his enraged leader, only to bump into something big and solid behind him. Er-Lan glanced over his shoulder and found a zombie general standing in his way. It was Ro-Zar, the most violent of the commanders.

The hulking monster glared down at him. He wore the most elaborate iron armor Er-Lan had ever seen, with decorative curves and lines carved into the metallic surface. Reaching up, he removed his pointed metal helmet, revealing his angry face. A thin line of black hair ran along the center of his scalp and extended down the back of his head. The short bristles almost seemed like sharp spikes, though Er-Lan knew they were just hair. Everything on this monster seemed dangerous; Er-Lan was terrified.

"Where is this zombie going?" the general growled.

Er-Lan swallowed nervously, then moved away from the massive zombie.

"How many villagers attacked the rear guard?" Tu-Kar asked. "Twenty? Thirty?"

"Four." Er-Lan's voice was soft . . . and scared.

"What?" the warlord asked.

"Speak up, zombie," Ro-Zar said, shoving the timid zombie forward.

"Er-Lan said four," he repeated.

"FOUR?!" Tu-Kar screamed. He stepped off the throne and approached. "These villagers must have been on horseback, heavily armed and extremely strong. How many of the enemy perished?"

"Well . . . none of the villagers perished, sire," Er-Lan reported, then cringed, expecting the fatal blow to strike. He closed his eyes and waited for the end to come.

No one in the hall spoke; it was absolutely silent. Footsteps echoed through the room as sharp claws clicked on the ground. Er-Lan cautiously opened one eye and saw Tu-Kar approaching him, a look of unbridled rage on his green face. The scar that ran down the front of his head seemed to pulse with each heartbeat. His milky-white eye that intersected the scar was looking off in the distance, but his lone, good eye was filled with such anger, it hurt to look at him.

"Is this zombie telling Tu-Kar that the four NPC warriors survived, and all the zombies were destroyed?" the warlord asked. "Only Er-Lan lives to tell the tale."

The small monster nodded.

"These warriors must have been great. It is good that Er-Lan thought to report this news." The warlord moved a step closer, the claws on each toe clicking on the cold, stone floor. "Were they huge? Tell Tu-Kar what was seen."

Er-Lan took a nervous swallow.

"They were not huge warriors, sire," the zombie said. "It was one warrior and three children."

Tu-Kar grew silent, his wheezing breaths quieting to a mere whisper; it made him seem even more dangerous.

"So, tell me if Tu-Kar understands this correctly."

Tu-Kar's voice was quiet as a graveyard. "My squad of zombies, some of the best fighters in the army, were destroyed by a single warrior and three children, is that correct?"

Er-Lan nodded. "When their skills with sword and bow were seen, this zombie thought it best to report to Tu-Kar."

"This zombie was a coward and ran." Ro-Zar growled like an angry beast. The towering commander moved closer to the little zombie, pushing him closer to his warlord.

"Is this so?" Tu-Kar asked.

Er-Lan shook his head, but lowered his gaze to the ground.

"Did this zombie even raise his claws in defense of his fellow comrades?" Ro-Zar prodded the little monster in the back with a sharp claw.

Er-Lan shook his head again.

"And what is the punishment for cowardice?" Tu-Kar asked.

"Death." Er-Lan's voice was weak, almost nonexistent. "But the NPC warrior was so good with his diamond sword, it was impossible for any to stand against him. This zombie felt it more important to tell Tu-Kar—"

"Did you say diamond sword?" Tu-Kar asked, interrupting the zombie.

Raising his head, Er-Lan looked up at Tu-Kar and nodded. "Yes, the warrior used a diamond sword with incredible skill."

Tu-Kar clasped his hands behind his back and paced back and forth for a moment, contemplating this information.

Er-Lan's heart pounded in his chest as he watched his leader. Cold beads of sweat formed on his forehead, some of them flowing into one of the many unhealed scars that dotted his face. It stung a little, but reminded Er-Lan he was still alive. Moving his eyes, he looked to the left and right. All the generals moved closer, their angry eyes focused on the timid monster. His weakness had been a stain on his family, and now it was a stain on this army as well. He was used to stares of resentment from other zombies; many thought he was pathetic because of his diminutive size and absent strength, but the looks he received from all these generals was something completely different. They hated him with every fiber of their being, as if he somehow tainted the very ground on which he stood.

Suddenly, Tu-Kar stopped his pacing and glared down at Er-Lan.

"This zombie will not be killed," Tu-Kar shouted in a loud voice.

Some of the generals moaned in disappointment.

"What is this zombie named?" the warlord asked.

"Er-Lan, sire."

"This zombie, Er-Lan will go forth and capture that diamond sword and return it to Tu-Kar," the warlord shouted in a loud voice. "Let all zombies cheer for Er-Lan!"

A couple of the zombie commanders cheered, but most of them just moaned. They all had a thirst for violence, and Er-Lan had been a ripe target. But for the moment, Tu-Kar had spared his life.

"It must be known to all," Tu-Kar proclaimed, "if this zombie ever returns to the army of the zombie warlord without this diamond sword, then let all zombies fall on Er-Lan until there is no HP remaining."

The zombie commander moved closer to the terrified Er-Lan. The smaller zombie shook in fright. Tu-Kar moved his mouth next to Er-Lan's ear and whispered. "Cowardice will not be tolerated in this army." The warlord's voice was strangely calm . . . it made him seem even more dangerous. "When the plans are complete, the Far Lands will belong to the zombies and will be ruled by Tu-Kar. Those who fail will face swift and brutal punishment. Now, go get that sword or be punished here and now."

"Yes, Tu-Kar . . . yes Tu-Kar," Er-Lan stammered as he slowly turned, and stepped away from the warlord and generals. The monster turned and shuffled out of the ancient church, then ran for his life before the great zombie warlord changed his mind.

CHAPTER 11

"Let's camp for the night," Cutter said.

They'd been following the zombie mob that had attacked the last village through the afternoon, and the sun was now nearing the horizon, splashing oranges and warm reds across the land.

"Not on the trail," Watcher suggested. "Let's go into the woods where we won't be seen. There might be more monsters about."

He hoped it would sound like a brave idea, but it came out sounding like a cowardly one. Planter gave Watcher a grin, then looked toward Cutter as the warrior stormed through the forest, not even bothering to comment on Watcher's suggestion.

"We'll camp here. This is a good place." The warrior pointed to a recession in the forest floor.

Cutter placed a block of wood on the ground, then struck flint and steel together. In no time, the wood was aflame. The campfire drove back the growing darkness as the sun settled itself behind the horizon for the night, allowing darkness to wrap around their little camp.

Blaster pulled out blocks of dirt from his inventory and built a wall between them and the trail. The barricade would keep the firelight from unwanted eyes on the road, but also act as a line of defense if necessary, though realistically, there were too few of them to have any hope of survival if the zombie mob returned.

Moving across the campsite, Planter pulled blocks of wool from her inventory and placed them on the ground, one for each NPC. It offered a soft place to sit and rest.

Cutter sat down and removed his armor, the plates clanking together, reminding Watcher of the sounds from his village's blacksmith shop.

I hope our blacksmith survived, Watcher thought.

Once his armor was off, the big warrior then pulled out an apple and ate. Planter sat next to the Cutter and smiled when he offered her a loaf of bread. She gratefully accepted. Watcher could just imagine her green eyes staring up at Cutter with admiration. She was probably impressed with his fighting skills back there on the road.

Watcher sighed, then placed his bow and quiver of arrows on the ground. He removed his chain mail and stretched, the knotted muscles in his back complaining bitterly in response. Reaching into his inventory, he pulled out a piece of melon and offered it to Planter.

"You want some more to eat?" he said to her.

Planter turned just as Cutter gave her a piece of cooked pork.

"Oh . . . uhhh . . . thanks, but Cutter just gave me this."

She held up the pork chop and smiled.

"I'll take it," Cutter said.

Picking up his diamond sword, he skewered the fruit with the tip of his blade and pulled it from Watcher's grasp.

With a sigh, Watcher pulled out another slice of melon and ate.

"So . . . ah, Watcher . . . right?" Cutter asked.

The young boy nodded.

"So, Watcher, why don't you carry a sword?" Cutter asked. "The girl here carries one."

"Her name is Planter," Watcher snapped.

"Right, Planter carries one, and so does he," he said, pointing to Blaster.

The dark-haired boy held a short blade in his hand. It was a curved thing and razor sharp, longer than a knife but shorter than a sword. Blaster held the blade in the air, then grabbed another and held both before him. The metallic edges reflected the light from the fire, making each seem as if they were coated with flames.

"This one has the two little short swords," Cutter continued. "Not very long, but at least they're sharp."

"They're long enough for me," Blaster said. "Besides, my weapon of choice is TNT."

"That's great, but tell that to a spider that's chasing you with their sharp, curved claws. They won't stand around and wait for your little blocks to blow up beneath them."

"Perhaps," Blaster replied with a wry grin, "or perhaps not."

He gave him a maniacal laugh that caused little square goose bumps to form on Watcher's arms.

"OK . . . we have the mayor of crazy-town here." Cutter stared at Blaster for an instant, then turned to Watcher. "But you. All you have is your little bow and arrow. Why no sword?"

"Well . . ." Watcher started to say, but Planter jumped in.

"He's great with that bow," she said. "Watcher's a better shot than anyone in our village."

He was embarrassed that Planter was defending him, but Watcher was a little intimidated by Cutter. The big warrior reminded him of Fencer back in his own village.

"It won't help much if a zombie is standing right in front of you," Cutter replied.

"They'll never get close to him because—"

"Planter, you don't need to protect me," Watcher said. "I've come to terms with this long ago."

She gave him a sad, understanding glance, then turned back to Cutter.

"I'm not strong enough to wield a sword, and besides, I'm too clumsy." Watcher glanced at the ground and continued. "I've tried lots of times, but a sword just feels wrong in my hands. Growing up, I always wanted to be a warrior, with diamond armor and a diamond blade—" he glanced at Cutter's sword "—but it was all too heavy for me. My weapon is the bow and I can make it sing like nobody else."

"So you thought you'd go after a zombie army with just your little bow there? Is that right?"

Watcher nodded.

Cutter laughed. "I hope you brought two hundred arrows with you, 'cause that's what you'll need to destroy all those monsters."

"I'm not here to destroy them all," Watcher snapped. "I'm here to rescue my friends. My father and sister were captured and I'm gonna find them and set them free."

"With your little bow and arrow?" Cutter laughed.

"I don't care what you say, I'll figure out how to do it and save them," he glared at the warrior. "They're my family, and you never give up on family. You see, my father taught me that—"

Suddenly, Watcher stopped speaking. He snatched his bow and arrows from the ground and stood, notching an arrow to the string and drawing it back.

"What are you doing?" Cutter asked.

"Shhhh," Watcher commanded.

He stepped around the edge of the dirt barricade and peered into the dark forest.

"Watcher, what are you doing?" Planter asked.

Watcher turned to look at his friend. Behind her, Blaster stood and put on his black leather armor, then drew his two knives and disappeared around the other edge of the dirt wall, melting into the darkness. Watcher faced the dark forest and drew his arrow back a little farther.

"I know you're out there," the archer said. "Come out and show yourself, and we won't hurt you."

He moved away from the wall and stood between two stout oaks. The sound of clanking metal filled the air as Cutter quickly put on his armor. Something moved up ahead. A shape passed through the moonlight, darting from one tree to the next.

Was that Blaster? he thought.

Moving deeper into the forest, Watcher scanned the darkness, looking for movement. Suddenly, there was the sound of a struggle up ahead, followed by a surprised growling shout.

"If you move, it's over for you," a voice said in the darkness.

It was Blaster.

Watcher sprinted toward the sound, keeping his arrow pulled back and ready to fire. Branches whipped him in the face as he charged through the forest, his keen eyes only able to make out the trunks of the trees in the darkness. As he ran, the familiar stench of zombies wafted through the trees. Following the odor, Watcher used his nose more than his eyes to navigate toward the creature. When he neared, he could hear Blaster's angry voice.

"What are you doing here, zombie?"

The monster only moaned.

"Blaster . . . over here," Watcher said.

And then he found them. Blaster was standing close behind the monster with both knives out, held at the ready. The zombie wore no armor, and carried no weapon, but Watcher knew it had a razor-sharp claw at the end of every finger.

A clatter of metal resonated through the woods as Cutter caught up.

"What is it? What's going on?" Cutter looked confused.

"We caught a zombie," Watcher said. "I sort of sensed it or smelled it or heard it moving through the woods and—"

"Good job catching that monster, Blaster," Cutter said.

"I was able to sneak up on him because of this armor," the boy said as he removed his black leather cap. "My dad always said, 'Stealth and silence are powerful weapons.' When I saw it was only one, I decided to capture him; maybe we could get some information."

"Good thinking," Cutter replied. "This monster is gonna tell us everything he knows."

"Maybe we should look around for more monsters." Watcher turned and peered into the darkness, probing the shadows with his keen eyesight. "There could be more."

"No, we'll question this one . . . now!" Cutter snapped. The tone of his voice made it clear there would be no more discussion.

"But there could be others out there in the forest, and we're not ready for them," Watcher said, but he was ignored.

We should be thinking first and acting second, he thought. *This is reckless.*

"Let's go, zombie." Blaster poked the monster in the back.

The creature grimaced as the sharp tip of the NPC's knife found vulnerable flesh. He shuffled forward with a sigh, an expression of resignation on his scarred face.

They led the monster back to the campsite. Planter was there, watching over the camp, her enchanted sword, Needle, drawn. When they emerged from the darkness, and stepped into the flickering circle of light cast by the fire, she smiled. Watcher felt the smile was meant for him and his heart soared.

"Cutter, you found them . . . good," she said.

His heart sank.

"Yep." The warrior's voice was deep, like rumbling thunder. "And we found a little friend as well."

Cutter shoved the zombie into the light, then grabbed the monster by the collar and guided him to an oak tree.

Reaching into his inventory, he pulled out a length of rope and tossed it to Blaster.

"Tie this . . . thing . . . to the tree," Cutter said. "Make sure it's tight."

Blaster wrapped the cord around the monster, pinning the zombie's arms to his side. He pulled the line taut and tied it at the back of the trunk, then moved back into the light. Glancing up at Cutter, the young boy nodded, then began removing his dark, leather armor.

"What are you gonna do with this zombie?" Watcher asked.

Cutter glared at the archer, clearly annoyed by the sound of concern in Watcher's voice, then drew his huge diamond sword. The zombie's eyes grew wide with excitement at seeing the blade, then grew fearful when Cutter brought the razor-sharp tip right up next to the monster's throat.

"What are you doing?" Watcher complained.

Cutter ignored him. Instead, he moved closer to the zombie, the tip of the shining blade scratching the monster's skin.

"Now, zombie, you and I are gonna talk." Cutter smiled at the monster. "And you better have something interesting to tell me if you want to survive till sunrise."

The monster glanced at Watcher, then brought his terrified eyes to Planter. The creature was in fear for his life.

This is wrong, Watcher thought. *We don't torture.* But he knew there was nothing he could do to stop this . . . at least for now.

CHAPTER 12

"This zombie means no harm, means no harm," the monster moaned. "The rope is tight . . . it hurts."

"Stop your complaining!" Cutter barked.

"What are you gonna do with him?" Watcher asked. "We can't torture this creature."

"We can't?" Cutter asked. "And why is that?"

"Because we aren't monsters," Watcher replied. "We're better than that."

"Oh really?" Cutter glared at the young boy. "And how do you think these zombies treated your friends and neighbors when they attacked your village? Do you think the zombies felt bad when they destroyed our soldiers, or when they murdered my friend, Fisher? No." He paused for a moment, then lowered his voice. "I'm gonna find out where they're taking our friends, and this zombie is gonna tell me." He lowered his voice to a whisper . . . it made it seem more threatening. "If you get in my way, then you must be on *their* side instead of *our* side."

"Maybe you should just let Cutter ask his questions," Planter suggested. "He's right. We need information."

"But he's . . ." Watcher started to say, but stopped when Blaster stepped forward and put a hand on his shoulder.

"Planter's right, we need to know where they've taken our friends and family," Blaster's voice was calm and reassuring. "I'll make sure things don't get out of control. Since you have the best eyes here, why don't you get up on the dirt wall there and keep watch for more monsters."

"I guess you're right," Watcher said.

It was a mistake, but he knew nothing could be done to stop Cutter. The warrior's rage was evident on his square face and nothing was going to deter the villager from questioning this zombie. This situation reminded Watcher of something his father Cleric was fond of saying: 'You can't put the milk back into the cow, but maybe you can make some excellent butter.' He couldn't un-capture this zombie or avoid turning the monster over to Cutter, but maybe they *would* learn something useful. Watcher just hoped the zombie wouldn't suffer.

With a nod, the boy set his bow on the ground, then pulled some blocks of dirt from his inventory. Building a set of steps, Watcher retrieved his weapons and climbed to the top, scanning the forest for motion, glancing down occasionally at their captive.

"Now talk, zombie. What are you doing out here?" The warrior moved closer to the monster, his diamond sword still pointed to the creature's neck.

The zombie's eyes stayed glued to the weapon. There was a look of fear in the creature's eyes, but there was something else there as well, like excitement or anticipation . . . Watcher wasn't sure. But it was clear there was something else going on here.

"This zombie has been exiled from the others," the monster said. "Er-Lan has no place to go, no home, no people."

"That's a sad story." Cutter smiled. "Tell that to all the NPCs your zombie friends destroyed in the last village."

"Er-Lan was not part of that raid," the zombie moaned. "Violence is a bad thing. Er-Lan only wants peace."

"That's easy to say when you're captured," Blaster said. "Everyone in our village wanted peace, and the zombies destroyed it all."

"That is sad, but Er-Lan is innocent. This zombie is not a fighter, and is too small and weak to be of any danger."

"Is that your name, Er-Lan?" Planter asked.

The zombie nodded.

"What are you doing out in the forest all by yourself?" Planter moved closer, her voice soothing some of his fears.

"Exiled. Er-Lan has been exiled." The monster's voice was sorrowful and sad. "This zombie has no place to be and no place to go. Er-Lan will never see family or friends ever again."

"That's so sad," Planter said. "It's just like us."

"Don't feel any sympathy for this creature," Cutter snapped. "It's a zombie and cannot be trusted."

Er-Lan looked up at Planter, a sad and lonely expression on his scarred face.

"Where are the villagers that were captured?" Blaster pointed one of his curved knives at the monster, then took a step closer.

"No knives . . . no knives," the monster said. "Er-Lan saw a large group of zombies moving along the trail. They were heading to the old church that lies along the path to the west."

"Our families are nearby?" Planter glanced up at Watcher as a tear trickled out of her eyes. "My mom and dad . . ."

"Where is this church?" Watcher asked from overhead. "Tell us everything you know."

"Er-Lan knows little . . . very little."

"Tell us!" Cutter growled into the monster's face. He stepped back, then dragged the tip of his diamond sword across the monster's chest. The razor-sharp point sliced through the monster's shirt and drew a faint scratch on the monster's decaying green skin.

"Er-Lan is scared. Er-Lan knows nothing. Er-Lan just wants to go home."

The monster made a moaning, growling sound as his gaze lowered to the ground. Watcher realized the zombie was so afraid that he was weeping.

"TELL US!" Cutter yelled, his face turning red with anger.

"Don't hurt . . . don't hurt. Er-Lan will tell; just keep the big villager away."

Planter stepped forward and grabbed Cutter by the back of his armor and pulled him back. The big warrior spun around quickly and glared at her. Watcher instinctively notched an arrow and drew it back, aiming at Cutter. The soldier look down at Planter, then glared up at Watcher. Slowly, he moved away from the zombie and sat on a block of wool.

The monster took a nervous swallow, then spoke. "They would be held in the large room beneath the church, but Er-Lan does not know if the villagers are still there. It is very dangerous. Many zombies, many zombies."

"Here's the deal, filthy zombie—" Cutter stood, his whole body tensed.

"His name is Er-Lan," Planter interrupted.

"It doesn't matter what his name is," Cutter growled, turning to face Planter again.

His rage was bubbling close to the surface. Watcher wasn't sure if this was just an act, or if Cutter was about to lose control.

"He's a zombie, he's the enemy, he's nothing," Cutter said. "Don't feel sorry for him. He took your families and friends."

"Not Er-Lan, not Er-Lan. This zombie is innocent, tiny and weak, yes, very tiny and very weak."

"Be quiet, monster," Cutter snapped. He moved closer to the creature and stared with his unblinking, steel-gray eyes into the monster's green face. "I'll allow you to live as long as you are useful to us. You're gonna to show us the way to this church, and then you're gonna show us this underground room. If you mislead us, my sword will take care of you." He raised the diamond blade and brought the keen edge close to Er-Lan's face. "If you try to warn any of the other zombies of our presence, or lie to us, or try any kind of deception, you will be destroyed . . . instantly. Do you understand?"

The zombie nodded his head.

"Good," Cutter said, his voice now calm. "We leave at dawn. All of you get some rest. I'll stay up and guard our guest."

"You can't just leave Er-Lan tied to that tree all night," Watcher said as he descended from the top of the wall. "He needs to sleep, too."

"The zombie stays there," Cutter replied without even looking in Watcher's direction. "It's been decided."

Watcher took a step toward Cutter, but Planter grabbed his sleeve and pulled him back.

"You need to get some sleep," she said, her blond hair reflecting the flickering light of the campfire, giving her a soft, golden halo. "Lay down close to the fire to stay warm."

She moved to the opposite side of the burning wood and lay down. Blaster removed his black, leather armor, then moved close to the fire and curled up on a soft patch of grass. He was quickly asleep.

Watcher glanced at Cutter, but the warrior was facing off into the dark tree line, lost in thought. He saw the big warrior clench a fist, his body tensing as if he were reliving some painful memory. He gave the zombie a quick look. There was an expression of fear in the monster's dark eyes, but also something else . . . like he had some kind of secret. The zombie relaxed, letting the ropes support his weight, his bald green head lolling to one side, dark eyes closed. In a minute, he was moaning in his sleep; it was likely the zombie equivalent to snoring.

Finally, Watcher laid on the ground as well, positioning himself so he could see Planter and keep her safe. As he relaxed, the relentless fingers of fatigue kneaded away at his body, causing one muscle after another to relax, his eyes growing heavier and heavier. But just before he fell asleep, he though he heard the zombie say something.

"Diamond sword, yes . . . diamond sword . . ."

And then finally, Watcher was asleep.

CHAPTER 13

Watcher was sure this was going to be the best day of his life.

The sun was high in the cloudless blue sky, shining down upon the young villagers that had assembled in the practice yard. Watcher glanced at his friends and gave them a smile, though many just laughed at him or sneered. He knew they resented his presence here, but he would not be deterred. Watcher wanted, more than anything, to be a soldier and protect the village. He'd finally reached the ripe age of twelve, and was now eligible to try out to be a cadet.

The drill instructor, a curmudgeonly old warrior by the name of Saddler, walked past the line of youths, his unibrow perpetually furled in an angry scowl. In his hands, he held a bundle of long, wooden sticks that were meant to be their practice swords. The warrior dropped one in front of each young NPC, then moved back to the center of the courtyard.

"Which of you pathetic recruits wishes to have the honor of facing me in combat?" Saddler drew a stick from his inventory and flourished it around his body as if he were blocking a dozen attacks, all at once.

Just then, Watcher remembered something his father had told him just before heading to the practice yard. Cleric had said, "Bravery does not come from strength of arm or skill with blade. Instead, it comes from an unwavering willingness to try, regardless of the odds." These words buoyed his spirit. Watcher knew he had no chance of defeating Saddler, but what he'd come here to do today was not to win a battle but to show the warriors the quality of his character and his ability to persevere, even when it seemed hopeless. He was sure the soldiers would see this and want him in their ranks.

"I will face . . . you," Watcher said, trying to make his voice sound strong and courageous, but his voice cracked on the last word, drawing more giggles from the other recruits.

"You?" Saddler asked.

Watcher nodded and took a huge step forward, but he forgot about the stick lying on the ground.

It all happened in excruciating slow motion.

His foot landed on the stick, causing it to roll out from under him. Losing balance, Watcher flung his arms out in the air, flapping them about to regain his balance; it looked as if he were trying to take flight.

None of the kids around him bothered to reach out and help. They just stood there and watched . . . and laughed.

Finally, the stick shot out from under his shoe, sending his foot into the air. Slowly, he fell backward, his feet flying upward. He screamed something as he fell, but was never really sure what he said. When he hit the ground, the air rushed out of his lungs; it felt as if a giant was stepping on his chest. Then the back of his head hit the ground with a thud, landing on a stone block. Pain erupted through his skull, as darkness started to wrap around him like a deadly fog. Watcher could hear the laughter of the other kids, their howl and jeers magnifying his shame until the darkness finally, mercifully, took him into unconsciousness.

It was the worst day of his life.

A voice pierced the darkness. It was a sweet voice, almost lyrical as it called his name. He thought it was probably the most beautiful thing he'd ever heard.

"Come on . . . Watcher, it's time to wake up."

He slowly opened his eyes, expecting to see the practice yard in their village, but instead, he was in a dark forest, stars shining down upon him overhead.

"Watcher . . . you need to get up."

Planter was gently shaking him, her hand pushing on his shoulder. Her touch felt magical, as if some kind of ancient enchantment was flowing from her soft hand and into Watcher. It was wonderful.

Slowly, he realized: he wasn't living through that terrible day again . . . it had just been a dream . . . no, a nightmare.

Sitting up, Watcher scanned their camp. The fire had burned itself out sometime during the night; they were completely cloaked in darkness. Blaster stood on the opposite side of the camp, but his legs seemed to be missing. Then he pulled his black, leather tunic over his head, and his chest disappeared, leaving his head floating in the air. Placing the dark, leather cap on his head, the rest of him vanished, leaving behind just his smiling face. The boy drew his knives, then disappeared into the woods.

"Let's get a move on," Cutter said as he collected his gear. "We're heading for the church where the villagers are being held."

"Er-Lan said the villagers *might* be at the church," the monster groaned.

"You better hope they're there," Cutter growled. He untied the ropes that held the monster to the tree, then wrapped them around the creature's body, pinning his arms to his sides. "If that church is empty, then you and me are gonna have another discussion, and it won't go as well as it did last night."

"Er-Lan does not lie," the zombie said. He turned and stared at Planter. "Pretty girl will protect Er-Lan, yes? Keep the warrior from hurting Er-Lan?"

"Don't worry, Er-Lan," Planter said. "Watcher and I will keep you safe."

"Ha!" Cutter said.

Watcher scowled at the big warrior as he stood. He quickly grabbed his weapons, then donned his chain mail. He checked the campsite for anything left behind; they'd gotten it all.

"Everyone ready?" Planter asked.

Watcher nodded.

"Where's the little one?" Cutter asked.

"You mean me?" Watcher asked.

"No . . . not you. I mean the one with the two curved knives."

"I'm here." Blaster stepped out of the darkness and removed his leather cap. "I was just looking around, making sure there were no unwanted visitors around. It looks like we're alone."

"Great, let's go," Cutter said.

They moved quietly through the forest, prisoner in tow. The eastern sky blushed deep shades of red as the sun peeked up over the horizon. The light pushed back the veil of night, causing the sparkling stars to disappear, giving way to the blue sky of morning. The occasional moo of a cow floated across the landscape, followed by the cluck of a chicken; the forest was beginning to greet the day.

"Where do you think the zombie warlord is taking our friends in such a hurry?" Blaster asked. "These monsters move faster than any zombie I've ever seen."

"Who knows," Watcher replied.

"I bet he knows." Cutter gestured over his shoulder at Er-Lan, then yanked on the rope, causing the little zombie to stumble to the ground.

"Cutter, you made him fall," Planter complained with an angry glare.

"Who cares, it's just a zombie." The warrior laughed.

"It's still a living creature and should be treated with respect," she said.

"What kind of respect did the zombies show our neighbors when they attacked our village?" Blaster asked.

"Er-Lan was not part of the attack." The zombie cast his eyes to the ground.

"Who cares what you say," Blaster snapped. "My brother was killed in that battle. He sent me to the forest to stay safe as he tried to protect everyone else." He paused for a moment as the painful memories replayed themselves through his mind. "He tried to fight off four zombies that were attacking my mother when he was . . ."

The young villager stopped speaking as he was overcome with grief. He glared at the zombie with a lust for violence in his brown eyes.

"Maybe the zombie knows where the warlord is taking our friends," Cutter said. "I don't believe this church is the final destination. There's something else going on here and you're gonna tell us, aren't you?" There was a violent threat in the tone of his voice.

Drawing his diamond blade, he hit the zombie in the back with the flat side of the weapon.

"You know anything about the warlord's plans?" the warrior asked.

"Er-Lan knows nothing," the zombie moaned.

"That doesn't seem very likely." Blaster eyes were stained red from fighting back tears. "You've probably been with this warlord for a while. I bet you know all of his hideouts." He slowly slid one of his curved razor-sharp knives from his inventory. The light from the morning sun reflected off the keen edge of the blade, making it seem to glow with deadly magic. "Maybe there's something I can do to help you remember."

"We aren't gonna hurt him!" Planter snapped, giving Blaster an angry glare. "I know you wouldn't cut him with your knife in cold blood. You're just trying to scare him." She glanced at Watcher, then pointed to the rope.

"Take the rope from Cutter. You and I will watch Er-Lan for a while."

Watcher moved nervously forward and reached out for the rope. Cutter stopped walking for a moment and just stared at Watcher. His steel-gray eyes glared down at the NPC as if he were daring him to take the rope from his grip. Suddenly, Planter moved between them and yanked the rope away, giving it to Watcher.

"Keep moving," the young girl commanded, then moved to the zombie, giving him a gentle push in the back.

The zombie shuffled forward, glancing nervously over his shoulder at Cutter.

Watcher followed Planter, keeping a firm grip on the zombie's leash. After everyone was moving along, Planter stepped to the monster's side.

"You know, we're just worried about our parents and friends, Er-Lan," she said. "This war, or whatever it is . . . it doesn't involve us."

The zombie grumbled something that none of them could really hear. Watcher moved forward to the monster's other side.

"What?" he asked.

"Er-Lan is not a warrior." This time, the zombie's voice was loud enough to be heard, but it was filled with a deep sadness.

"Me neither," Watcher said. "I'm just here because of my father and sister. My sister is named Winger. She's super annoying, always taking my stuff and getting me in trouble. I think, because she's older, Winger likes to boss me around." He paused for a moment as they emerged from the trees and turned to follow the grassy stone trail. "She and my dad Cleric were captured a while ago. I miss them a lot and hope they're okay."

Watcher turned away as thoughts of his family suddenly overwhelmed him with emotions. A faint sound escaped his lips and his sadness grew, but he refused to cry, especially in front of Cutter. Clenching his fists, he dug his fingernails into the palms of his hands, the pain driving away the sorrow. A chuckle came from Cutter as Watcher wiped a lone tear from his cheek.

He imagined himself spinning around and yelling at the warrior. Cutter was just like every other bully in the village—in all the villages, in fact—picking on him because he was small and weak and couldn't hold a sword. He wanted to yell at him, but he was afraid. He felt rage and frustration from years of teasing and bullying and abuse, and wanted to just erupt and let it all out on the big warrior, but Watcher knew he wouldn't do anything. It wasn't his way to just lash out at people, even though everyone did to him. Instead, Watcher liked to think everything through and approach a problem with a calm mind. Some interpreted that to be cowardice on his part, but Watcher knew that wasn't true . . . at least he didn't think it was.

"My mom and dad were also attacked," Planter said. "They were . . ."

She paused for a moment, letting a memory of her parents play through her mind.

"Er-Lan, do you have any family?" Watcher asked.

The zombie looked at Watcher, surprised.

"Of course Er-Lan has a family."

"Well, who are they?" Watcher asked.

"My father is a 'P.' His name is Pe-Lan," Er-Lan said.

"What do you mean a 'P'?" Blaster asked, moving closer, a look of curiosity in his brown eyes.

"A zombie's rank is shown by the first name," Er-Lan explained. "The closer to 'Z,' the higher the rank, but there has not been a 'Z' amongst the zombies for centuries. Er-Lan heard there was once an 'X,' but that was not in the Far Lands."

"So your father is a 'P.' Has he always been a 'P'?" Planter asked.

"Of course not," Er-Lan replied. "When a zombie does some great deed, the clan leader will promote that zombie to a higher rank. My father is Pe-Lan, and my brother is Ko-Lan."

"Lan is your family name?" Mapper asked.

Er-Lan nodded.

"This is all *really* interesting," Cutter said, sarcastically.

"Ignore him." Planter smiled at the zombie.

"Your mother's gone?" Watcher asked.

Er-Lan nodded again, then lowered his gaze to the ground.

"Mine too," Watcher added.

The zombie glanced up at the boy, and for a brief instant, there was a connection between the two of them, a feeling that only comes with shared grief.

"Er-Lan thinks the destination of the warlord might be known," the zombie said in a low voice.

Watcher stopped breathing for just a second. *Did I hear him correctly?* he thought. "What?"

"Er-Lan thinks the warlord is heading for the zombie fortress." The monster's voice grew even softer. "Tu-Kar will go to the old church first, gather all the prisoners, then head for the fortress. All prisoners from all over the Far Lands are being brought to the fortress; there will be many villagers there. That is what Er-Lan thinks."

Cutter moved closer to the zombie, but Planter held up a hand, stopping the warrior. Instead, the big NPC just followed along down the trail, scanning the trees for threats.

"The old zombie fortress," Blaster said. "You mean the one with the two towers on either side of the entrance?"

Er-Lan nodded his scarred green head.

"You know where this place is located?" Cutter asked.

Blaster shrugged. "Maybe. But the problem is that it's a huge place. The villagers could be kept anywhere."

"Er-Lan thinks the warlord will keep the prisoners in the courtyard that sits on one side of the fortress." The zombie looked up at Watcher and the villager gave him a smile. "There is a secret entrance, a hidden entrance. If the villagers enter there, then they can get to the prisoners and escape, if they move quick and quiet."

"And what if we aren't quick and quiet?" Blaster asked.

"A large number of zombies are there, many with armor and iron weapons," Er-Lan explained. "Perhaps sneaking into the courtyard at night will make it safer."

"That's a good plan," Planter patted the monster gently on the back.

Er-Lan flinched at first, then relaxed when he realized it was not an attack.

"But what if he's lying?" Blaster said. "How do we know we can trust this creature?"

"My little friend makes a good point," Cutter replied.

"You have a better idea?" Planter glanced at Cutter, then Blaster, waiting for a reply, then continued. "We can't just charge in there and challenge all of the monsters to a fight."

"You're right," Cutter said. "It would be a disaster with all of you tagging along. Me and Blaster would have to do all the fighting."

Watcher felt the sting of his implied taunt; he wasn't strong enough to help. With a sigh, he lowered his gaze to the ground, feeling frustrated and ashamed, as usual. He felt another tear trying to make its way out of his eye, but Watcher would not set it free. With all his strength, he choked back his emotions and refused to weep in front of the others.

"Then it's a plan," Planter said. "We'll check the church for any villagers and free them if we can. Then we'll go to this zombie fortress and free the rest of the prisoners." She turned to Cutter. "After they're freed, Er-Lan will be released . . . agreed?"

The big warrior glanced at Blaster, then back to Planter.

"Of course . . . the monster will be set free when we save our people." Cutter gave her a wry smile.

For the first time, they had a plan, and it seemed to make the companions feel optimistic. But something about it all nagged at the back of Watcher's mind. There was something amiss here, some flaw in the plan, but he couldn't quite see it. And not knowing seemed to make that uncertainty slowly turn into an unknown and unseen danger, waiting to devour them all.

CHAPTER 14

The sky was alive with color, the reds, oranges and yellows of dawn creating a masterpiece of hues across the eastern horizon.

"That's incredible, don't you think?" Watcher pointed at the rising sun.

"It's just the sun," Cutter grumbled as he walked past.

Watcher shook his head. *All Cutter can see are enemies and battle,* the boy thought. *He's missing everything else around him.* He actually felt sorry for the warrior.

The party moved quietly through the forest, approaching the dilapidated church from the west. They'd traveled along the road for an hour, maybe less, when they saw the tall tower of the church sticking up above the trees. When he saw the structure, Cutter led them off the road and approached from the cover of the forest, hoping to keep any unwanted monsters from spotting the NPCs before the NPCs spotted the monsters.

They moved from tree to tree, using the trunks to hide their presence. Watcher held on to the rope tied around Er-Lan, keeping the monster close. The smell of the creature was terrible, and at times Watcher tried to get upwind from the monster to reduce the odor. Unfortunately, it did little to alleviate the stench.

"Everyone stay here for a minute," Blaster said.

The boy removed his black leather armor and replaced it with armor colored forest green. He then ran toward the edge of the forest, fading into the background. In minutes, he returned with a smile on his square face.

"I don't see any guards around the church," Blaster said. "In fact, the whole place looks deserted. The top floor is dark, but the bottom floor has a huge chandelier hanging from the ceiling. I could see it through the huge windows in the side of the church."

"Hmmm." Cutter turned and faced his prisoner. "Where are all the zombies?"

The zombie shrugged. "Er-Lan does not know. Perhaps they headed for the fortress already, but Tu-Kar had to come here and collect all the NPC prisoners that were already captured. The zombie warlord might still be here with many soldiers." He turned and faced Planter and Watcher. "All must be very careful."

"Great advice." Blaster gave the group a mischievous grin.

"Were there any guards on the entrance to the church?" Cutter asked.

Blaster shook his head. "No, all the entrances were sealed with cobblestone. If we're going in through the main entrance, then we'll have to dig our way through with pickaxes."

"We can't do that—everyone will hear us," Watcher said.

"You have a better idea, professor?" Cutter asked.

Watcher moved to the edge of the forest and looked up at the church and tower. It was built from stone brick, some of the cubes cracked with age, while others were green and mossy. Vines hung down much of the structure, giving it a sad and forgotten look. Dotting the sides of the tower were small pieces of stone and wood that stuck out ever so slightly, likely the remains of some kind of decoration. These strange protrusions wrapped around one of the towers of the church, climbing up the walls until they reached the top. Behind some of the cracked windows torches flickered, casting a warm yellow glow.

Surveying the structure with his keen eyes, Watcher searched for a path that would allow them to gain entrance into the church . . . and then he saw it.

"Of course . . . we can jump," he said to himself.

Turning, he sped back to his friends.

"I figured out a way we can get in without being noticed," Watcher said. "We won't need to dig through any stone and we'll be completely silent."

"Oh really?" Cutter asked. "Tell us your magical strategy."

"Here's what I think we do." Watcher lowered his voice. "We climb up the outside of the tower. There are vines and small blocks we can stand on. We'll use these to climb up the sides of the building, then jump onto the roof. There is an opening on the top floor."

"I like that plan." Planter patted her friend on the back.

Watcher beamed. He felt as if he were charged with electricity.

"What do we do with him?" Blaster asked, pointing at the zombie.

"He stays here." Cutter grabbed Er-Lan and pulled him to a tree, then wrapped a rope around the prisoner and tree, tying him tight. "When we're done, we'll come back and get him, but we aren't gonna have this monster give us away in there."

"Er-Lan will stay quiet," the monster moaned. "It is not necessary to tie up this zombie."

"Be quiet!" Cutter snapped. "You're staying here."

The warrior pulled out a cloth and tied it around the zombie's mouth, making it impossible for him to speak.

Er-Lan looked at Watcher and Planter, his dark eyes pleading for help.

"Don't worry, Er-Lan," Watcher said. "We'll be back for you."

"Yeah," Planter added. "It'll be okay. In no time, we'll return and set you free again."

The monster nodded as a tear slowly dripped from his eyes. Watcher could tell Er-Lan was afraid. Maybe it was fear of being tied up, or being left alone. They had formed a bond with the zombie in their short time together, and found they had more in common than not. Er-Lan, like Watcher, felt alone in his zombie community. Being small and weak, everyone felt the monster was worthless; it was an attitude Watcher knew all too well.

"Just be calm, Er-Lan," Watcher said. "We'll come back soon."

"How cute, the little villager trying to keep the little zombie from being afraid," Cutter said. "How pathetic."

"Be nice," Planter scolded, but Cutter had already turned his back and was heading for the church.

Watcher sighed, then followed the big NPC toward the church tower.

They sprinted across the clearing that circled the structure, each of them glancing to the left and right, watching for monsters. Cutter was the first to reach the building. Instantly, he began climbing the vines that ran down its rocky sides.

"No, not there," Watcher said. "You can't make it to the top from that spot. Over here."

The young NPC ran around the tower until he found the spot he'd identified earlier. The vines led upward to a small piece of stone sticking out of the brick siding of the church. Watcher was the first to climb, scaling the wall as if he were walking down a path. When he reached the end of the vines, Watcher climbed to the top of the stone slab, then sprinted forward a step and jumped out into the open air. He landed on a wooden post that jutted out from the wall, then jumped to the next one, and then the next, slowly rising up the side of the tower. Behind him, his friends were doing the same, Blaster and Planter following along easily. It was like the game they used to play as children, jumping from tree to tree in the forest. But Cutter looked uncertain and afraid, though Watcher knew the big villager would never admit it.

They moved slowly up the side of the tower, switching between the parkour jumps to climbing the vine-covered walls. It was arduous work, Watcher's muscles screaming at him with fatigue. Finally, after one last terrifying leap, Watcher made it from the tower to the sloped roof of the church. There was a small opening near the top that would give them access to the second floor.

"Look out!" Blaster landed with a thud right next to him.

"Thanks for the warning."

Blaster patted him on the back, then scurried up to inclined roof and stood near the opening.

Planter came next. She climbed up the vines that extended up the side of the tower, then pushed off and sailed through the air. Her blond hair flowed like a golden flag as the light of the morning sun reflected off the long strands. Landing with the grace of a dancer, she gave Watcher a smile, then moved quietly up the sloped roof to stand at Blaster's side.

"Come on, Cutter," Watcher said, motioning to the big warrior.

The soldier was to the last jump, but he looked nervous.

"Hurry up. Planter and Blaster are already at the entrance to the second floor. If any zombies spot them, they'll be in trouble. We need you . . . now!"

The warrior gave Watcher a scowl, then grasped the vines. He climbed carefully, a look of apprehension on his square face. At the top of the vine, he paused and glanced down. A fall from this height would likely be fatal. Watcher could see the fear in the big warrior's eyes; he must be afraid of heights.

Watcher reached out a hand. "You can do it."

Cutter glanced at the boy, then gritted his teeth and pushed off from the side of the tower. But when he released the vine, his foot slipped, and he tumbled in the air.

"He's not gonna make it," Planter yelled from behind.

Watcher gripped the edge of a block and extended his body out over the edge of the church roof. He reached out as far as he could. As the big villager came near, Watcher grabbed at his outstretched hand. They met and both held on, but almost immediately, Watcher's grip started to slip; he wasn't strong enough to hold Cutter for long. The weight of the soldier was too much to bear.

"I can't pull you up," Watcher said, gritting his teeth. "You have to climb."

Cutter glanced up at the boy, a look of uncertainty in his eyes. He swung his body until his boots touched the wall, then he used them to push himself up. Climbing Watcher's arm like a rope, he slowly moved higher and higher until Cutter's fingers reached the edge of the stone wall. He grabbed the edge with his other hand then pulled himself upward. With his free hand, Watcher grabbed the edge of Cutter's armor and yanked hard, helping the soldier up onto the ledge. Finally, he made it safely to the top.

"You two done playing around up there?" Blaster asked.

Watcher lay on his back, breathing heavily, sweat dripping down his face. His wrist throbbed with pain, the skin red and sore.

"You okay?" Watcher asked.

Cutter stood up and glanced at his two companions, then back to Watcher. "Why shouldn't I be okay?"

Adjusting his armor, Cutter moved up the sloped roof to the opening where Planter and Blaster stood.

"Hey archer, are you coming or what?" Cutter said.

"Yeah." Watcher sighed, then lowered his voice. "You're welcome." But of course, no one heard him.

Standing, Watcher climbed the sloping roof and stood near his friends. Inside, the church was dark, with only one torch lighting this top floor. Moving to the opening, he listened for monsters but heard nothing.

Cutter pushed his way forward and leaned into the entrance. "I don't hear anything. Let's go in."

"Wait."

Watcher placed a hand on the big warrior's chest. Cutter looked at his small hand, then glared at the boy. Slowly, he removed his hand from the soldier's chest.

"Why should we wait?"

"Can't you smell it?" Watcher asked.

Cutter glanced at Blaster and Planter, then brought his attention back to Watcher. "Smell what?"

Watcher inhaled, then made a disgusted face as the smell of rotten and decaying flesh wafted into his nose. "I smell zombies."

"You smell zombies?"

Watcher nodded.

"Nonsense." Cutter started to charge into the room.

"I think we should go slowly and be careful," Watcher said.

"There's nothing to be afraid of." The warrior gave Watcher a scowl over his shoulder. "I can take care of anything in this building."

"I'm not afraid, I just think we should be cautious and think this through."

"There's time enough to think after all our friends are free," Cutter said with a sneer.

The warrior moved farther into the dark room, the sound of his boots echoing off the walls.

"We should slow down," Watcher whispered, but no one answered.

Cutter moved deeper into the church, Planter and Blaster right on his heels. They passed through a narrow doorway, into the rear of the building. Sunlight streamed through the narrow windows, casting sunlight in spots on the dusty wooden floor. But the rest of the room was cloaked in darkness. It was as if some kind of magical enchantment was present, driving away most of the sun's rays.

The stench of rotten flesh was getting worse.

Just as Watcher was about to take another step, the sound of something sharp scraped across the wooden floor. Everyone froze. Watcher stared into the darkness, looking for movement, but the corners of the room were pitch black, and he couldn't see anything . . . But he knew they were there; the smell was terrible.

"Zombies," Watcher whispered. "They're here, but I can't see any of them."

No one replied.

Blaster removed his forest green armor, and put on his favorite, black. He then darted off into the darkness, his leather boots hardly making a sound. Suddenly, light flared on the opposite side of the room. A torch had been placed on the ground, the burning stick forming a circle of illumination. The light struggled against the darkness, it's radiance weaker than normal. The shuffling of leather scraping the ground off to the right, then another torch came to life. More torches appeared as Blaster darted across the center of the room.

In seconds, the entire center of the room was lit, the walls remaining cloaked in darkness. Still, no zombies could be seen. Blaster put the torches away and drew his two, curved knives.

"I don't think there are any monsters here at all," the boy said.

Just then, a moan floated out from the shadows to the right. It was a sorrowful wail that spoke of pain and suffering, and a hatred of living things. Another came from the left, this one more of a growl than a moan.

"They're along the walls," Watcher said. "I told you I could smell them."

Zombies stepped into the light from the flickering torch. Razor-sharp claws extended from their fingers, reflecting the light from the torches. Sharp claws scratched the ancient floor behind them as more monsters advanced.

"We're . . . surrounded." Planter's voice cracked with fear.

Watcher glanced at the monsters approaching from the right, then turned to those from the left. A group of decaying creatures moved across the floor and blocked the opening they had used to get in. They had nowhere to run . . . they were trapped!

Watcher drew an arrow and notched it to his string but didn't know where to shoot. There were at least a dozen monsters in the room, if not more. It was hopeless. Slowly, the creatures shuffled forward.

Fear lit every nerve, causing Watcher to shake as panic slowly overtook his courage, driving it deeper into the back of his soul. His heart beat faster and faster as his breaths grew shallow. Glancing at Planter, he saw the same expression on her face . . . terror. He'd failed his father and sister, and now he'd led Planter to her doom.

Looking to the left and right, Watcher knew the situation was impossible. This was the end, and all he could do was wait for his doom.

CHAPTER 15

The zombies moved closer, their sad moans getting louder and angrier. Cutter glanced at the others and smiled, then drew his diamond sword and charged forward. At the same time, Blaster dashed between two monsters and disappeared into the darkness along the edge of the room.

Swinging his sword with practiced ease, Cutter tore into the monsters. Zombies screamed in pain, but still drew closer. Planter drew Needle, her blade, then pulled the enchanted shield from her inventory as well. She moved to Cutter's side. Her weapon glowed with a purple luster that made the zombies hesitate for an instant . . . that was their first mistake. Planter took advantage of their hesitancy and attacked. At the same time, Cutter attacked the monsters around him, kicking them aside as he slashed at arms and legs.

Watcher pulled out blocks of cobblestone and built a small tower, three blocks high. He fired his bow from the perch, aiming at monsters sneaking up behind his friends. His bow string hummed as the arrows streaked through the air. The pointed shafts found monster after monster. At times, he pulled out two arrows and notched them at the same time. Firing both, he did double the damage in a single draw.

"Cutter, behind you!" Watcher yelled.

He fired a pair of arrows at a zombie, striking it at the same time as its claws reached out for Cutter. The big warrior ducked, then spun around and struck the monster with his diamond blade. The creature disappeared, a sad moan on the monster's lips.

Suddenly, the approaching horde shouted out in pain, even though they were not within reach of Needle and Cutter's blade. Watcher continued to fire at the monsters, but was surprised by the confusion amidst the zombies.

"Blaster," he whispered.

A zombie charged at Planter. Watcher fired at it before its dark claws could reach his friend. At the same time, Blaster emerged from the darkness and attacked with his curved knives. The monster groaned, then disappeared. Planter glanced over her shoulder and gave Watcher a smile, then charged at a zombie trying to sneak up on her companion.

Cutter and Planter fought side by side while Blaster wove between the monsters, slashing at exposed arms and chests. Watcher's arrows tore into the creatures like deadly hail. With at least ten zombies destroyed, the rest of the horde chose to retreat. They fled out of the room and into one of the towers that loomed high over the structure, their shuffling feet scraping the ground as they ran down its spiral staircase.

Blaster put torches along the walls, lighting the edges of the massive room and checking for any zombies hiding in the shadows. They were all gone.

"We did it!" Planter put away her sword and turned to Cutter. "That was incredible. I was so scared, but I saw you all calm and confident, and I just kept on fighting."

"Did you see how surprised they were when I came out of the darkness?" Blaster removed his black leather cap. "Their eyes got all big and surprised . . . it made me laugh. It reminded me of—"

"We aren't done," Watcher said. He jumped down from his perch and approached his friends.

"What are you talking about?" Cutter put away his diamond sword. "They ran away."

"No, they just went down stairs," Watcher said. "We have to go down there and find our friends and families. Er-Lan said the prisoners were kept in an underground chamber. That means we need to go down stairs and face the ones that are left."

"They won't be that tough," Cutter said. "I think they'll probably just—"

An angry, guttural scream echoed through the church, making the walls of the structure vibrate. The booming voice was piercing, with a gravely, scratchy edge to it.

"What was that?" Planter drew Needle again.

Watcher moved closer to his friends and spoke in a low voice. "We have to go down there, but I don't like the sound of that monster."

"I do," Cutter said. "I recognize that voice—it's been in my nightmares every night." The others looked up at the big NPC. "It's the same monster that slew my friend and commander, Fisher. I'd recognize that voice anywhere." He gripped his sword tight, his knuckles turning white as he squeezed the hilt. "It's time for revenge."

"Wait, we should make a plan." Watcher ran ahead of Cutter, then turned and tried to stop him, but the big warrior just walked past.

"I already have the only plan I need. I'm gonna destroy that zombie so Fisher can finally rest in peace. You can stay here if you're afraid."

"I'm not afraid."

Cutter didn't reply. He just stormed through the room toward the front of the church. A doorway stood open on the left side, leading into one of the two towers that stood on either side of the structure. Stairs went down into the darkness, spiraling to the lower floor. Cutter marched down the steps, a soft, enraged growl coming from between clenched teeth as his feet pounded the stairs.

"They'll know he's coming," Watcher said. "The way he's stomping his feet, it's like he's advertising his arrival."

"What should we do?" Planter asked.

Watcher glanced at her, then turned to Blaster and smiled. "I have a plan."

He quickly explained what he wanted Blaster and Planter to do. They followed Cutter down the stairs, trying to catch up with the big warrior. When they reached the last step, they found Cutter charging through a room filled with tall stone pillars, the chamber surprisingly empty. Before they could reach him, the warrior stormed into the next room. The sound of his blade crashing into armored monsters rang out.

Watcher sprinted past the pillars and slipped quietly through the door into the main hall. He was shocked by what he saw. Cutter was completely surrounded by zombies, his massive diamond blade swinging in great, deadly curves, striking multiple creatures. This was keeping the monsters back for the moment, but Watcher knew the defense couldn't last.

He moved beneath the massive chandelier that hung from the ceiling. Placing blocks of dirt under his feet, he slowly ascended upward until he could jump on the hanging structure. The chandelier was made out of wooden fence, creating a grid of torches that lit the chamber. Watcher moved across the structure, jumping from post to post, avoiding the torches. When he reached his position, he shouted.

"NOW!"

Blaster and Planter charged through the doorway. At the same time, Watcher opened up with his bow. He fired down upon the monsters that were trying to attack Cutter from behind. His arrows rained down upon the creatures, the mob so tightly packed together that he couldn't miss. Cutter never glanced up to see who was helping; he just fought as hard as he could, tearing into the zombies.

Turning his aim to his other friends, Watcher carved a hole through the zombie formation with his pointed shafts, allowing Blaster and Planter to come to the warrior's aid. Blaster's curved knives flashed from monster to monster, and the zombies howled in pain as Needle tore through the decaying creatures with savage precision. Zombie swords swung toward Planter, but her shield seemed to have a mind of its own, moving just in time to block attacks, even though some were coming from behind.

Slowly, the villagers chipped away at the zombie horde. The monsters were clearly growing afraid of the three villagers as they saw how viciously they fought, but many of the creatures were also glancing over their shoulders at their general, screaming commands at them.

"Fight harder, fools." The zombie commander stomped back and forth through the shadows. "Destroy the villagers. Let none survive."

With a great swing of his diamond blade, Cutter carved through the remaining zombies before him, leaving the rest of the creatures for his companions. The gap in the monster horde allowed the big warrior to pursue his true enemy.

"Where is the zombie coward that took the life of my friend?" Cutter stormed through the zombie lines, knocking arrows out of the air.

Watcher turned and found a group of skeletons on the side of the room. Quickly, he fired on them, sending a stream of arrows at the bony creatures, their return fire sticking to the chandelier and leaving Watcher untouched.

"Are you hiding, coward?" Cutter bellowed. "You ran from me once in the forest. Do you have the courage to face me now?"

Watcher peered into the darkness at the far end of the chamber; a similar enchantment as the one on the upper floor bathed the far side of the room in shadow.

"Where are you, zombie?"

"So, the villager returns after the last failure in the forest," a deep, scratchy voice said from the darkness.

Watcher leapt down from the chandelier and moved near Cutter, watching his back. The remaining zombies were finally destroyed, allowing Planter and Blaster to stand with Cutter.

"Come out and face me, zombie. You don't have all your pathetic soldiers to protect you this time. Fisher's diamond sword thirsts for revenge."

The zombie stepped into the light, his dark eyes fixed on the blade in Cutter's hand. A thin line of dark hair ran along his bald head and down the back, the bristly strands standing straight up like tiny spikes. He wore iron armor that was ornately decorated with sweeping curves and dark ridges, thin lines of magical enhancements running across the metallic surface like arteries pumping blood.

Watcher gasped when he saw the armor; it looked like a relic from the ancient times in the Far Lands; Cutter had to be careful.

"Yes . . . Ro-Zar remembers that pathetic villager begging for mercy after being abandoned." The zombie general stepped forward and drew his enchanted iron sword. The glowing blade splashed iridescent light on the walls of the abandoned church.

"I didn't abandon him!"

"That villager had to fight alone, I remember." He took another step forward. "Explain, villager, how was it that Ro-Zar could so easily deliver the fatal blow to your comrade? Was it because the doomed villager was alone, with no one to watch his back?"

"No!" Cutter shouted.

The zombie laughed. "First this warrior abandons his friend in the forest, and now he leads these villagers with him to their doom. Who is the bigger fool: the one that leads his friends to their destruction, or the idiotic NPCs that follow him?" He glanced at the shadows to his left and right. "Skeletons!"

The clattering of bones filled the room as a group of skeletons emerged from the darkness. Watcher and his companions gasped. At least six of the creatures moved into the light, their bony faces all staring at Cutter.

"Oh no," Watcher said.

Cutter glanced over his shoulder and glared at Watcher, but the young archer ignored the warrior. Instead, he glanced at the skeletons, taking careful note of their positions, before turning to sprint for the shadows near the wall.

"It figures," Cutter growled. "I always knew you were a coward, Watcher."

"Ha ha ha," Ro-Zar laughed. "Now, it is time for your destruction. Skeletons . . . ready." The skeletons raised their bows. "Aim . . ." They drew back their arrows and pointed them at Cutter.

Suddenly, Watcher's pointed shafts streaked out of the darkness. He stood on a small tower he built, and was firing as fast as he could draw his string back. The skeletons were shocked by the sudden barrage and returned fire into the darkness, even though they were not sure where their target was standing.

Cutter and Blaster took advantage of the confusion and charged at the bony monsters. Blaster disappeared into the shadows, slashing at the skeletons while Planter advanced, arrows bouncing off her glowing green and white shield. A few arrows clanged harmlessly off Cutter's iron chest plate, and the NPC ignored him. His eyes were glued to Ro-Zar as he advanced.

Their swords clashed together, making a deafening sound that shook the entire church. The monster tried to kick at Cutter with a booted foot, but the big warrior stepped out of the way. His diamond sword flashed through the air, striking the monster's ornate, iron armor.

"You have no place to run this time, zombie," Cutter growled.

Ro-Zar moaned, lowering his guard for just an instant. When Cutter advanced, the zombie stepped to the side and brought his sword down onto Cutter's shoulder. The NPC screamed out in pain, then blocked another attack as he moved away.

While the two behemoths battled, Blaster tore into the skeleton's HP while Watcher fired down upon them. Planter, with Needle held out before her, ran toward the skeletons.

"Planter . . . no!" Watcher screamed.

But she didn't heed his warning. Instead, she charged at the monsters. Some of the skeletons turned their bows from Watcher to her, but her shield was nearly impenetrable. She crashed into the monsters, using her shield as a battering ram, knocking monsters to the ground. With a flick of her wrist, she moved her narrow blade at incredible blades, knocking the arrows from the air. Slashing with all her strength, the young girl fell upon the closest skeleton, tearing into the monster's HP. The skeleton tried to fire back in defense, but her sword was too quick, swatting away the projectiles like harmless flies. With one last swing of Needle, Planter took the last of the monster's HP. Screaming out in pain and despair, he disappeared with a pop, confusion and sadness in his dark eyes.

Watcher fired at the next skeleton, his arrow destroying that monster's HP. Without hesitation, he turned his bow to the other skeletons while Blaster worked on them from behind. In a minute, all the skeletons in the room were destroyed, leaving only the general and Cutter, locked in a dance of death.

Notching an arrow to his bowstring, Watcher drew it back and aimed at the commander, but the combatants were moving around too quickly; he was unable to get a clear shot off.

Jumping down from his perch, he approached with

an arrow ready to fire. Cutter saw him out of the corner of his eye and shook his head.

"None of you interfere," the big warrior commanded. "This monster is mine. I'm the one that will punish him for hurting all those villagers."

The zombie growled, then lunged at Cutter's chest. The villager spun to the side, deflecting the sword with his diamond blade, then slashed at the beast. Ro-Zar retreated, bringing his sword up in defense, but Cutter's blade was already there. Watcher looked on in amazement as Cutter advanced with a flurry of attacks that were so fast they were difficult to even see.

The general kept retreating, but he had no place to go. Cutter kept up the attack, slowly destroying the monster's ancient armor. The iron chest plate fell to the ground, a large section cracking into pieces. Pushing his attack, the NPC continued to strike the zombie, tearing into his iron leggings, then attacking the monster's chest and side. Screams of pain filled the chamber as the two warriors battled, the zombie landing the occasional hit on Cutter, but the villager connecting four times for every one he received.

Finally, with the zombie on his last legs, Cutter knocked the monster's enchanted sword from his hands. It skidded across the ground. "You move and it's over," Cutter said in a loud voice.

The zombie general froze in place and waited for the final blow to arrive.

"We have questions, zombie," Blaster said. "And if you answer them, you will survive to see another day. But if you lie to us, it will go poorly for you."

Cutter stepped forward and kicked the monster's fallen chest plate across the room. It skidded across the wooden floor, then clunked into the wall. Putting his diamond sword back into his inventory, the big NPC moved closer to the zombie general, a look of anger glowing in his steel-gray eyes.

"Are the prisoners still here?" Cutter asked.

"Go look and see what you find." Ro-Zar's raspy voice was weak.

Blaster pressed one of his knives against the zombie's side, reminding the monster of its sharp tip.

Blaster whispered into the monster's ear. "Answer him."

The zombie general mumbled something, but it was too soft to hear. Ro-Zar looked up at Cutter, then mouthed something so quietly that it was barely a trickle of sound out of the zombie's mouth.

"What did you say?" Cutter asked.

The zombie mumbled again, his deep, guttural voice impossible to understand.

Cutter moved closer as the monster general continued to mumble. He turned his head to bring his ear close, straining to hear. Suddenly, Ro-Zar shoved Blaster backward, hard, sending him flying. He then reached into his inventory and drew another iron sword with lightning speed. He raised the weapon, its keen edge heading for Cutter before the big warrior could draw his diamond sword.

Suddenly, an arrow zipped in front of Cutter and hit the zombie. It was followed by two more shafts, piercing the last of the general's HP. He disappeared with a pop, a confused look being the last thing that was on his scarred face, his sword clattering to the floor.

Cutter turned and glared at Watcher. "I was supposed to be the one to destroy him."

"He would have hit you with his sword. I just fired out on instinct."

The warrior glared at Watcher, anger filling his eyes. "Well, next time, have a little better control of your instincts."

The big NPC stood and stomped away.

Blaster moved to the zombie's iron sword and put it into his inventory, then kicked the enchanted blade to Watcher.

"What am I supposed to do with that?"

Blaster shrugged. "There might come a time when you need a sword. It's better to have one and not need it, than the other way around."

"I guess." Watcher bent over and picked up the blade, then stuck it into his inventory.

"There's a set of stairs over here," Cutter said from the far side of the church. "I'm going down to check it out. Maybe that's where all the prisoners are being kept."

"Wait for us," Watcher said, even though he knew Cutter wouldn't listen.

The three companions ran to the far side of the church. In the corner, they found a tunnel carved in the floor, plunging into the darkness. There were no torches in the passage, and only the sound of Cutter's descending boots floated up from the opening.

"I guess we need to go down and see if any of our friends or families are still there," Watcher said.

He glanced at Planter. The expression on her face mirrored his own . . . *What if they were . . . dead?* The thought pounded away at his courage, but he knew they had to find out. Gripping his bow tight in his hand, he took a first step, but before he'd gone further, Cutter emerged from the shadows, an expression of frustration and anger on his square face.

"It's empty," the warrior said. "They're all gone."

"What?" Watcher's hopes sank. "My dad and sister?"

"I told you, there's nothing down there." Cutter stepped out of the stairway, Watcher on his heels. "No villagers and no items. The zombies already took the prisoners to their next destination."

"The zombie fortress," Blaster said.

"Probably." Cutter glared at Watcher. "And our zombie prisoner is gonna take us there. Now let's get going. We still have a warlord to catch."

CHAPTER 16

Tu-Kar watched as a zombie guard swung his sword at the villager, hitting the exhausted captive with the flat side of the blade and making him stumble to the ground. An NPC with long brown hair, a young girl, reached down and helped the man to his feet. She then slung an arm over her shoulders and helped him to walk.

The collection of prisoners had grown since the last two raids. Other zombie groups had brought their prisoners to the church, as instructed, adding to the total number. Now, the prisoners neared a hundred in size, almost as many as the zombies.

If they try to rise up and fight, it will be difficult stopping them, Tu-Kar thought. The zombie warlord glared at the rabble as they passed, each NPC averting their eyes.

He chuckled at their cowardice.

"These prisoners move too slow." Tu-Kar turned to one of his zombie generals. "They must be made to move faster."

"It is the weak and injured that slow progress." The commander stood tall in his iron armor, a razor-sharp blade in his hand. "If the army goes too fast, some will die."

"Tu-Kar does not care! The army will reach the zombie fortress soon, but many of these villagers will be too weak to be of any use to Kaza. It will be dangerous if the zombies bring that hateful king NPCs that cannot dig and tunnel."

"Why must the prisoners be brought to Kaza?" the general asked.

"Tu-Kar thought the arrangement was clear," the zombie warlord replied.

The zombie just shrugged, his tiny brain apparently unable to remember the plan.

"The more gold that is given to Kaza, the more iron weapons and armor are given to the zombies," Tu-Kar said. "When the zombie army has enough iron for all warriors, then Tu-Kar will lead the horde across the Far Lands, and take over everything. With this enchanted chain mail that was a gift from Kaza, all zombies will work together and flock to my side. Soon, we will have the greatest zombie army ever seen in the Far Lands.

"From the ancient histories, it is known that the villagers have risen up against the monsters countless times. Tu-Kar will not let the NPCs sneak up on our zombie-towns and attack our wives and children. This time, the zombie nation will be ready. Keeping our families safe from the aggression of the villagers means everything, and Tu-Kar is going to make it happen. But to defeat the villagers and the other monsters, weapons and armor are needed. Kaza is the key to getting what we need."

"This zombie understands," the general said, though Tu-Kar could see the idiotic monster was still confused.

It's too bad this magical chain mail couldn't make the zombies smarter as well as obedient, the zombie warlord thought.

"We must move quicker. Tu-Kar has a command for all zombies." The warlord's enchanted chain mail grew bright as he spoke the order. "If there are any villagers too weak to walk or to work, they are to be left behind. Let them starve."

His armor pulsed once, sending the command to all his zombies. Instantly, the monsters began pulling the elderly and the grievously wounded villagers out of formation, then pushed them to the edge of the road.

Tu-Kar turned and scanned his collection of prisoners. He spotted an old man that was nearly bald, a paltry ring of gray hair around the edge of his scalp. A tall villager in a cleric's smock, white with a gray stripe, and a young girl dressed in forest green with a brown stripe, were helping the old man to walk, but it was slow progress. "There, that one," Tu-Kar said, pointing with a sharp black claw. "Leave that one behind."

A group of zombies approached and yanked the old man from the formation and shoved him to the ground.

"Please, leave us some food," one of the wounded villagers said.

"Food . . . ha." Tu-Kar pointed his iron sword at the exhausted NPCs. "No stew for you!" The zombie glanced at the guards. "Give none of the decrepit villagers any stew nor bread; it will not be wasted on those that cannot work." He glared at the discarded prisoners. "Blame your ancestors for attacking the monsters over and over. It's time for payback."

The warlord motioned to one of the zombies. The creature approached the villager, then kicked him hard with his iron boot. The NPC fell back, flashing red one last time, then disappeared.

"Archer . . . NO!" An NPC woman started to run to the fallen villager, but her friends held her back.

Tu-Kar glared at the woman, pointing at her with a dark claw. He then spoke in a low, raspy voice, but none had trouble hearing his words. "Get back in line and keep walking."

The other villagers quickly pulled the woman to them, then turned and continued walking down the road, the zombie guards around them growling and moaning.

"Make them speed up," the warlord shouted. "These

prisoners are due at our fortress, and nothing will be allowed to delay us, not even the life of a villager."

The zombies growled excitedly, then poked the prisoners with the tips of their claws, urging them toward their doom.

CHAPTER 17

Blaster, in his green leather armor, ran silently ahead of the company, looking for threats along the grassy trail. After leaving the church, they quickly found evidence of the zombie horde. Now they followed the monster trail, moving fast to catch up to their prey.

Footprints from the zombies were clearly evident on the ground, their clawed feet tearing tufts of grass from the soil, leaving them scattered about. He was about to run farther ahead when a moaning sound floated out of the forest. He glanced back at Cutter, then drew his knives and crossed them over his head.

Instantly, the other three ran forward with weapons drawn. Cutter charged down the center of the road while Planter took the right side, leaving Watcher to the left. The archer pulled on the rope tied to Er-Lan, forcing the zombie to keep up.

"What is it?" Cutter whispered as he neared.

"I heard moaning in the forest, over there." Blaster pointed with one of his knives.

Then the moan came to them again.

"That is not a zombie moan," Er-Lan whispered to Watcher.

The boy pulled the zombie to Planter, then handed her the rope.

"Er-Lan says it's not a zombie." Watcher drew an arrow and notched it to his bow. "It must be a villager who needs help."

"Don't believe anything that zombie tells you." Cutter glared at the creature. "All those creatures can do is lie."

But Watcher didn't wait. He moved into the woods, his sharp eyes searching the shadows for movement. A green shape streaked through the forest to the left; Watcher figured it was Blaster. Stepping carefully around shrubs and fallen branches, he continued his quiet approach. Light from the afternoon sun streamed through the overhead foliage, at times looking like shafts of gold as they pierced the canopy. All the animals in the forest seemed eerily quiet as the rustling leaves stilled; it was as if the forest itself was holding its breath. But then, the sound of banging iron broke the silence as Cutter blundered ahead, his armor like a loud bell.

A weak voice spoke out. "Over here."

Watcher turned toward the sound and approached, arrow ready to fire.

"It might be a trap," a voice said next to him.

Glancing over his shoulder, he found Blaster grinning at him, his green armor merging almost completely with the leafy background.

They approached the voice, weapons held at the ready. The sounds of clanking iron moved away; likely Cutter hadn't heard the voice with all the noise he was making.

"I'm here."

Blaster turned and sprinted off to the right, circling around the voice while Watcher kept going straight. A trickling of water could be heard over the rustling of the leaves; a stream flowed nearby. Watcher moved behind a large oak, then peered around the trunk. There was movement on the banks of the stream ahead. He ran to the next tree, carefully stepping around leaves and twigs. The sound of the stream was getting louder.

"Help me. If someone's there, please . . . I need help."

Watcher stepped around the tree and moved into the clearing that lined the banks of the stream. He pulled his bowstring back, ready to fire. Then he stepped out from behind the tree and took aim.

Lying near the edge of the stream was an old man dressed in a tan smock, a red stripe running down the center. He was almost completely bald, with a thin ring of gray hair running around the sides and back of his head. By the clothing, Watcher knew this was a mapper.

Slowly, he approached, glancing at the shadowy woods surrounding them.

"You heard me . . . thank you," Mapper said. "I didn't know how long I would last. My health is almost—"

Blaster crashed through the trees behind the old man, startling him.

"There's nothing else around." He put away his curved knives and took off the green leather cap. "We're safe here."

Watcher lowered his bow, then rushed to the old man's side as he shouted, "Planter, Cutter, we're over here. Come quick."

The boy pulled out a piece of steak and handed it to the old man, then offered him a loaf of bread. Mapper devoured the food like he hadn't eaten in weeks.

"Are you okay?" Watcher placed a block of wool on the ground, then helped the man lean against it. "What happened to you?"

"Well, you see . . ."

"Maybe we should wait for the others," Blaster said.

"Good idea."

The sound of clanking iron grew louder.

"Over here . . . we're over here." Blaster banged on the side of a tree with the hilt of a knife. It made a dull thud that was easy to hear.

Cutter crashed through the undergrowth, his diamond blade held ready for battle. When the warrior saw the two youths on the ground next to an old man, he put away his weapon with a sneer.

"I thought there were monsters around."

"You *always* think that," Watcher said quietly. Blaster elbowed him in the ribs.

Twigs broke and leaves were crushed as the sound of shuffling feet reached them. Cutter drew his weapons again, but Watcher only stood and waited. He could smell Er-Lan approaching and knew Planter would be with him.

She emerged from the shadows with the zombie in tow, her blond hair glowing in the light of the afternoon sun. When she saw the old mapper on the ground, Planter tossed Cutter the end of the rope leading to Er-Lan. She ran to the man's side and knelt, checking him for wounds.

"I'm all right, child, just bruised and hungry." Mapper took another bite from the bread, then accepted a bottle of water from Blaster. "There were some much worse off than me. They didn't last very long."

"What happened to you?" Planter asked.

Mapper glanced at Er-Lan, then spoke in a low voice. "The zombies . . . they attacked my village."

"We know, they attacked ours as well," Blaster said.

"After the attack, they rounded up all the villagers and sent us on a forced march through the forest. Some NPCs tried to make a run for it, but without any weapons, they didn't stand a chance." Mapper stopped for another bite of bread, then continued. "We ended up in the basement of an old church. I think that structure was left over from the ancient times. By the architecture of that building, I think it was one of the old wizards' meeting places. You can tell from the—"

"Enough with the history lesson," Cutter interrupted. "How did you end up here?"

Mapper glanced up at the big warrior, a concerned look on his wrinkled face. "They're running out of food."

"What?"

"The captive villagers . . . they're running out of food." Mapper struggled to his feet, Watcher and Blaster offering help. "That terrible zombie warlord . . . I don't remember his name—"

"Tu-Kar," Er-Lan said.

"Right . . . Tu-Kar, that's it. Anyway, he took the old and the wounded, and just left them on the roadside. He said if a villager wasn't strong enough to work, then they wouldn't waste any stew on them. So they threw all of us to the edge of the trail, leaving us to starve. I think I'm the only one that survived. If you hadn't come along when you did, I'm sure I would have died as well."

"That Tu-Kar is despicable," Planter said.

"On that we can agree, child." Mapper pointed to Er-Lan. "You seem to have a zombie with you . . . there must be an interesting story there."

"Er-Lan is a friend," Watcher said. "He's helping us find the captive villagers."

"He's a friend, yet you have him tied up?" Mapper turned his gaze to Watcher, the old man's brown eyes, with their flecks of gold, boring into the young boy.

"Well, we thought it best to play it safe and—"

"The villagers do not trust Er-Lan," the zombie said. "It is understandable. Zombies and villagers have many differences."

"Like how they smell," Cutter said. "And you stink. It's time for a bath."

The big warrior pulled Er-Lan to the stream, then shoved him into the chilly water. The zombie splashed water in all directions, struggling to keep his head above the surface.

Planter rushed to the zombie's aid. "He'll drown with his arms tied to his sides." She splashed into the stream and pulled the creature's head out of the water.

Cutter waded into the stream and rubbed his hands across the monster's clothing, knocking loose pieces of dirt and filth that had long been stuck to him.

"Be careful," Planter complained.

"I'll be careful after the stink is gone from this zombie." Cutter rubbed harder, using the nails on his stubby, square fingers to dislodge clumps of dirt from the monster's pants and shirt.

Satisfied with his work, Cutter then dragged Er-Lan from the stream and let him lie on the grass to dry in the sunlight.

"That was mean," Planter complained.

"It's just a zombie . . . who cares?"

"*We* care." Watcher moved to the zombie's side. "All living creatures deserve to be treated with respect."

"Tell that to all the villagers who died at the hands of these zombies," Cutter replied.

"Er-Lan is not a fighter." The little zombie stared up at Cutter, then cast a glance to Planter and Watcher. "Er-Lan has never been a fighter. That is why Er-Lan is homeless. Brother and father were great warriors, but not Er-Lan. This body and these arms were always too small and too weak to be of any value to the clan." The zombie sighed and glanced down at the ground. "Father and brother, Pe-Lan and Ko-Lan, say Er-Lan is a disgrace to the family and to the clan. They say Er-Lan is not worthy to carry the name Lan, but it cannot be changed according to zombie law."

"That's a terrible thing to say to a family member." Planter put a reassuring hand on the monster's shoulder. "I'm sure they didn't mean it."

The zombie shook his head. "It was meant. Pe-Lan told this zombie to leave the family home. They blame Er-Lan for not defending mother in the last spider attack."

"Your mother was killed by spiders?" Watcher asked.

The zombie nodded. "They discovered the entrance to our zombie-town and attacked. Er-Lan was fixing the water supply, making it flow more efficiently so the clan might have more clean water. The attack happened on the opposite side of the cave, where the zombie-town resides. By the time Er-Lan reached our home, mother was grievously wounded. She died in Er-Lan's arms."

"Er-Lan, that's terrible." Planter put her arms around the zombie and gave him a hug. "It wasn't your fault."

The zombie sighed. "Er-Lan knows that, but father and brother felt differently, and demanded this zombie leave the zombie-town. After wandering the forest alone for a long time, Er-Lan found the zombie warlord. Tu-Kar forced Er-Lan to be a part of his zombie army."

"I'm so sorry that happened to your mother," Watcher said. "That must have been terrible."

The zombie nodded. "But the strange thing was what mother said before her death."

Er-Lan struggled to his feet, then shook loose the last of the water that dripped from his clothing.

"Well?" Blaster took a step closer. "What did she say?"

"She said, 'Value should not be judged by the sharpness of one's claws, but by the sharpness of one's mind. The zombie nation will soon need thinkers and not fighters. Remember that when the time comes for you to choose the right path.' And then she died. Er-Lan has pondered her last words, but is unsure as to her real message."

Planter put an arm around the zombie's shoulder. "That is so sad."

Er-Lan nodded.

"I think it's clear what she was trying to say," Mapper said. "Worth should not be based on strength or skill in fighting. It should be based on what you can create with your mind. Destruction is always easier than creation; if we focus on the sword, then we will only be left with ashes."

"That's ridiculous," Cutter said.

"No, it's not." Watcher stood tall, glaring at the NPC. "Each of us have a skill that can help others. If all we do is focus on fighting, and not solving the problems before us, then we are lost."

"Ha ha." Cutter laughed a sarcastic laugh. "How did your skill help people when we were surrounded by zombies? Your little bow is useful when things are far away, but face-to-face, it's worthless. The real measure of a villager is what they do when the enemy is standing up close, and you're staring into their hateful eyes. If you can't push back when they're within arm's reach, then you aren't very important."

"Sometimes, true capabilities remain hidden until needed," Mapper said. "Sometimes, we don't know what we can do until we are called upon to act. Then, it is not the strength of our arms that is important; rather, it is the strength of our character."

"I can't believe we're wasting time with this discussion." Cutter grabbed the rope wrapped around Er-Lan and tossed it to Mapper. "It seems everyone is rested, and the zombie no longer stinks. We're heading for the zombie fortress, and your little friend is going to show us the way." He gave Er-Lan a hateful stare. "If you play any tricks, I'll make sure you will suffer."

"If we're not careful, I fear *all* of us will suffer," Watcher said.

Cutter glared at the archer, then turned and headed back to the stony trail, the rest of the party following, all of them knowing they were heading toward danger.

CHAPTER 18

The party followed Er-Lan along the forest trail as the sun gradually sank in the west. The trees cast long shadows across the rocky path, giving it a striped appearance that looked odd in the distance. Ahead, a large hill jutted up from the forest, the path climbing up the side and disappearing over the top.

"The fortress is just beyond that hill," the zombie said.

"How do we know you aren't leading us into a trap?" Cutter drew his diamond sword and pointed it at the monster.

Er-Lan glanced at the weapon. His dark eyes seemed to light up for just an instant, but then he looked at Watcher and Planter and sighed.

"This zombie does not want violence. These villagers have been nice to Er-Lan. Only desire is to find their families and friends. Er-Lan wants peace between zombies and NPCs, not war."

"That's a very reasonable thing to strive for, Er-Lan." Mapper had been tasked with holding on to the monster's leash. "Soon, when we find our friends, you will be free to go on your own way. Maybe go back to your home in your zombie-town."

"Er-Lan has no home."

"That's so sad," Planter said.

"Don't feel sorry for it," Cutter snapped. "None of them can be trusted. His monsters attacked our villagers and took our friends captive. I don't believe for a minute that he wasn't involved. Zombies can't be trusted . . . they can never be trusted."

"Maybe we should keep our voices down," Blaster said. "There could be monsters anywhere around us."

Watcher nodded, then glanced at Cutter, speaking softly. "He's right, we need to keep our voices down."

"Okay, we go up the hill, quick and quiet," the warrior whispered.

They climbed the hill, jumping from block to block, the sounds of the forest and the clanking of Cutter's armor the only thing they could hear. Cows mooed somewhere off to the left. The leaves rustled on the oaks. Tree branches creaked as they bent in the wind. It was all peaceful and calm, but knowing there was a zombie fortress nearby made the quietude seem almost frightening.

"Why can't we hear any monsters?" Planter asked in a low voice.

Watcher shrugged, then whispered. "Maybe we got here before they did?"

"I'm gonna go ahead and look around." Blaster put on his green leather cap, then darted up the hill, his armor allowing him to merge with the grass as if he were a ghost.

When they reached the top of the Hill, Watcher glanced around at the forest. The trees were densely packed, as was common in the Far Lands. Patches of oak trees butted up against sections of spruce, with the bright green of jungle wood trees peeking through the haze in the distance. The square face of the sun was beginning its gentle caress of the western horizon, the sky blushing a deep crimson, while stars peeked through the darkening sky to the east.

"Stop the sightseeing and get moving," Cutter's deep voice said.

Turning, Watcher followed the stony trail. It led down into a narrow valley with trees lining the steep slopes. The grass between the stone blocks that made up the trail was trampled by many feet, the blades still bent and struggling to stand tall again.

"Look at the grass," Watcher whispered. "A lot of creatures came by here recently."

"It's probably the zombies and their prisoners." Cutter glared at Er-Lan. "Our friends better be okay."

The zombie remained silent.

The companions followed the trail through the valley, the sides walled in with trees. Moonlight from the east cast a silvery light on the landscape, giving it an almost magical appearance, but it did nothing to ease their tension over the eerie silence that had gripped the terrain. Watcher's eyes darted about the area, looking for movement. Images of monsters emerging from behind trees and bushes flitted through his mind. They drove his fear to even higher levels, making the boy's nerves feel stretched to their limits.

"Look, up ahead." Planter drew Needle from her inventory. The purple glow of the enchanted relic lit the ground around her feet.

Watcher moved to her side. The valley ended at what looked like the gates to a gigantic castle. Two huge towers stood on either side of the valley, the cobblestone structures cracked from lack of care. A gigantic opening stood in the center of the wall, the remnants of some kind of gigantic iron gate hanging along the sides of the opening, the rest of the barricade destroyed by the ravages of time.

They passed through the gate and were shocked by what they saw. Sitting on a large grassy plane was a massive fortress with fortified walls ringing the structure, turrets dominating the corners. Parts of the wall were collapsed, the blocks lying on the ground in disheveled piles. Tall grass covered the grounds, making it easy for the party to move unseen. They ran along the edge, using the oak trees and thick foliage for cover. As they moved around the corner of the building, Watcher spotted a hole in the ancient wall.

"There, we can get in there." Watcher pointed with his bow.

He sprinted for the opening, the rest of the companions following closely behind. The hole looked as if some gigantic beast had taken a bite out of the structure.

When they moved through the broken wall and into the actual castle grounds, the stench of zombies became overpowering; there were clearly a lot of monsters nearby. A large doorway stood off to the right, and through the opening, dark wooden steps led up into the castle. To the left, an old stable stood tucked into the side of the castle. No horses remained, having likely fled long ago. Along the wall to the left, another opening led to a curving passage that quickly disappeared into shadows, the whole structure ominously silent.

"I wonder if this was the Wizard's Keep we read about in school?" Watcher asked.

"You mean the one where the Great War started?" Planter said.

Watcher nodded.

"Quit it with the history lesson. All that matters is finding a way to sneak in." Cutter shoved his way past Mapper and Er-Lan and stood at Planter's side.

"The passage to the left will lead to the back of the castle." Er-Lan pointed with a sharp claw.

"You mean the dark and scary passage?" Blaster asked.

The little zombie nodded. "It will lead to the back courtyard."

Before anyone could move, a growling sound came from the flight of stairs to the right. They could hear clawed feet scraping across the wooden steps and a group of zombies approaching.

"Quick! Follow me." Watcher sprinted into the dark tunnel, the others following.

They sprinted through the curving passage, and the sound of zombies slowly grew quiet behind them. The corridor ended in a large courtyard. Steep walls ringed the area, a huge opening carved into the tallest side. Wide steps led through the opening with a large balcony overhead, shielding the entrance from the elements. Strong iron bars ringed its sides, giving it the appearance of a large jail cell.

"I think I saw something moving up there, in the balcony," Blaster said.

Watcher looked where he was pointing with his curved knife. And then he saw it for himself; there was something behind those bars. Was it one of the NPC prisoners?

Er-Lan moved to the boy's side in the courtyard. "This is the rear entrance to the castle. Possibly, entrance can be gained here if all are quiet." He pointed to the huge opening in the wall.

A series of steps led to a raised porch made from black and purple blocks of obsidian. The darkness seemed to hug close to the obsidian, merging with the shadows. Glancing over his shoulder, Watcher spotted a large gate that opened in the fortified wall, leading to a narrow trail. The path led away from the castle and into the darkness.

Planter moved next to Watcher, Needle held firmly in her hand. The enchantment from the weapon cast a purple glow across her beautiful face. Watcher glanced at her and could see her eyes were filled with fear.

"Don't worry, Planter. It'll be all right," Watcher said.

"Be quiet," Cutter whispered, giving the archer a scowl.

Watcher wanted to return the look, but instead just turned away.

They moved closer to the obsidian platform, each of them peering into the darkness, looking for threats. As Watcher slowly crept closer, he thought he smelled something rotten, but figured it was probably just Er-Lan.

That bath seemed to erase the stench from Er-Lan, Watcher thought. *So why would I be smelling him now?*

"Oh no," he whispered.

"What is it?" Planter asked.

"Zombies."

Suddenly, a dozen monsters charged out of the opening in the huge wall, their clawed feet scraping against the hard, obsidian surface. The monsters growled and snarled as they approached, many wearing iron or chain mail armor. Some held swords while others had bright shining axes. They charged straight at the intruders, hateful expressions on their scarred faces.

Cutter didn't hesitate. He stormed straight at them, swinging to the left, then lunging to the right. Blaster snuck around the monsters' flank, then attacked them from behind while Planter moved to Cutter's side, her sword and shield held at the ready.

Watcher pulled out blocks of dirt and placed them under his feet, forming a small tower. From there he fired upon the monsters, his bow string singing. He drew two arrows and let them go at the same time, the shafts easily finding targets amidst the horde. Drawing another arrow back, Watcher fired at a zombie approaching Planter from the side. She likely didn't see the monster. He quickly fired twice more, silencing the monster, then turning toward Cutter to attack a monster to the left of the NPC. Watcher's arrows took HP from the zombies before the defenders, making it possible for Cutter and Planter to destroy them with a single strike.

In minutes, the zombies were destroyed, leaving behind many glowing balls of XP and discarded weapons and armor.

"That wasn't so bad," Blaster said with a smile.

Suddenly, a hacking, scratchy sort of laugh floated across the clearing. It had a vile, angry feel to it, as if that laugh had never known joy, only pain. Watcher's nerves felt electrified as panic filled his mind. His heart pounded in his chest as he held his breath, afraid the wheezing sound might give him away.

"That was just the beginning," the scratchy voice growled.

Torches burst into life all along the top of the wall that ringed the courtyard. Each circle of light revealed multiple zombies. They growled from atop the battlement, their dark claws glistening in the flickering light. More torches ignited along the back of the fortress, showing a huge zombie wearing enchanted chain mail. It sparkled with an iridescent glow, as if it were made from a million glittering stars. The monster had a long scar running down one side of its face, one damaged eye milky white, the other black as pitch.

A group of zombies stepped through the opening, each wielding an iron sword and wearing armor. They growled as they stepped into the torch light, hateful expressions on their scarred faces.

Watcher glanced around, terrified.

"What do we do?" Planter asked.

"There's too many of them," Blaster said, his black armor now visible in the torchlight.

More torches burst into life in the enclosed balcony. NPC prisoners stood silent in the barred cell, staring down helplessly at the small party, their monstrous guards glaring at them with weapons drawn. Watcher saw his father and sister in the crowd, their faces covered with tears; they knew what was about to happen, and they were already mourning.

"I think this is . . . the end," Watcher said, shaking with fear as the zombie warlord focused his hateful stare upon him.

CHAPTER 19

The zombies ringing the courtyard gave off an angry growl that was half moan and half excited wail. Watcher glanced at Er-Lan, who was now lying on the ground mumbling to himself.

"Please . . . not Er-Lan's fault," the zombie wept. "Surrender and be safe."

Cutter glared at the little zombie, then turned and faced the zombie warlord. He pointed at the monster with his sword.

"Ahhh . . . the diamond sword. Er-Lan did well to bring it here." The warlord laughed another hacking, raspy laugh. "Tu-Kar thought it was time to destroy Er-Lan, but now that this great diamond sword has been brought to the zombie warlord, all is forgiven. Welcome home, Er-Lan."

"No . . . no, Er-Lan not home. Er-Lan *was* home with new friends." The zombie looked up at Watcher and Planter, an expression of despair on his green face. "No betrayal, only wanted to help find families and friends."

"Well, we found them all right," Blaster said, staring up at the balcony.

"You see, never trust a zombie." Cutter glared at

Watcher. "All they do is lie and cheat . . . they should be exterminated."

"Ha . . . good luck with that." The zombie warlord stepped forward, his enchanted chain mail sparkling with a million points of light. "But it is time to get to business. Drop all weapons and armor, and Tu-Kar will let all the invaders become slaves in the service of the great Kaza."

"Kaza—what's a Kaza?" Blaster asked.

Just then, a strange chill seemed to settle across courtyard. It was as if a cold, wet blanket had been draped across all his skin. Watcher glanced around, looking for the source. When he turned back to the fortress, he was shocked by what he saw.

A wither slowly entered through the doorway, floating on its stubby spine. Dark, charred ribs stuck out from the shadowy backbone, giving the creature the appearance of something just risen from the cold ashes of a deserted campfire. But the most terrifying thing was the creature's heads. Three of them sat atop the monster's broad shoulders, the center head wearing a golden crown dotted with small black skulls.

"Tu-Kar, are these more recruits for me?" the wither's center head asked.

"Tu-Kar . . . was unaware that Kaza, King of the Withers, would be arriving." The zombie warlord bowed before the floating monster.

"I came to inspect the flock of volunteers you have for me." The center head swiveled until it was staring straight at Cutter. "That one seems strong. Likely he will be good for digging."

"He may be too big for the tunnels," the right head added. "Maybe we should starve him a while until he is more suitable in size."

"I do like the look of that diamond sword." The left wither head gave an eerie smile. "It will look nice next to our throne in the Capitol."

"The sword will belong to Tu-Kar, as per our agreement." The zombie warlord stared up at the monster.

"The zombies bring gold to the king of the withers, but all armor and weapons belong to Tu-Kar. That was the agreement."

"That was the agreement." The right skull nodded.

"Very well," Center replied.

"I don't care what the agreement was; no one's getting my diamond sword," Cutter declared.

Watcher moved to the warrior's side and aimed his bow at the terrifying monster. The bow shook frantically, fear ruling the boy's body.

The left head on the wither laughed. "We should just destroy these fools."

"No, they might have valuable information," Right growled. "One of them might know the location of more villages."

Planter and Blaster moved next to Watcher, weapons gripped firmly in their hands. Mapper stood close behind.

"No," Center snapped. "These fools are a distraction from our plans. We have enough villagers to torture for information. I'm sure some of our captives will gladly tell us where the other villages are located after we destroy a few of their friends. Perhaps we will start with these five here as an example."

"That is a good idea," Right said.

"Of course you would say that, Right," Left added. "You always agree with Center. It's as if you two are conspiring against me all the time."

"That's ridiculous," Right replied.

"Enough bickering!" Center commanded.

The wither turned and faced the zombie warlord.

"Destroy those fools, then take your prisoners to the Capitol. We have some mining for them to do."

"When do we get paid?" Tu-Kar growled.

"You get paid after you deliver the prisoners to my castle," Kaza barked. "I gave you that armor so you could rule this rabble of zombies . . . now rule them! Destroy these five fools as an example to the other villagers, then take the prisoners to the Capitol. If you delay, you will be destroyed and I'll find another zombie warlord who *can* follow my commands."

Tu-Kar growled, then turned to Watcher and his companions. The monster's chain mail glittered with an iridescent light, as the enchantment on the armor reached out to the minds of the other zombies, making them helplessly obedient to him.

"Zombies, destroy these five as an example to the other prisoners." He glared up at the NPC captives on the second floor balcony. "Let all understand, there is no hope for any of the prisoners. No one will get away, and no one will elude punishment for trying to escape. All villagers are now under the command of Tu-Kar, so that they may serve the great Wither King, Kaza."

He turned back to the five companions.

"Zombies . . . attack!"

CHAPTER 20

Zombies charged at them from the fortress steps as monsters climbed down from the walls surrounding the courtyard. But even more terrifying was the zombie warlord himself. Tu-Kar sprinted toward Cutter, his one, good eye fixed on the diamond sword, and his deep, guttural battle cry filling the air.

"Let's get out of here." Watcher fired an arrow at a zombie, then drew and fired again. "We can still escape . . . out the back gate."

"Right, everyone follow Watcher," Planter said.

But Cutter didn't listen. Instead, he shouted back at his enemy. "Zombie warlord, you have hurt and killed untold numbers, and now it is time for you to be punished. I will destroy you just like I destroyed that cowardly zombie general back at the church."

Tu-Kar screamed, then drew a massive iron broadsword that was bigger than any blade any of the NPCs had ever seen before. The keen edge gleamed in the moonlight as the warlord held it over his head. Swinging with all his strength, the monster attacked. Cutter ducked, the weapon zipping just over the top of his iron helmet. Moving in quickly, the NPC slashed at the zombie's legs, then jabbed at his ribs. Tu-Kar screamed, then brought the huge blade down on Cutter's shoulder. It glanced off his armor, but tore a huge gash in the metallic coating.

"Cutter, come on, we need to get out of here." Watcher fired arrows as fast as he could. Off to his right, Blaster and Planter were fighting back to back as they moved closer to the gate, Mapper standing between them. "We can't win this battle. It's better to run."

But again, the big warrior was lost to the fever of war.

"No one interfere," Tu-Kar bellowed. "This villager is mine."

Their blades crashed together, the diamond sword taking a chunk out of the zombie's massive weapon. They clashed again, sparks flying in the air when the two blades met. Watcher moved closer to the combatants, wanting to cover Cutter's escape. Tu-Kar grunted when the diamond blade sliced into his arm. Cutter shouted when the massive broadsword crashed down on to his back. The two behemoths were fighting to the end and there was no stopping them.

But then, an arrow shot out of the darkness and zipped past Cutter's head. Watcher saw a skeleton step into the light and fire again. Drawing back his own arrow, he fired at the bony creature, then again and again, but he was too late. The skeleton had released a second pointed shaft that hit Cutter in the hand, causing him to drop his diamond sword. The big warrior stared down at the tumbling weapon, forgetting the attack about to come down on his head from Tu-Kar's sword.

Watcher sprinted toward the battling giants, firing his arrows at the zombie warlord. His first shot struck the zombie in the shoulder, causing him to lower his swing; the massive broadsword hit Cutter in the side instead of hitting his head. Firing more shots, Watcher drove the zombie back. Meanwhile, Cutter's blade had disappeared amidst the chaos.

"Cutter, we need to go . . . now!" He pulled Ro-Zar's enchanted weapon from his inventory and shoved it into his friend's hands. "Come on."

Watcher grabbed him by the armor and pulled him to the courtyard exit. Cutter looked at him, then glared back at the zombie warlord, the monster waving Cutter's diamond sword in the air.

"Zombies . . . don't let them escape." Tu-Kar's enchanted chain mail flashed bright just for an instant, causing the warlord to shout in pain. "Destroy them."

Cutter turned and started to run.

Monsters were climbing down the walls, trying to cut them off. Blaster streaked out of the gate with Planter at his side, Mapper trailing behind. They fell on the zombies before they could reach the ground, destroying them with shocked expressions on their scarred faces.

"Cutter . . . hurry." Watcher drew an arrow and fired it at a monster trying to close in on them. The shaft hit the creature in the arm, then the next two arrows took the rest of the creature's HP. "Blaster, Planter, take Mapper and head through the gate."

The duo stopped fighting and ran for the courtyard exit, Mapper holding the gate open. When he reached the arched exit, Watcher glanced over his shoulder. It seemed as if the entire zombie army was pouring out of the fortress, all of the monsters snarling and growling. The wither king, Kaza, watched from the obsidian platform, pleased expressions on its three heads.

"Which way do we go?" Planter asked.

Sorrowful moans could be heard on both sides of the walls; the zombies were trying to get at them from the left *and* the right.

"We can't get out the same way we came in," Watcher said. "I can hear monsters in that direction."

"Follow this path. It must lead somewhere, and anywhere is better than right here." Blaster shot down the rocky path, the rest of the party following close behind.

The trail led between two large and steep hills.

Watcher could see it would be impossible to climb up; their only choice was to continue following the path. They ran a short distance, the light from the ascending moon not yet reaching above the hills, leaving the trail in shadow.

"Wait . . . STOP!" Watcher skidded to a halt with his arms outstretched.

"What are you doing?" Cutter asked. "The monsters are following."

"Look, the trail ends." Watcher pulled out a torch and held it into the air. "We need wings if we want to keep going."

"I can't believe you were able to see that," Planter said. "Everything is so dark."

"Stay away from the edge. It's a sheer drop." Watcher peered over to look down. The ground was lost in darkness, but he thought he could hear something . . . a trickling sound.

The companions stood in a tight group, shoulder to shoulder, peering into the black that nearly swallowed them all.

"So, the invaders are trapped."

Watcher turned and found the zombie warlord slowly approaching along the narrow path, a host of monsters at his back.

"These four villagers will make excellent slaves," Tu-Kar said. "But I think the old one will be of no use. Kaza, the great wither king, would never accept a slave as pathetic as that one. Perhaps the river should devour him."

Some of the monsters chuckled a growling sort of laugh.

"So Kaza is the one behind all of this," Watcher said. "I thought zombies did what they wanted, and weren't just subordinates? I never knew they would take orders from a wither."

"Do not play games with Tu-Kar, boy," the zombie growled. "The zombies do what Tu-Kar orders." His enchanted chain mail pulsed for just an instant. "The time for villagers attacking zombie-towns is over. The zombie nation is rising up and taking what rightfully is ours . . . and that's everything. If following Kaza for a while helps Tu-Kar reach this goal, then so be it." The zombie warlord took a step forward and glared at the villagers. "The NPC prisoners have been given over to Kaza, and soon, slavery will be the fate for these intruders as well . . . or maybe even death."

"You'll never make us slaves. We'll fight to the end before we surrender." Cutter held the enchanted sword from the zombie general before him, the blade sparkling with unknown enchantments.

Tu-Kar glanced at the blade, then cast his gaze on the other villagers. "Very well. If surrender is not an option, then there is only one other outcome."

Something the zombie warlord said suddenly made sense to him. Watcher glanced over the edge of the cliff and peered into the darkness. There was that trickling sound again, but it could be coming from anywhere, carried in on the wind from some distant location. It was a big risk, but it was also their only hope.

"No, zombie, I think we actually do have another option." Watcher turned and faced his friends. "All of you need to trust me. This is our only chance."

"What is it?" Cutter asked.

Watcher put away his bow and extended his arms. "Everyone get ready to jump."

"Jump?"

Without further warning, he ran toward the cliff, his arms outstretched, forcing his friends with him. At the last instant, they all turned and leapt as Watcher pushed them off the cliff, falling away into the darkness.

CHAPTER 21

His nerves screamed, causing waves of panic to spread throughout Watcher's body. Watcher stared down as he plunged through the night, hoping with every fiber of his being that he hadn't just doomed all his friends. Time seemed drawn out, moving at an excruciatingly slow pace. Above, he could hear the growls of zombies; one in particular stared down at him, a sad expression on his face. It was Er-Lan.

A thought bubbled up through the back of his mind, but before he could wrap his brain around it, daggers of chilling cold stabbed at him from all sides as he was enveloped in a watery embrace.

"I'm alive!" Watcher coughed.

He was underwater, and talking probably wasn't the best idea. He kicked upward. His lungs burned, starving for oxygen. When his head found air, he coughed again, then scanned the river for his friends. The water was still, and no square heads poked up from the chilly surface.

Did they all miss the water? Watcher's thoughts turned dark. *Are they . . .*

Just then, Planter shot up to the surface, gasping for air. She was shortly followed by Mapper and Blaster. They coughed and sucked in deep breaths, then glanced around.

"It's okay, we're in a river." Watcher swam toward Mapper, who was struggling to stay afloat, his frail body not very buoyant. "Mapper, put an arm around me."

The old man reached out for Watcher. The pair made for the bank, where Blaster was already climbing out of the water. Just then, Cutter emerged from the water, the zombie general's enchanted sword still in his hand. He glanced up at the top of the cliff. The moans of zombies floated down to them, the cliff's edge masked in darkness. Swimming to the river's edge, the big warrior crawled out of the water then glared at Watcher.

"What do we do now?" Planter asked.

"I don't know." Watcher helped Mapper onto solid ground, then sat next to the old man. "Did you see how many zombies the warlord had? How are we supposed to get past all those monsters so we can save our friends?"

"There were hundreds of them, and that's not even counting the wither," Blaster said. "Who knows how many of those three-headed monsters he has in his army."

An uneasy silence lingered on the river bank between the group, and only the trickling of water and the angry moans from zombies high overhead filled the air. The image of Cleric and Winger appeared in Watcher's mind. His father and sister had looked gaunt and haggard behind those iron bars, as if they were starving. Their clothing had been tattered and dirty, with scratches and bruises on their faces. But worst of all had been the look of terror on their faces as they'd stared down at him in that courtyard. They'd been so close, but he'd failed to save them, just like he'd failed in so many other ways. Watcher felt tears welling up in his eyes, but he refused to set them free. Instead, he choked back his emotions.

"I get the impression that the wither was in charge, and not the zombie," Mapper said. "But there was certainly something interesting about the zombie warlord . . . interesting and important."

"Who cares about the warlord right now?" Cutter stepped onto the river bank. "Watcher, what were you thinking?" Cutter put away the sword, then shook his head. Water droplets flew in all directions. His voice grew louder. "You could have killed us. That was careless and stupid."

Watcher stood. "Well . . . I . . ."

"There's nothing you say that will justify what you did."

"But I . . ." The young boy's posture slumped.

Cutter interrupted again. "You just made a choice for everyone and then acted on it without saying anything."

"He did say '*jump*,'" Blaster said with a smile.

The big warrior glared at the dark-haired boy. "Be quiet." He turned back to Watcher. "You've made no effort at all on this quest, Watcher. In that church, you ran away at every chance you had."

"But . . ." Fear nibbled at the edge of Watcher's mind.

"In that courtyard, back there, you were useless. And then you endangered all of us by pushing us off a cliff when you didn't know what would happen. Were you trying to make us all commit suicide, or were you just running away again, like usual?"

Watcher looked up Cutter. His fear of the big warrior was like a lead blanket weighing on his soul. Anger was growing in Cutter's eyes and Watcher wasn't sure what the warrior was going to do. He waited for some of his friends to come to his defense, but they all remained silent.

Maybe they all feel the same. Watcher glanced at Planter, but she only looked away, avoiding his gaze. He then turned toward Blaster, but the boy had already started to take off his armor to dry it out. The only one that would look him in the eyes was Mapper, and the old villager had a smile on his face as if he was keeping some kind of secret.

"Well," Cutter said, his voice growing louder. "What do you have to say for yourself?"

He was so afraid. Watcher glanced at Planter again; she was still looking at the ground, as was Blaster . . . he was alone.

"I'm waiting!"

But then something happened within his soul. The fear that was overwhelming his mind seemed to morph into something else . . . frustration. Watcher had been there many times, pushed up against the wall by the bigger kids, cornered by the bullies, teased by the new trainees in the army . . . he'd been in this situation many times, alone and waiting for the punishment to begin. But the frustration of the moment he now found himself in was too much.

I refuse to be the victim, he thought, frustration boiling over and becoming anger. *I refuse to be bullied just because I'm smaller and weaker. I refuse to accept the insults and the humiliation.*

Just then, he remembered something his father told him long ago: *"Courage is an elusive creature. It hides behind fear and despair, and sometimes prefers the shadows of self-doubt. But when the things most important to you are at risk, your courage can become the brightest of beacons that will light the darkness and turn night into day."*

Moans from the zombies high overhead floated to them again, but this time a little quieter, and a little less scary. Watcher glanced at Planter as she too looked up at the source of the terrifying sound. An expression of fear covered her beautiful square face.

I refuse to let them hurt her. Watcher turned and faced Cutter. *I'm not gonna let Cutter do this to me. I won't fold up and say nothing. I refuse to give in.*

Courage blossomed within him, flowing throughout his body, making him feel as if he were a giant. He was tired of being stepped on, pushed aside, bullied . . . he was tired of it all, and it was time that stopped . . . now.

He glared up at big warrior, then stood a little taller. He put his hands on his hips and squared his shoulder.

"Let me tell you something, Cutter." Watcher kept his voice low and controlled. "While you were fighting the zombie warlord, surrounded by hundreds of zombies, *I* was shooting them with my bow. When you dropped your sword, *I* stopped Tu-Kar from killing you."

"Now you listen here—"

"No, *you* listen, Cutter," he snapped, then grew calm again, lowering his voice to barely a whisper. "You think that just because someone doesn't charge straight ahead, they're a coward. Well . . . you're a fool."

Planter and Blaster both gasped, but Watcher didn't back down. In fact, he took a step forward.

"In that church, I destroyed dozens of monsters with what you call my little toy. I can hit a bat from twenty blocks away with my bow. I can cut the petals off a flower. What I shoot at, I hit. And when the zombie warlord was up close . . . *I* was the one who pushed him back."

Cutter's body tensed while Watcher's slowly relaxed. He took another step closer, now almost toe-to-toe with the warrior.

"Cutter, I pushed everyone off the edge of the cliff because I knew there was a river down here." He paused so they could all hear the trickling of the river. "Didn't you listen to the warlord?" Watcher pointed to his ears. "He told you it was here."

"I heard it," Mapper said.

"Yes, he did say something . . ." Planter said, remembering.

"I don't care about what that pathetic Tu-Kar said. All I care about is—"

"All you care about is fighting, Cutter." He shook his head slightly. "You don't think and you don't plan." Watcher turned and faced away, leaving his back exposed to the warrior. "You could do these things if you only started trying, but every time there's an opportunity to think, you just barrel forward with your blade swinging."

"That's what a good warrior does . . . he fights battles!"

"No, Cutter. You're wrong." Watcher's voice grew strong and confident. He turned and stared defiantly up into the big NPC's eyes, chest out and head held high. "A good warrior doesn't *fight* battles; a good warrior *wins* battles. And sometimes, a battle isn't won with the arms . . . it's won with the head."

"But I . . ."

"The zombie warlord told us about the river. I heard . . . I thought . . . then I acted."

Cutter stared down at Watcher, an expression of uncertainty on his square face.

"And I noticed something else . . . and I thought . . . and now, I'm gonna act."

"What are you talking about?" Cutter asked.

Watcher pointed at Mapper. "You know what to do, don't you, Mapper?"

The old man nodded his head. "Tu-Kar controls his zombie army with that chain mail he wears. It's an ancient relic called the Mantle of Command, and it controls the minds of the zombies. If we take that armor, then we can get rid of the zombies."

"But that's not all," Watcher added. "After we destroy Tu-Kar, then we're gonna destroy the wither king, Kaza. He's the real enemy here; the zombie warlord is just an obstacle in the way."

"You want the five of us to destroy the zombie warlord, then attack the king of the withers?" Cutter shook his head. "How do you suppose we're gonna do that? We don't have enough swords to do that job."

"We aren't gonna use swords . . . we're gonna use our minds and *think*." Watcher placed a hand on the big warrior's sword arm. "But Cutter, we'll need your help.

All those villagers back there are now probably heading toward the Capitol, and they need your help as well." He looked up into the villager's eyes. "Are you with us? Are you gonna think first and act second? Or are you just gonna keep swinging your sword, fighting battles instead of winning them?

Cutter looked down at Watcher, glanced at the other companions, then nodded. "What's your plan?"

Watcher smiled. "Blaster, how many sets of leather armor do you have?"

"A lot, plus some iron armor as well."

Watcher smiled again. "It's time we stopped just fighting and started crafting. Here's what I have in mind."

And the young archer explained his plan, the others smiling and nodding their heads. And for the first time, a feeling spread across the company of adventurers that they hadn't felt for a long time . . . hope.

CHAPTER 22

Er-Lan glanced to the east as the sun slowly crept up from behind the distant horizon. The little zombie was still stunned by everything that had transpired.

The villagers are gone. The thought ripped through Er-Lan's mind like a tornado. *Was this Er-Lan's fault?*

He'd brought them to the fortress in hopes of finding the family members of Watcher, Planter, and Blaster, and helping them to escape. He hadn't expected them to be captured, and he certainly hadn't wanted them to end their lives by jumping off the cliff.

"It's all wrong . . . all wrong."

Er-Lan had stared down at his new friends, in shock, as they fell and were engulfed by the darkness. There was no doubt in Er-Lan's mind about their fate.

"They had been Er-Lan's friends," the zombie growled to himself. "For the first time, Er-Lan actually had friends, and now they are . . ." He didn't want to finish the thought.

The little zombie struggled to his feet. He was sitting in a dark corner of the courtyard, the rope from Cutter still wrapped around his arms. In the confusion of the battle and the aftermath from the incident at the cliff, the zombie warlord had forgotten about Er-Lan.

Grief washed over the zombie—terrible, debilitating grief. Er-Lan had never felt so empty and alone. His friends had filled a place in his soul, and now that they'd been torn from him, he burned with loneliness. He'd never been this sad in his life, probably because he'd never been accepted by others before those villagers. Guilt mixed in with the grief, creating a maelstrom of emotions that tore through the zombie's soul.

"Er-Lan cannot endure these emotions." He squared his shoulders, then stepped out into the light, heading straight for the zombie warlord.

As he crossed the courtyard, the yellow face of the sun crept up from behind the distant horizon. It cast ruby red light upon the landscape, creating deep oranges where there should have been greens. The stars overhead faded from sight as the blue sky of day pushed them aside.

From the side of the cobblestone structure, Er-Lan watched as Kaza slowly rose in the air, his three-headed black body looking like a dark hole in the fabric of Minecraft. Likely, the King of the Withers was heading back to the Capitol, getting ready for this new crop of slaves. Er-Lan pitied those villagers; their fate was to toil in the mines until they fell from exhaustion and their HP faded to nothing.

"No fate can be worse than Er-Lan's." The zombie lowered his gaze and shuffled across the grassy yard. His voice grew soft, barely a whisper. "They were my friends . . . my friends . . ."

"There is the exile." A nearby zombie grabbed him by the edge of his shirt and held on as if he were stopping the little monster from escaping.

But escape was not his plan, instead, it was atonement. The zombie pushed Er-Lan through a crowd of monsters, growls and wails of anger levied at the little creature.

"Tu-Kar, here is the exiled zombie." The monster's voice was loud and scratchy.

He shoved Er-Lan through the crowd, pushing him to the ground at Tu-Kar's feet. The zombies in the court-yard growled and moaned, all of them hungry to see punishment delivered.

"Er-Lan was told returning would be punished by death. Does Er-Lan remember?" Tu-Kar's milky white eye was painted with orange light from the rising sun.

"Yes, Warlord, Er-Lan remembers." He lowered his head, but felt no fear. There wasn't room for that emotion in his heart; it was already full with sorrow and guilt.

The zombie warlord moved a step closer. "Does this zombie have anything for Tu-Kar?"

Er-Lan shook his head.

"The puny monster should be destroyed," one of the monsters shouted from the crowd.

Tu-Kar glanced up from Er-Lan and sought out the malcontent.

"There is no diamond sword in this zombie's hands," the monster continued. "Er-Lan was a captive and a failure to the zombie race. Destruction is a just reward."

"Destruction is indeed a just reward." Tu-Kar grabbed Er-Lan by the arm and lifted him to his feet. He then pushed through the crowd, pulling on the rope still tied around him.

"That zombie even *smells* like a villager," a monster called out. "There is no stench to Er-Lan. That zombie is trying to be like the NPCs. He should receive the same fate." The discontent monster stared straight at Tu-Kar, a look of determination on his scarred face. "Er-Lan returned from exile without the diamond sword. That is a violation of Tu-Kar's law. Death is the only reward."

Suddenly, Tu-Kar reached into his inventory and pulled out something blue, the object shining bright as it reflected the morning light. He struck down the bois-terous zombie, hitting him once, then again and again. The monster's armor fell to the ground, the surprised zombie unable to react. Tu-Kar then struck him again and again until the creature disappeared, a look of surprise and fear on his green face.

Extending his arm up high, Tu-Kar held aloft the diamond sword dropped by Cutter. The zombies gasped in surprise and awe at the magnificent blade.

"Behold, the diamond sword that was demanded by Tu-Kar was delivered by Er-Lan." The zombie warlord walked in a circle around Er-Lan so all could see the weapon. "The foolish villager dropped it in battle, and now it belongs to your warlord."

He turned and faced Er-Lan.

"Now, what do we do with Er-Lan?"

Tu-Kar raised the blade higher, then brought it down in a powerful stroke. Er-Lan closed his eyes, welcoming the end to this terrible grief. The blade whistled past his ear, then sliced through the ropes that wrapped around his body. The monster horde held their breath for just an instant, then cheered as the ropes fell away, freeing Er-Lan from his bonds.

"This zombie did the impossible and brought the diamond sword of the villager to Tu-Kar!"

The zombie warlord held the glacial-blue weapon high in the air. The mob growled and moaned excitedly.

"Er-Lan is to be rewarded for the deviousness in which the villagers were brought here." Tu-Kar patted the little zombie on the back. "This zombie tricked the villagers to come to our fortress, and then we drove them off the cliff, to their deaths. It is a great day!"

"Er-Lan didn't do anything," the little monster said, hanging his head low.

"This is a great warrior, and all zombies can learn from Er-Lan's example," Tu-Kar said. "Do the unexpected and victory will be at hand."

Er-Lan's voice grew softer. "I did nothing . . . I am nothing . . . I am alone, again."

The zombie warlord patted him on the back again, then sheathed his newly acquired diamond blade.

"Come, brothers and sisters, it is time to march the prisoners to the zombie hideout. And after that, they'll go to the Capitol, where they will find the end of their days."

The zombies cheered and followed their warlord, leaving Er-Lan standing there, still mourning the loss of his only friends.

CHAPTER 23

After crafting everything they needed, the companions moved through the forest quietly, their inventories bulging with wooden stick-figures.

"You sure this is gonna work?" Cutter looked uncertain.

"We have to do something that'll even the odds a bit, Cutter." Reaching into his inventory, Watcher readjusted one of the items so it wouldn't poke him in the stomach. "I'm betting this will get most of the zombies out of the warlord's hideout, leaving him alone and vulnerable. Once that happens, you get to do your sword thing."

Cutter smiled.

"Mapper, tell us more about the armor the warlord is wearing," Planter pressed.

"Well, the Mantle of Command was made ages ago, when the NPC wizards and the monster warlocks were feuding. Scholars, myself included, agree the Mantle was likely a very important magical tool during the war. The wearer could direct a huge host of monsters and make them follow any command. Some books suggest that the Mantle of Command almost tipped the war in favor of the warlocks, but something happened—exactly what is not clear—that brought the advantage back to the wizards."

The old NPC glanced at Planter. "That sword you carry is also from the ancient times; I can tell by its shape. It doesn't have the broad and heavy shape that Cutter's sword has; it's nimble and swift. I wouldn't be surprised if there wasn't some kind of enchantment on it to make the weapon feel extra light, but still be incredibly strong."

"You're right." Planter drew the blade from her inventory. Instantly, she was engulfed in the weapon's iridescent glow. "I've always marveled at how easy it is to swing."

"The ancient wizards used powerful magic to not only make them easier to use, but also make them connect to the wielder's mind. This let the sword act *for* the owner, the blade moving before the thought was ever given. It's written that these smart weapons will only *connect* with someone that was a descendant of the great wizards. To regular people like you and me, it's just a sword."

"That's really interesting, professor, but how does it help us defeat the zombie warlord?" the big warrior asked sarcastically.

"Cutter, if we can lure the zombies away from the hideout, I have no doubt Tu-Kar can be defeated, as long as we work together." Watcher glanced at the warrior and stood tall. He refused to be intimidated. "We must not forget who the real enemy is."

"And who's that supposed to be?" Cutter asked.

"The wither king. He's the puppet master, pulling all the strings." Watcher cast his gaze across all his companions. His blue eyes, for a change, were bright with confidence. "Kaza is the one that's the real threat, and we need to know his plans so we can stop him."

Cutter looked down at the boy. His steely gaze would normally make Watcher shrink and look away, but the young boy stared back, relaxed and self-assured.

"I'm surprised to say . . . I agree with Watcher." Cutter patted the boy on the back. "We take out the zombie warlord, then we get to the Capitol and teach that wither a thing or two about messing with villagers."

Planter smiled. "Alright."

Suddenly, a mottled brown and black figure emerged from behind a tree trunk. Planter jumped with a start as Watcher strung an arrow and pulled it back, ready to fire. But when the huge grin grew across the square face, he realized it was just Blaster.

"The hideout is just up ahead." The boy removed his brown cap, his dark, curly hair going in all directions as usual. "It'll be night soon. That's when we should plan our little surprise."

"I agree." Cutter adjusted his inventory, the uncomfortable stick figure poking him in many places. "I'll be very glad to be rid of these things."

"I found the perfect place for our skinny little friends." Blaster put the brown leather armor away and replaced it with his favorite, midnight black. "Come on."

They followed the stealthy boy as the sun slowly caressed the horizon, turning day to night.

Normally, the dark forest would have made Watcher nervous, but instead of reacting to everything and feeling as if he was being pushed around by his surroundings, he was the one driving the chain of events. For the first time in his life, he felt in control, not because he was the strongest or the bravest, but because his idea would hopefully help them to defeat the zombie warlord.

"Here," Blaster whispered. "Put them here."

The NPC had led them to a clearing in the forest that faced the entrance to the warlord's hideout. Majestic birch trees ringed the perimeter. Tall blades of grass swayed in the breeze, occasionally masking the presence of the bright yellow flowers that dotted the field. Long shadows stretched across the grassy plain as the moon slowly rose in the east. It was nearly an idyllic scene, except for the massive horde of monsters sheltered nearby in the zombie warlord's hideout.

Blaster stopped in the middle of the clearing, then reached into his inventory and pulled out a contraption made of sticks, with a thick stone base on the bottom. He placed it on the ground, then hung a set of leather armor on it.

"This was a clever idea." Blaster decorated the stick man with green armor, then placed another on the ground. "Using armor stands to trick the zombies will be fun."

Watcher smiled, then pulled out his own armor stands and put them on the ground, spread out as if they were just entering the clearing. Any spare armor he had was hung on the wooden frames, simulating a squad of soldiers.

"Put some near the edge of the clearing," Cutter said. "We want to make them think there are more out in the woods."

Planter nodded, then moved to the back of the clearing and placed her stands between the trees. She hung leather armor on one, and iron armor on another. The rest of the party did the same, positioning at least two dozen armor stands across the clearing. Those near the tree line only received partial armor, as their legs were hidden by blocks of dirt and wouldn't be visible to the zombies from far away.

Blaster placed blocks of wood around the clearing, then stepped back to survey their creation. In the dark evening light, the scene they'd created looked just like a squad of soldiers was walking out of the woods and across the meadow.

Watcher smiled. "You sure you're gonna be alright out here on your own?"

"Someone has to light the wood on fire," Blaster said. "They won't see me with my black leather armor. I'll join you right after the foolish zombies get out here."

"Okay, everyone follow me." Watcher took out his bow and notched an arrow.

They ran through the dark forest, leaving Blaster behind. Watcher knew it was imperative to be in position when Blaster got the attention of the zombies; they had to be out of the monsters' path or they'd be overrun. The companions wove around the trees, keeping to the shadows whenever possible.

As they approached the hideout, the sounds of monsters grew louder, their sorrowful moans and angry growls causing chills to run down Watcher's spine.

"I wonder if any of those sounds are from Er-Lan," Planter whispered.

Watcher shrugged, but had the same concern. He hoped the young zombie was okay.

"What if we see him on the battlefield?" Watcher asked.

A horrified expression grew on Planter's face.

He shook his head. "That's not gonna happen, so let's not worry about it. I'm sure Er-Lan is safe somewhere in that hideout. I bet he'll just stay out of the way when the fighting starts."

"Let's hope so," Mapper added.

Cutter grunted.

The companions reached the edge of the tree line. Before them stood a gigantic wooden structure built from spruce logs and oak planking. A moat ringed the structure, the channel filled with water. Anyone falling in there would never be able to climb out.

A wall at least six blocks high ran around the building, with a tall watchtower standing next to the open gate. Behind the wall, another tower stood even higher than the first, but no motion was visible within.

Between the moat and the fortified structure sat an encampment of colorful tents, some striped blue and black, others red and white. The fabric fluttered in the gentle breeze, masking the sound of the NPCs' approaching footsteps.

Running along the edge of the forest, Watcher found a recession in the ground near the bridge that spanned the moat. Tall grass covered the area, creating an ideal hiding spot. Watcher checked the hole. It had a solid stone bottom and steep sides. That, coupled with the tall grass, would easily hide them from the horde of monsters that would move past them any second. He glanced at his friends as they followed him into the hole, trying to give them a reassuring smile, but fear nibbled at the edge of his senses, making the grin look more like a strained grimace. Suddenly, a light flared to life in the forest, and they could hear something clanking against a piece of metal.

"Come on, soldiers, we have a zombie hideout to attack!" a voice shouted. They all knew it to be Blaster.

More shouts came from the forest, each in a different sounding voice, to simulate multiple villagers calling to each other.

The moans from behind the walls changed to angry growls as zombies poured out of the gates and charged across the wooden bridge that spanned the moat.

"Destroy them all!" Tu-Kar shouted, his unmistakable deep, scratchy voice blaring over the sounds of the other zombies. "Capture any that surrender, but I want their iron. Bring Tu-Kar some new armor."

The zombies growled and snarled as they charged out of the gates, heading straight for the fires that lit up the clearing in the distance. The monsters didn't even bother to look around, their thirst for violence overwhelming any other thoughts. Watcher sensed something next to him. Turning, he found Blaster breathing heavily, his dark armor making him almost invisible.

"Everyone ready?" Blaster gulped another lung full of air.

They all nodded.

Cutter placed a hand on Watcher's shoulder. "I think it's time you lead us into battle."

Watcher swallowed as beads of sweat trickling down his square face. He looked up at the big warrior, then gripped his bow firmly, and jumped out of the hole, running for the bridge. Crossing it in seconds, the group passed through the now-deserted encampment.

I wonder if there are any weapons or armor in those tents? Watcher thought, but knew they didn't have the time to search. Instead, he headed straight for the fortified wall. Without slowing down, Watcher charged through the open gates, an unknown number of monsters likely waiting on the other side.

CHAPTER 24

Zombies came pouring out of the watchtower that loomed high over the gate, their swords gleaming in the moonlight. Watcher knelt and fired arrows as fast as he could draw and release, aiming for exposed points between pieces of armor. They fell to his barrage while the others continued to advance.

Cutter descended upon the monsters, his enchanted iron sword cleaving great paths of destruction through the mob. At the same time, Blaster wove between the creatures, slashing at zombies as he passed, never standing still long enough for any of them to hit him. Planter moved to Cutter's side, Needle glowing bright with magic. She swung the blade faster than any of the creatures had thought possible, her glowing green shield deflecting zombie blades.

"Watcher, look what I found," Mapper said.

He looked over his shoulder for a second, taking in the scene, then continued to fire.

The old man opened a chest that stood next to the gates. He reached in and took out multiple items, stuffing them into his inventory. A growl sounded behind him. Before Mapper could turn, Watcher fired three quick shots into the monster, eliminating it from the Far Lands.

"Mapper, stay behind me." Watcher started to advance, continuing to launch his pointed shafts at the few remaining monsters.

Blaster attacked two zombies at the same time, extending his curved knives, then spinning like a top. His blades found soft flesh, erasing their remaining HP.

Quickly, the companions destroyed the guards from the towers, leaving only those within the fortress.

"That's that last of them." Cutter put away his sword and allowed some of the XP to flow into him. "Let's go inside."

"Wait, I have something for each of you." Mapper reached into his inventory and withdrew a handful of bottles, each with a dark purple liquid sloshing about. "These are night vision potions. Each of you drink. When we get into the main building, destroy any torches; the darkness will be our ally."

"That might even the odds a bit." Watcher slapped the old man on the back. "What are those other potions?"

Mapper held what looked like a pink splash potion of some kind in his hand. "A little surprise for our friends." He gave Watcher a devious smile.

With a shrug, Watcher drank his purple potion. Instantly, spirals of dark blue hovered around his head as his surroundings grew sharper and easier to see.

"I like it," Blaster exclaimed. "Let's do this. I'll take care of all the torches."

"I'll help," Planter added.

Cutter nodded, drank his potion, then charged toward the entrance to the wooden building.

As soon as the doors were opened, they were all overwhelmed by the stench of the place. It smelled as if someone had left meat out in the hot sun, allowing it to rot. That could only mean one thing . . . zombies, lots of them.

Their moans confirmed their suspicions. Cutter ran into the room, drawing his sword to attack. The chamber was brightly lit, a torch placed in the middle of each wall, casting wide circles of light across the chamber. Tall columns of wood lined one side, holding up a portion of the roof, while a solid wall covered the other. Watcher knew there would be zombies on the other side of that wall; he could hear them. Blaster and Planter dashed through the room, destroying the torches. He faced the opening to the side room and readied his bow.

Cutter's blade could be heard crashing into armored monsters, their shouts of pain and fear filling the air. A pinging sound stood out in the cacophony; Watcher knew what it was from.

"I need some help with an annoying skeleton," Cutter said.

Watcher turned and scanned the room. He found the skeleton hiding in the corner, the monster likely hoping the darkness would protect him . . . that was a fatal mistake. Notching two arrows, he fired them both at the bony creature, then quickly drew and fired again. One of the first pair hit, then the second landed. The skeleton scanned the room, but by now all the torches had been extinguished and it was impossible for the creature to see. Watcher drew another arrow and took aim. He had to hurry; monsters would be coming through that doorway any second, and he wasn't sure if he could stop them all by himself, even if he had the advantage of night vision.

Suddenly, Blaster entered the fray, his knives slashing at the monster. The skeleton tumbled to the ground, now just a pile of parched-white bones.

With a sigh of relief, Watcher turned back to the doorway, ready for the zombie reinforcements. But instead, he found Mapper standing directly in the way.

"Mapper . . . move." Watcher reached out and tried to push the old man aside.

"Don't worry," he said. "I got this."

"Are you crazy?"

Mapper glanced over his shoulder, a devious smile plastered on his square face.

The sound of angry monsters was the first thing to come out of the doorway, followed by razor-sharp claws and pointed fangs. The monsters charged out of the side room and headed straight for Mapper. Watcher tried to take a clear shot, but his friend was right in the way, the pink splash potion still in his hand.

"Hello zombies." Mapper laughed. "So nice to meet you."

The monsters growled, looking confused. Then, the old villager threw the potion. It flew through the air and shattered on the lead monster. The liquid splashed in all directions, covering half a dozen creatures. Instantly, they fell to the ground, writhing in pain. Mapper threw another potion at the next wave of zombies. They fell just like the first, screaming in agony as their bodies flashed red, taking damage.

"See Watcher, I told you I had this." Mapper laughed and threw another potion, coating the last few monsters. "Healing potion . . . it's poison to undead creatures."

"Of course," Watcher said with a nod.

He was about to say more, but stopped as a new sound emerged among the clashing of swords on armor. It was a faint clicking, as if someone were tapping hard pieces of wood or stone together. But there was an anger to the noise, something that caused a chill to run down his spine . . . spiders.

"There are spiders in the room."

Watcher looked around him. The combat was still focused at the front of the chamber, zombies charging at them from the darkness. And then he saw them; eight points of angry red light slowly moving down the walls.

"The spiders are coming down the walls!" Watcher shouted. "Watch your backs."

Focusing on the first set of eyes, Watcher fired a stream of arrows at the monster. It dodged the first one, but misjudged the next projectiles. They hit the spider, quickly destroying its HP. Watcher didn't wait for the monster to disappear, instead he turned and found another target. More spiders were crawling down the wooden pillars holding up the roof. Watcher moved to a corner and knelt, then fired as fast as he could, not even pausing to breathe. His arrows were like a continuous stream of wood and flint, the pointed shafts like deadly rain.

Gradually, Watcher destroyed the rest of the spiders as his companions shattered the zombie ranks. The last few monsters tried to flee, but Blaster was on them with his curved knives, giving quarter to none. It looked as if they'd won when suddenly, something blue moved quickly through the darkness.

"Cutter, look out." Watcher fired an arrow over the big warrior's shoulder, but it was deflected away by a diamond sword.

"So, the villager returns to try to claim the diamond sword." The zombie warlord placed a torch on the ground and glared at Cutter. "Tu-Kar took this blade from the pathetic villager. Now it will be used to take Ro-Zar's weapon back as well . . . and then it will end your life."

"You talk too much, zombie." Cutter slashed at the monster, his sparkling iron sword flashing through the air like a bolt of metallic lighting.

The zombie blocked the attack, then swung the diamond blade at Cutter's head. The NPC ducked, then slashed at the monster's legs, scoring a hit against the zombie's left thigh. Groaning in pain, Tu-Kar stepped back and glared at his adversary.

Just then, Watcher stepped into the light, an arrow pulled back and aimed at the zombie warlord. Blaster moved in from the left, his curved blades ready for combat. The glow from Needle painted a purple splash of light on the floor as Planter approached the monster from behind.

They started to close in. Tu-Kar growled, glancing at all the villagers.

"No!" Cutter raised his hand, stopping his companions. "I need to do this . . . for Fisher. . . and for me."

His friends stepped back as Cutter approached the zombie warlord alone.

"Ahh . . . the NPC has some courage. The original owner of this sword could have used some of that bravery when he was destroyed. Ro-Zar said that the villager begged for mercy like a child . . . how pathetic." Tu-Kar laughed. "That NPC was abandoned, sealing their fate." The zombie pointed at Cutter with the diamond blade.

"I know what my faults are, zombie. I don't need you to lecture me." Cutter took a step closer. "I've come to terms with my mistakes in life." He glanced at Watcher, then turned back to the monster. "I've misjudged people, and I've treated people poorly, but I won't hide from those mistakes, and you can't use them as a weapon against me."

"Blah . . . blah . . . blah . . . villagers talk too much when they're afraid." Tu-Kar glared at him. "Begging for mercy will probably come next. All you villagers are pathetic."

The zombie smiled a toothy grin, then charged. Cutter stood his ground, deflecting the attacks with his enchanted iron blade. But for the first time, instead of trying to use strength to overcome his attacker, he merely allowed the monster to tire himself out. When opportunities appeared, he stabbed at the warlord, his razor-sharp tip jabbing at the monster, scoring hit after hit.

It seemed as if Cutter was going to defeat the zombie warlord, and by the look on Tu-Kar's face, the monster knew it as well. Landing a strong kick into Cutter's chest, the monster pushed the NPC back, then quickly reached into his inventory and draped the Mantle of Command over his shoulder.

"He's gonna bring all the zombies back!" Watcher shouted.

"If he does that, we're doomed," Planter added.

"Zombies." Tu-Kar smiled as he backed away from Cutter. "Come back to the—"

Suddenly, a green creature dashed out of the darkness and collided with the zombie commander, hitting Tu-Kar hard in the chest and knocking the wind out of him. The monster fell on the floor, another smaller zombie on top of him.

"Er-Lan . . . it's Er-Lan." Watcher sprinted forward, firing arrows at the zombie warlord. "Planter, protect our friend."

The two of them closed in on Tu-Kar while the two zombies wrestled. The warlord pushed Er-Lan off, then raised his sword and swung at the defenseless monster. Watcher fired arrows as fast as he could while Blaster and Planter closed in, their blades inflicting wicked damage. At the last minute, Cutter grabbed Er-Lan and pulled him back, then brought his big sword down upon Tu-Kar. The warlord's face changed from one of rage to uncertainty and fear. He disappeared as a sorrowful moan escaped his lips, leaving behind his items: enchanted chain mail, the three balls of XP.

Watcher bent down and picked up the chain mail, then handed the diamond sword to Cutter. The warrior took the weapon by the handle and stared down at it as if it were an old friend.

"You earned this." Watcher nodded his head. "Fisher would be proud of you."

Cutter nodded, then put the weapon away.

"I think it would be best if we ran, in case the warlord was able to get his command out to his army." Mapper bent down and retrieved some of the warlord's items. "I don't relish the thought of being here when a hundred zombies return looking for a fight."

"Perhaps you're right," Cutter agreed.

"Wait . . . Er-Lan." Planter rushed to the zombie's side. "Are you okay?"

The monster looked up at Planter, then saw Watcher and Blaster approaching. He smiled. But then he saw Cutter approach, and his smile turned to a frown. The big warrior gently pushed the others aside, then held out a hand to Er-Lan, helping him to his feet.

"We probably owe our lives to you." Cutter dusted him off. "You stopped the warlord from issuing that command. If you hadn't, we'd probably be . . ."

"All these friends would have done the same for Er-Lan," the zombie said.

Cutter nodded. "Let's get out of here. We have a date with a wither."

"We do indeed," Watcher agreed. "Kaza, you're next."

CHAPTER 25

Kaza floated over the collection of zombies and prisoners as they trudged toward the coastline. The aroma of salt permeated everything, smelling clean and fresh; it was a welcome relief compared to the stench of these pathetic zombies.

The company of monsters and their prisoners crested the last hill and passed by the ancient watchtower that guarded the fishing village nestled on the coastline. The dark ocean, with its rippling waves and splashing squid, stretched out into the darkness, the distant edge engulfed by the night. The only land mass visible on the rippling waters was an island upon which was built a tall stone and brick castle: the Capitol. A large seawall, made of the same bricks, stood in the water, forming an enclosure where ships sat empty, abandoned since the wither king had taken everything over. This site had been a prominent figure in the history of the Far Lands, and until recently, the seat of power for the NPCs. Now, it stood as a reminder of how violence could change the fortunes of anyone.

"Hurry up," the right head of the wither king growled. "You're too slow."

"But the zombies are tired," one of the monsters

complained. "Marching all through the night has brought many to exhaustion."

"You need to rest?" Left asked. "Very well."

Suddenly, a pair of flaming black skulls shot out of Kaza's left head and slammed into the complaining zombie, exploding. Instantly, black swirls formed around the zombie's head as the wither effect took over the monster's body. Kaza knew the monster could no longer tell how much health it had left, which made the creature afraid. Left loved this part, when their victim panicked.

"Just finish him off and stop torturing the monster," Right grumbled.

Center nodded in agreement.

Left gave a sigh then fired another flaming skull at the monster. The blast from the projectile took the last of the monster's HP. With a look of terror on its green face, the monster disappeared, a sad wail leaving his lips.

"Let that be a lesson to all of you," Center shouted. "March too slowly and you will be destroyed."

Some of the zombies growled, but they all shuffled faster down the trail. The army of monsters moved along the stone pathway, down to the sloping beach and into the fishing village that sat nestled along the shoreline.

The coastal village was like a ghost town, the NPCs having been captured long ago and put to work in the mines until their HP ran out. The doors to some of the homes still sat open, items of clothing and children's toys lying on tables in the buildings. It was as if the community had been frozen in time, devoid of life.

"I remember when these villagers came to the Capitol in hopes of stopping our takeover." Left laughed a harsh laugh. "It was fun blasting them out of the water."

"Yes, many were destroyed." Center glanced at Left. "The greater surprise was what we found down in the secret vaults, below the great castle."

"That was a great day," Right added. "I'd never seen that much gold in one place."

"The caretaker of the Capitol thought that gold was left over from the ancient war between the wizards and the warlocks." Center glanced at Right, then glared down at the prisoners that were moving onto the docks. "It was that pile of gold that caused me to come up with our great plan."

Left lowered his scratchy voice. "Just think, when we have the gold we need to awaken all the other withers, then we can destroy all these villagers once and for all."

"We can also destroy the zombies as well." Right's voice was soft and lyrical. "It will be good to be rid of that terrible stench."

"Absolutely," Left added.

"We will destroy them all, but not until I say so." Center glared at the other heads. "When we see our sleeping brothers and sisters arise from their subterranean prison, then we will have achieved our goal. Until then, the zombies and villagers are to remain untouched." The tone of his voice made it clear that neither head should dare to object.

The zombies forced the prisoners into a fishing village and out onto the docks.

"Villagers, get into the boats," one of the zombies growled. "Head for the dock on the edge of the island. Any boats heading away from the island will be destroyed."

The villagers, terrified and half-starved, obediently piled into the small rowboats and paddled toward the nearby island, the main building looming tall over the rest of the Capitol. A few NPCs made a run for it, turning their boat away from the coast and trying to flee out into the ocean. Kaza quickly destroyed the fools, his flaming skulls making an example of the slaves and extinguishing any hope of escape.

When they reached the loading docks, the villagers climbed out and moved into a central square, empty homes silent and deserted around them. Zombies moved out from between the buildings, their swords and armor gleaming under the waning light of the setting moon.

Once all the villagers had successfully disembarked onto the island, they were led through the ghost village, the zombies goading them along with their sharp claws. Some wept as the possibility of escape or rescue became more remote. They knew they'd likely never leave the island alive.

At the edge of the village, a steep set of stairs ascended along the edge of the mountain that formed the core of the island. Halfway up, a lone NPC sat huddled in an iron cage, the pathetic man begging for mercy.

"Please, release me," the gaunt villager said from behind iron bars.

"We will never release you." Left glared at the prisoner as he floated up the steps.

"You know too much about the Capitol," Right said. "We cannot let you run free. You were the caretaker here for a long time, and your knowledge of the Capitol is vast. Instead, I think we'll keep you here in case we need any information."

"But I'm barely alive," the man moaned.

"We know, but we'll make sure you get enough food to stay alive." Center laughed. "Have we ever failed to feed you?"

"Please . . . just let me die."

"You'll die when we give you our permission." Left scowled at the sickly villager. "Until then, suffer."

The new prisoners glanced at the imprisoned villager as they climbed the steps, moving past him. When the captives reached the gates of the huge castle, they swung open, revealing more zombie guards. The solders escorted the NPCs down a flight of steps and into the mines, a place many villagers entered but few ever left.

"Where is my general!" Center's voice boomed through the castle as he floated near the entrance to the mines. He had no desire to go down into the cramped tunnels; withers hate confined passages. Open spaces were what Kaza always preferred.

"Here is So-Mal." A fat zombie struggled past the stream of prisoners heading down the steps into the mines.

"Stand before us." Kaza floated closer to the ground. Right glanced upward, making sure there was still room to rise if anyone attacked. Left scanned their surroundings, watching for threats. "We bring new prisoners. They must be put to work right away. We are nearing our goal, but still need more gold. You will put these slaves to work and find us the gold we need."

"Yes, Kaza." So-Mal bowed low, his large belly making it difficult. "The new slaves will work hard."

"I hope so, for your sake." Left's voice was scratchy, a not-so-subtle promise of violence in his statement. "I'm sure there are other zombies that can do your job."

"The slaves will dig with all their strength. So-Mal will see it done." So-Mal bowed again, his iron armor creaking under the strain. Turning, the zombie pushed one of the prisoners into the descending passage, yelling at the top of his lungs.

"Soon, brother and sister, we will have the gold we need." Center glanced at the other two heads, his eyes bright with anticipation. "And then we can put the next part of our plan into action."

The three heads chuckled, each in a different tone, creating a symphony of malicious laughter, adding to the sad and hopeless wails of the NPCs.

CHAPTER 26

The comrades walked in pairs of two, each scanning either the left or the right, looking for hidden monsters or traps. After the battle with the zombie warlord, their spirits had been high, but as they drew nearer to the Capitol, each grew more and more nervous.

"We should be able to see the Capitol after this next hill." Mapper pulled out an apple and ate it as he walked. "But before that, I think it's best we come up with a plan."

"There will be zombies . . . many zombies." Er-Lan walked next to Planter, his arms no longer bound by rope. "It will be impossible to just fight through them."

"Zombie, aren't you worried about us killing your fellow zombies?" Cutter asked.

"His name is Er-Lan." Planter scowled at the big warrior.

"Ahh . . . right, whatever."

The zombie gave Cutter a nod. "Er-Lan has been an outcast for a long time. The other zombies hate Er-Lan because Er-Lan is not the same. Er-Lan is not strong. Er-Lan is not a fighter. Because of these differences, Er-Lan has been despised by other zombies. Only when it seemed as if Er-Lan betrayed these villagers was this zombie accepted. But it was still clear, many zombies still have hate in their hearts." He reached up with a claw and scratched his bald head. "Er-Lan has no love for other zombies . . . best to be alone."

"Or maybe with friends that appreciate you," Planter added, placing a hand on his shoulder.

The zombie smiled and nodded.

Cutter guffawed then rolled his eyes, drawing a glare from Planter. The big warrior didn't respond.

"Let's go into the jungle and talk." Watcher turned and climbed over blocks of leaves. Long vines hung down from the jungle wood trees, making it difficult to see anything . . . which is just what he wanted. Once they'd moved deep enough into the verdant growth, he found a place where the group could talk without being easily seen.

"The sun will be up soon." Cutter removed his iron helmet and rubbed his stubby hair. "I understand we need to use boats to get to the Capitol. I'd rather cross the sea while it's still dark."

"Agreed," Blaster said.

"What do we do about all the zombies?" Watcher put away his bow and pulled a loaf of bread from his inventory. He took a bite.

"The Mantle of Command should help us," Mapper said. "But I think it would be wise to test it out before we're faced with a hundred monsters who all want to kill us."

Cutter nodded. "I agree."

"I'll test it." Watcher removed the mundane chain mail he was wearing and put it away in his inventory, then pulled out the sparkling armor dropped by the zombie warlord.

"Come, Watcher . . . sit here." Mapper motioned to a leafy block next to a jungle wood tree.

Watcher sat down, removed his leather cap, then slowly lowered the enchanted mail over his head. He gasped as images formed in his head. Instantly, he was submerged into an inky blackness that wrapped around him like a funeral shroud. The darkness reached into his soul and a great emptiness filled him with such fear that it was almost too much to bear. Just as Watcher was about the surrender to the shadows and lose himself to the magical armor, the darkness parted and he could see monsters with his mind's eye.

"What do you see?" Planter asked.

"I can see zombies moving through long tunnels. They're guarding the prisoners as they dig."

"What about spiders?" Cutter asked. "Are there any spiders?"

As soon as Watcher thought about spiders, the image changed to that of a huge cave. Lava spilled down one wall, casting an orange glow across the chamber. Hundreds of dark, spotted eggs covered the ground, each nestled between blocks of spider web. One of the spiders was larger than the rest, with long, wicked-looking claws at the end of each leg. Instead of having eight red eyes, one of the eyes on this creature was a deep purple, and seemed to pulse as if alive with some kind of magic.

"I see a nest of spiders, with tons of eggs all over the place." Watcher took a calming breath. "Hopefully, that place is far away. I wouldn't want to be there when all those eggs hatch."

"Can you see any skeletons?"

The image changed again, moving at the speed of thought. Instantly, his vision was of a long room built underground. Tall columns of quartz stretched up from the ground to the ceiling, redstone lanterns ringing each. Hundreds of the bony creatures moved about, one of them much larger than the rest.

"Yes, there's some kind of hall with tall pillars made of something white. The ceiling is impossibly high and there are hundreds of . . ."

But then the image faded from his mind. It was as if the magical armor had lost its power. Suddenly, the Mantle of Command reached out for the nearest source of energy to recharge its magical enchantments . . . and that source was Watcher himself. Pain exploded through his body, the Mantle using the wearer's HP for energy. Watcher flashed red as more health was torn from his body.

He groaned and slumped to the side, his shoulder resting on the tree next to him.

The vision grew even brighter as the newly energized Mantle projected the images into his head. Somehow, Watcher could feel connected to the skeletons, and knew he could issue a command to them if he desired. But for some reason, the thought scared him.

The image grew dim again, as before, and again pain spread through his body like a raging inferno. Watcher gasped as fingers of agony wrapped their torturous grasp around his body. He knew it was the armor doing this to him, draining his health and pumping the energy into the enchanted relic; he could feel his health flowing into it. He had to take it off.

Slowly, he reached up, but his arms felt as if they were made of lead. He could barely move. Another blast of pain flooded through him, every nerve feeling as like it was on fire. Using every bit of strength, he raised his arm again, but before he could reach the armor, it was pulled off his shoulder.

It felt as if a million pounds had been lifted off his body. Watcher collapsed, falling to the ground.

"Watcher, are you okay?" Planter was helping him up. "What happened? You flashed red and groaned, then were quiet."

He tried to speak, but was too weak.

Mapper reached into his inventory and brought out a splash potion of healing and threw it on the boy. The glass shattered on his shoulder, splashing pink liquid across his body, rejuvenating his HP and bringing color back to his skin.

"Watcher, are you all right?" Cutter helped the boy to his feet.

"I thought . . ." Watcher took a breath. "I thought if I didn't get that thing off me . . . I was going to die." He took another huge breath, then finally relaxed a bit.

"What happened?" Mapper picked up the sparkling armor off the ground and handed it back to the young boy.

Watcher looked at it like it was a poisonous monster. "I think it uses the HP of the wearer to give it power. The images started to fade away, like the armor was running out of energy to keep working, then it felt as if the entire coat of chain mail was stabbing into my skin and sucking out my health."

"That's terrible," Planter said.

"There are hints that many of the magical creations from the wizards and warlocks came at a great price," Mapper said. "I think we now understand what they meant."

"For a moment there, I thought it was going to pull out my soul." Watcher shook for a moment. "There was a great emptiness in that armor, like it wanted more power, and there would never be enough to satisfy it. I don't know what will happen if I use it again. I'm afraid I'll get lost in that dark emptiness and never escape."

"Maybe it's too dangerous to use," Planter said.

"Well . . . if we don't—" Cutter started to say but was interrupted.

"I'm okay now." Watcher stood up straight, not wanting to look weak in front of Planter. "I think we need to get moving. The wither king thinks we're dead; we have the element of surprise on our side. While it's still dark, let's go sneak into the Capitol and rescue our friends."

"I agree," Cutter said. "Everyone follow me. We'll steal some boats from the fishing village and get onto that island."

He turned and stepped through the bushes, parting vines with his hand as Cutter headed for the shore, the rest of the party following close behind.

When they reached the docks, each climbed into a boat and shoved off. Watcher took in a huge breath, the salty, clean air driving some of the lingering pain from his head, then glanced at the moon. It was just starting to kiss the western horizon. Day was coming soon; they had to hurry. But as they rowed, Watcher thought about something his dad, Cleric, was fond of saying: *"Wanting to do something, without forming a plan, is the same as making an empty wish."*

Is that what we're doing, trying to free our friends and families without any real plan in place? Watcher shuddered as the thought bounced around in his head. It gave him a feeling of dread that seemed to chill his very soul. He felt they were missing something. Just sneaking around in the dark might not be good enough, but they had no choice. So instead of speaking out, Watcher continued to row, while a maelstrom of fear slowly built in his mind.

CHAPTER 27

Silently, the companions stepped out of their boats and ran across the wooden dock, each staring up at the massive castle that loomed over the island. Their boots pounded against the wooden planks, the muffled thuds like thunder in the still night air. Watcher ran next to Er-Lan, the tiny zombie surprisingly quick on his feet. When they reached the end of the dock, they moved behind the closest building in the tiny village to catch their breath where no one could see them.

"Everything seems so empty." Planter stood on her toes and peeked through a glass window. "I can see a few items lying on the ground. It's like the people living here had to leave in a hurry."

"The wither king invaded with many monsters," Er-Lan said. "Likely the inhabitants were either driven off or destroyed."

"You sound pretty casual about that," Cutter said.

Er-Lan gave the big warrior a fearful glance.

"It's not his fault, Cutter." Reaching into his inventory, Watcher drew an arrow and notched it to his bowstring. "Er-Lan cannot be held responsible for the actions of all the other monsters. Besides, he did help us out back there with Tu-Kar."

"Well . . . I guess." Cutter glanced at the little zombie. "It's just . . . I'm not used to being around zombies."

"You mean, you aren't used to being around zombies and not trying to kill them." Blaster gave him a smile.

"Well . . . yeah, I guess that's right."

"Then that's something we need to work on," Planter added.

"Let's get this done." Blaster adjusted his black leather cap, then drew his two knives. "Follow me."

Moving like a shadow, Blaster ran from one deserted home to the next, using the structures for cover whenever possible.

Watcher peered through the window of each building as he moved past. They were all masked in darkness, with no torches or redstone lanterns anywhere to offer illumination. Moving to the next building, he peeked in.

"I thought I saw something move." Watcher gripped his bow tight, fear tingling along his nerves.

"What was it?" Cutter's voice was quiet, less than a whisper.

"I don't know . . . it's too dark." Watcher glanced at the west. The moon was sinking behind the horizon; they had to hurry.

"Watcher, you were able to smell the zombies before," Mapper said softly. "Can you smell anything now?"

The young archer shook his head. "All I can smell is the salty air from the ocean."

Just then, a moan floated to them on the breeze. It sounded as if it came from very far away, something they didn't need to worry about . . . for the moment. But it still caused tiny square goosebumps to form on Watcher's arms and neck.

"I see some steps at the end of this village." Blaster turned and glanced at the others. "I say we make a break for it and get up those stairs. We can't be caught down here after sunrise."

"Okay," Cutter said. "Lead on."

They ran through the deserted village, moving from building to building as before.

The moaning grew louder.

Watcher glanced around, looking for the source, but with the moon almost down, and the sun not up yet, it was incredibly dark. He thought the sad moan was maybe coming from the castle high overhead. But then Watcher heard it from behind him. Stopping in the middle of the village, he turned and looked back at the dock. An inky blackness seemed to cover everything, erasing the details of the village gate and boats and ocean. Another moan, this one louder, then came to them from off to the left, then another from the right.

"Is the wind playing tricks on my old ears?" Mapper asked.

"I don't . . . know." Planter's voice cracked with fear.

A sour, putrid smell drifted across the abandoned village. It was the odor of something rotting from neglect, like spoiled meat or curdled milk. It drove the salt air from Watcher's nostrils and filled them with a stench he instantly recognized.

"Zombies." The boy didn't bother to whisper.

Now the moans grew louder, intermixed with angry growls and hungry snarls.

At the foot of the steps up ahead, shapes moved across the path, their arms outstretched. Sharp claws scratched across stone blocks as the creatures filled in the village.

Suddenly, a torch flared into life, then another and another, illuminating the stairs. Before them, at least a hundred zombies were piling down the steps, some of them falling off the stairway as their clumsy feet missed the next step. They growled and snarled as their dark, lifeless eyes stared straight at the invaders.

"Oh no," Planter said.

"That's a lot of zombies." Blaster adjusted his black armor. "I think we need a better plan."

"Many zombies . . . Er-Lan said many zombies." The tiny monster shook with fear.

"We hear you, zombie . . . I mean Er-Lan."

The monster stopped shaking for just an instant.

"Watcher, you have any ideas?" Mapper asked.

But the young archer was paralyzed with fear.

CHAPTER 28

A large zombie, clad in iron armor and wielding an enchanted sword, stepped forward and pointed his blade at Watcher and his friends. He snarled, making a sound like that of an enraged beast, then charged, yelling at the top of his voice. "ATTACK!"

The horde of fangs and claws surged forward.

Blaster instantly went into motion, darting between the buildings. Cutter moved to the front and waited for the tidal wave of hatred about to crash down upon them. Planter moved to Watcher's side, Needle held at the ready. Mapper and Er-Lan stood at the rear, determined looks on their faces. The old man had splash potions in each hand and Er-Lan's small, dull claws were extended, though they would likely have little effect.

Everyone was ready for battle except Watcher. The whole scene seemed to blur as time slowed, stretching the terror into a long, drawn-out moment that consumed his mind.

What do I do? Have I failed my family? Have I led my friends to their deaths? Thoughts of uncertainty circled his soul like vultures around a wounded beast. Self-confidence . . . clever ideas . . . courage . . . they were but distant memories. The Watcher that he knew was gone.

But then, a voice spoke, soft and lyrical. It was from the deepest recesses of his mind; something from long ago when he was very young. Chills ran down his spine when he realized the words were from when his mother had been so terribly sick. They were her last words, though at the time he'd been too young to understand them.

"Watcher, a great NPC is not defined by skill with a blade or accuracy with a bow. They are not the strongest or the fastest or the bravest. A great NPC is the person that's willing to take a risk and step into the darkness, in hopes of making the world just a little better for everyone else."

He shook almost imperceptibly as he fought back a tear.

"Mom . . ." Over the years, Watcher had forgotten what she looked like, but now her image was burning bright in his mind. "Step into the darkness . . ."

He knew what he had to do.

Time returned to normal as the growls and moans of the zombies filled the air. Planter was shouting something, but he couldn't understand. Cutter was slashing at the lead zombie, the two warriors locked in deadly combat.

Dropping his bow, he removed his armor, then reached into his inventory and pulled out the Mantle of Command.

"Watcher . . . no." Mapper's voice sounded so far away.

He lowered the sparkling chain mail over his head, then closed his eyes and stepped into the darkness of his mind.

Instantly, pain engulfed his body as tiny little needles dug into his soul; the armor was energizing and drawing out his HP.

It doesn't matter what happens to me as long as I can save my friends. Watcher was without fear.

He concentrated on the zombies. Instantly, he felt connected to every monster on the island. Before he lost his nerve, he sent the command that he hoped would save them all.

"Leave this island . . . now!" Watcher's voice sounded weak, but he could hear the sounds of battle pause for just a moment.

Pain blasted through him again. He sank to his knees. Something wet splashed against his back, easing the agony just a bit, causing his connection to the zombies to slacken. Focusing his will, he reached out and could sense every zombie, projecting the magical power of the Mantle to them. The monsters appeared to glow with a soft purple radiance in the darkness of his mind, but one was slightly different. They had an ancient feel to them, as if they were from another time, but they were also brighter and filled with hope. They were all staring at him now, listening to his command.

But there was also another thing high up in the castle he could feel, a thing wrapped in a darkness deeper than even the void. It was a strong source of magic and hatred, not weak-minded like the zombies. The strength of that creature's mind would not allow the magical armor to control it; that dark monster was immune to the Mantle of Command. Watcher pushed aside the shadowy thing and focused on the zombies.

"Leave this island . . . NOW!"

Some of the monsters around them stopped growling and grew silent. His entire body felt as if it were wrapped with fire as anguish spread through every nerve.

Watcher lifted his head and stared at the monsters. His eyes glowed with a purple radiance, casting his magical gaze across the horde like enchanted laser beams.

"LEAVE THIS ISLAND . . . NOW!"

A blast of magical energy burst from him, knocking some of the zombies to the ground.

The monsters before him stopped attacking, turned, and shuffled toward the wall that ringed the village.

Using their sharp claws, they climbed the rocky barricade, then jumped off, landing in the water. Watcher could feel the zombies deep underground drop their weapons and leave their posts, climbing the long stairs that would lead the guards out of the mines and off the island.

A thought flashed through his mind. "Er-Lan . . . stay."

His connection to the zombies faded. Watcher tensed, ready for the Mantle of Command to take the last of his HP and end his life. But the million-pound weight that pressed down upon his soul was lifted off his shoulders, relieving his pain at the very last moment. Then he collapsed, his life hanging on by a single thread.

CHAPTER 29

A deluge of salt water crashed over his head, the chilling liquid instantly pulling the boy into consciousness.

"He's coming around."

Watcher reached up and wiped the water from his face, then slowly sat up.

"What happened?" The NPC looked around, confused.

"You sent all the zombies away." Planter had a joyous smile on her face. "You saved us!"

"Good goin', kid." Cutter slapped him on the shoulder, almost knocking him over.

"Take it easy on him," Blaster cautioned. "He just saved us all with some quick thinking."

"Sorry." The warrior glanced at his companions. "We need to get moving and find our friends."

"I know where they are." Watcher shook his head, throwing a spray of water on his friends, then slowly stood. "And I also know what's nearby."

Mapper moved to the boy's side. "What do you mean by that, Watcher?"

"The wither king—I could feel him through the enchanted chain mail. Our friends are somewhere underground, but that monster is close."

"All the more reason to get moving," Cutter said.

"Where are we going?" Planter asked. "We have no idea where the mines are located. Our friends could be anywhere."

"Well, I know for a fact we aren't gonna find them out here, near the outer wall," Cutter said. "Let's get closer and we'll figure it out."

"I agree," Watcher said. "But first, where's Er-Lan?"

"Here . . . Er-Lan is here."

The zombie stood away from the rest of the group, uncertain if he was still welcome after the confrontation with the monster horde.

Watcher motioned for him to come close. With his eyes to the ground, Er-Lan shuffled up and stood at the boy's side.

"Er-Lan, I could sense you when I used that magical armor."

The zombie nodded.

"You're not like those other zombies. There is no hatred in your heart."

The monster looked up at Watcher.

"You have been an outcast from your people, not because you aren't strong or vicious, but because you're a peace-maker. I could see, in your heart, that you want happiness, not conflict. You want to give and not take. The zombie people, I think, are not ready for a zombie as advanced as you . . . but one day, they will be. For now, you're part of our family."

The zombie smiled. "Really?"

"Of course." Planter put an arm around the monster. "You're one of us, now and forever."

The zombie glanced at the other NPCs, then turned his gaze to Cutter. The big NPC returned the look, then sighed and nodded. Er-Lan's smile grew even bigger.

"It's time to move . . . now." Watcher patted the zombie on the shoulder, then spun and headed for the stairs.

The young archer walked slowly at first, but as his head cleared he began to run. Sprinting up the steps,

Watcher kept a cautious eye on the surroundings. The sky was blushing a deep crimson as the sun rose in the east, driving away the sparkling stars and the dark sky. The surroundings grew brighter, making it easier to spot any stray monsters who might have refused his command with the Mantle. Thankfully, they found none.

As he approached the top of the stairs, a weak and scratchy voice spoke a single word. "Help."

At the top, Watcher found a villager in an iron cage. He looked bone thin, as if he hadn't eaten in an eternity. Pulling out his pickaxe, he went to work on the iron bars. When they finally shattered, he quickly handed the man a piece of cooked pork.

"Are you all right?" Planter helped the man to his feet.

"Yes, yes, Sweeper is all right." The villager had a crazed expression on his face. "Been there a long time, I have, but now I am free. The wither king will be furious . . . ha ha ha . . . yes, yes, furious."

Watcher glanced at Planter. The old villager sounded a little crazy.

"Your name is Sweeper?" Watcher asked.

The villager nodded.

Watcher gave the man an apple. "Why were you in that cage?"

"Sweeper knows everything about the Capitol. The caretaker, I was. Kaza didn't want my secrets to get out, but he still needed information every now and then . . . like the combination to the Great Vault."

"The Great Vault?" Blaster asked.

The old man nodded. "Yes, yes, the Great Vault. That's where Kaza's gold is stored. When he has enough gold, the treasure will awaken the ancient wither army that existed in the days of the wizards. When that happens, the end of the Far Lands will be near."

"That doesn't sound good," Watcher said.

Cutter stepped forward. "How do we find the vault? Do we go through that huge castle up there?" The warrior pointed to the gigantic stone structure that loomed overhead.

"No, no, no . . . anyone going through will be attacked by monsters."

"Not to worry, we got rid of all the zombies." Watcher stood a little taller and smiled.

"Ha . . . zombies are not the problem." Sweeper leaned forward and spoke in a low voice. "Zombies are not the only creatures here. There are spiders and skeletons and creepers. The front entrance of the castle is well guarded. Anyone entering that way . . . their life will be sacrificed." He glanced around, as if looking to see if anyone were watching. "There is a back entrance to the vaults, yes, yes, a back entrance. Go through Mr_man12's house and you will find the secret entrance, yes you will. Ha ha ha."

Watcher glanced at Cutter, a worried expression on his young face. Cutter just shrugged.

"Go into the back entrance and find the minecart tracks that go deep underground. Sweeper put a slime block at the bottom of the shaft. You can jump straight down without taking any damage. Ha ha . . . Kaza will never know you are there."

Is Sweeper insane? Watcher thought. He wondered if anything the old man was telling them was the truth, or if he had just lost his mind.

"Take the back entrance and you can get to Kaza's gold." Sweeper moved closer to Watcher and whispered. "Destroy his gold and you destroy his plans. The army of withers must not be awakened."

"Yes, I'm sure you're right but—"

"You need better weapons and stronger armor to defeat the royal guards. Plus, you'll need TNT to destroy the gold."

"What?" Blaster pushed Cutter aside and moved next to Sweeper. "What did you say about TNT?"

"Before Kaza took over the Capitol, I hid weapons, armor, potions, and TNT in various shops and homes." Sweeper laughed manically. "Find the quarters of Quadbamber, Arp97, Mr_man12, Benma98, and devLuca. There is a sign outside each shop or home with their name on it. Inside, I've hidden chests with loot in them. These things will help you destroy the gold and hopefully allow you to escape with your lives as well."

"Do we need to know anything else?" Planter asked.

Sweeper turned away from Planter. He tilted his head as if he were listening to some invisible companion speaking to him. With a nod of his head, he turned back.

"One last thing . . . the vault is sealed with a combination lock, if it even still works." Sweeper smiled, his teeth stained and decaying. "Kaza made Sweeper promise not to tell, but I *will* tell the nice girl."

The crazy NPC paused as if waiting for something.

"Well . . . what's the combination?"

"Ahh . . . oh yeah . . . the combination is 1638." Sweeper smiled. "Once the vault doors are opened, the Royal Guards will know you are there, so be cautious but also be fast. If Kaza catches you in the vault, his flaming skulls will destroy you all. And watch out for the Royal Guards."

"Thank you, Sweeper, for your help." Watcher handed the old man a slice of melon. He devoured it.

"One last thing . . . one last thing."

"What is it?" Cutter asked.

"Remember the crown—he draws his power from the crown." Sweeper turned and headed down the stairs. "Must destroy the Crown of Skulls so that the wither's power can be extinguished." His voice grew softer. "Yes, yes . . . the crown must be melted, must be melted. Remember the crown . . . remember the . . ."

The old man reached the bottom of the stairs and ran for the docks, his voice too soft to hear any longer.

Watcher looked at his friends. They all had surprised expressions on their faces.

"You think anything he said was true?" Mapper asked.

"We'll find out soon enough," Blaster said. "Everyone choose a different name and go find their home. We need that hidden loot."

"Right, everyone, pick a name." Watcher glanced at them. "I'll take Quadbamber's house. Meet back here as soon as you can. Move quick and quiet—there may still be monsters about."

They all nodded and dispersed, leaving Er-Lan next to Sweeper's shattered cage.

As Watcher ran, he thought about that dark presence he'd sensed within the castle. He was sure it was Kaza; the incredible hatred and thirst for violence that creature emanated seemed to burn a hole in his mind. They would have to face that creature eventually, but would better weapons or enchanted armor make any difference? He shook almost imperceptibly as he thought about that inevitable confrontation, fingers of terror squeezing his soul.

CHAPTER 30

The companions returned to Er-Lan with arms full of items. They laid loot out on the ground so everyone could see everything that had been found.

"What are those?" Watcher pointed to arrows with large red tips and tiny crimson sparkles dancing around the shafts.

"Those are arrows of healing." Mapper picked one up. "They heal whatever target they hit."

"So, they're like the splash potions you used on Watcher?" Planter asked.

Mapper nodded.

"And just like the ones you used on the zombies in Tu-Kar's hideout." Watcher picked one up.

Mapper nodded again.

"Interesting . . . I'll take all those, and the enchanted bow." Watcher held the sparkling weapon in his hand. He could tell by the way his inventory reacted, it had the *Infinity* enchantment. And by the way it pulsed, he figured the bow also had the *Punch* enchantment as well; Watcher would know for sure when he fired the first shot. He also grabbed an iron helmet and placed it on his head.

Blaster smiled as he picked up stacks of TNT, piles

of redstone dust, and redstone repeaters. "I know just what to do with all of this."

Cutter took the enchanted iron armor, while Mapper scooped up the many potions. Planter removed her normal chain mail and took the enchanted mail, its purple glow casting a lavender circle on the ground. Watcher doubted the armor was the same as the Mantle of Command, but he still watched her cautiously for any signs of pain. With a smile, Planter gave him a nod, signaling it was okay.

Everyone took something from the pile of loot, except for Er-Lan. The small zombie just stared down at the items, unsure what to do.

"Er-Lan, you need some weapons." Watcher picked up an iron sword and extended it to the zombie. "Take something."

"Well . . . Er-Lan has not earned . . . um . . ."

Cutter lifted an iron chest plate off the ground, the armor decorated with jagged streaks of black and white that looked like lightning bolts. The big warrior raised it over the monster's head and settled it onto his shoulders. "You earned this when you helped me with Tu-Kar. No one can dispute that. And if they do . . . they must deal with me." He then grabbed an iron helmet and placed it on his head. "Now you look like a proper warrior."

Er-Lan smiled, as did the rest of the companions.

"Okay, it's time." Watcher adjusted his helmet, the metallic cap wobbling about, a little too big for his head. He reached up and straightened it again. "Let's find that secret entrance to the vaults. With all that TNT Blaster has in his inventory, we could destroy Kaza's gold. I don't like the idea of a wither army being awakened."

"Good idea." Cutter drew his diamond sword. "I found Mr_man12's home, follow me."

"Then lead on," Watcher said, gesturing with his sparkling, enchanted bow.

The warrior nodded, then took off running, his heavy boots thudding on the stone path. They followed, eyes shifting from left to right, searching for stray monsters. The stone pathway branched off in many directions, but Cutter followed the one that led directly to their destination, Mr_man12's house.

They stopped at an arched entrance, multi-colored banners hanging high overhead. A sign next to the entrance marked the owner's name; they were in the right place. They entered the structure, passing an ornate fountain ringed with iron bars. Next to the flowing water, Cutter found an open door.

They followed the big warrior into the room, weapons held at the ready.

"This looks like some kind of dormitory or something." Planter pointed to the many beds lining one wall. "This must have been where all the soldiers lived, before . . ." She grew silent.

"You mean before Kaza invaded, and destroyed them all," Watcher added.

Planter nodded.

"We're gonna make him pay." Blaster drew one of his knives and tested the keen edge with his thumb.

"Which way do we go?" Mapper asked.

Watcher glanced around the room. There was a large passage that plunged down a set of wide stairs, but the passage was dark and foreboding.

"I don't like the look of that corridor." Blaster pointed with his knife. "Let's follow the one that's lit up. I like being able to see what's trying to destroy me."

"Agreed." Cutter headed through another narrow passage, the rest of the party following.

After about a dozen blocks, they were outside of the building, near the back of the castle which soared high into the sky.

"There are some steps there." Planter pointed with Needle. "I bet that's the rear entrance."

They sprinted up the steps that wrapped around the back side of the castle. The stairway ended at a wide gate that stood open; likely Kaza figured no one was crazy enough to try and break into his fortress. A gravel path led from the gate and into a small courtyard ringed with tall stone-brick walls. The entrance to the main castle was blocked off with iron bars. Watcher smiled . . . that meant any monsters in there couldn't get to them, but they could still see them if they looked this way.

A clicking sound floated out of the castle accompanied with the rattling sound, like someone rubbing dry sticks together.

"Spiders and skeletons," Blaster whispered.

Watcher nodded.

The sounds echoed off the many stone walls, making it impossible to tell how many monsters were guarding the fortress. But it didn't matter. Everyone in their company knew they had to see this through in order to save their friends, and possibly save the Far Lands as well.

Watcher motioned the others to hug the walls and stay away from the barred opening; if they were spotted now, it would be a problem. The path split in two near the bars, with the second path leading into a small building. Watcher peeked through the door and saw it was empty, then entered.

"Over here." Blaster stood in front of a set of minecart tracks that spiraled downward into the darkness. "I can't see the bottom. Those tracks must go down really far."

"Do we just walk on the tracks to get down there?" Planter whispered.

Watcher shook his head. "If a minecart comes down the tracks while we're on the rails, we'll be in serious trouble."

"The caretaker, Sweeper, said something about slime blocks," Mapper said.

"Yeah, he said he put the slime blocks at the bottom of this shaft." Blaster peered down into the darkness again. "He said we could just jump."

"But what if the monsters took out the slime blocks after they imprisoned Sweeper?" Planter glanced at her friends. "That fall would be fatal."

"One of us needs to try," Mapper said.

"Here's what I'm gonna do." Cutter spoke in a quiet voice. "I'll jump down there. If I survive, I'll tap the tracks with my sword so you know it's okay. Then, all of you—"

Er-Lan pushed through the group of villagers and stood at the edge of the vertical shaft. He glanced over his shoulder and gave his companions a toothy grin, then jumped.

"Er-Lan!" Planter reached out to the zombie, but he was already gone.

They waited. It seemed to Watcher as if an eternity had passed, but finally, a dull thud sounded from the shaft, followed by another and another. Then, a tapping echoed up the passage, the sound running up the minecart rails.

Planter breathed a sigh of relief. "He made it."

"One at a time, let's go." Cutter jumped into the hole.

After fifteen seconds, another person jumped, then another and another. Watcher waited at the end, an arrow notched to his bow. He stared into the darkness of the chamber, the clicking and rattling bones still at a murmur . . . for now.

Watcher stepped to the edge of the shaft and looked down. All he could see was darkness below. For some reason, he took a big breath as if he were diving into a pool . . . and then he jumped.

The minecart rails spiraled around him as he fell. Glancing down, something green came into view as he fell: the slime blocks. Watcher bounced high into the air when he hit the spongy blocks, then bounced again and again until he finally came to rest.

He climbed off the minecart track and into a long, high-ceilinged passage. Instantly, a dusty, dank smell invaded his senses. This tunnel felt as if it were hundreds of years old, which was probably about right. Watcher knew the Capitol had been built during the Great War between the wizards and the warlocks. Probably, many of the great wizards had walked these very halls back then. The thought made Watcher nervous for just an instant, but for some reason, he felt at home in the hallowed passage.

A long passage stretched out before him, with blocks of netherrack burning perpetually behind sets of bars. The flames lit the passage with flickering light, making it easy to see the footsteps of his comrades on the dusty floor. Watcher followed the passage, turning to the left and right, until he found himself before the door to the vault. His friend stood before a large keypad on the wall, numbers beneath each stone button.

"Anyone remember the combination Sweeper told us?"

"I think he said it was 5 2 3 8." Blaster reached up and pressed the buttons.

"Did anyone check out the door to the vault?" Watcher gestured to the huge hole in the iron bars that had, at one time, blocked the passage. "I don't think we're gonna need that combination after all."

They moved through the opening in the bars, and down a long passage, with Cutter leading the way. The big NPC led them past a set of double iron doors. Above them, a sign said "Security Offices" and "Authorized Personnel Only." Cutter ignored the doors and kept going, his boots echoing off the stone walls.

At the end of the passage a single torch burned. When they neared, the companions found two stairways, one going to the left, the other to the right.

"Which one?" Cutter glanced at Watcher.

One of the stairwells was well lit, with torches on the walls. The other was masked in darkness.

"I say we keep following the torches," Watcher said.

Without waiting for a response, the young archer ran down the stairs to the left. They turned once to the left, then to the right, ending at a wall made entirely of wooden planks. Large glass windows lined the wall, allowing Watcher to peer into the room on the other side. It was empty, lit by a single, flickering torch.

Watcher stepped in through the door a few blocks down, sweeping the room with his sensitive vision; it was indeed deserted. Moving cautiously forward, Watcher drew back an arrow and slid his back along the wall. Even though he couldn't hear anything, the young archer felt as if there were monsters nearby.

Inching along, he finally came to a large arched opening. On the other side of the archway, a huge chamber taller than anything he's ever seen stretched out before him. Chests were stacked from ground to ceiling, with columns of wood on either side, and ladders on the wooden columns that gave access to the upper storage and topmost chests.

Watcher stepped into the room, stunned by the immensity of it. There really were hundreds of chests, stacked from floor to ceiling all throughout the chamber, with ladders climbing all the way up into the darkness high overhead. It was an incredible construction, but the thought of why someone needed this much storage was even more confusing.

What did they do here, in the Capitol, in the ancient times? Watcher shook his head in disbelief.

"Look," Planter whispered.

Watcher turned and found his friend pointing to the end of the storage chamber. Another arched opening sat at the far end of the chamber, leading to a room made of bright white quartz. Blocks of nether-quartz created intricate patterns on the walls, adding occasional splashes of red. A golden glow spilled out of the chamber, the edge of some gold blocks just barely visible.

"That's the treasury room and Kaza's gold . . . come on." She sprinted toward the opening.

"No . . . wait!"

But it was too late. Planter charged through the storage chamber, heading for the gold, the rest of the party in hot pursuit. As their boots pounded on the ground, Watcher picked up on a strange sound. It reminded him of Er-Lan's claw tapping on the minecart rail, a hollow and angry sort of noise.

They were a dozen blocks from the treasury chamber.

"Slow down," Watcher warned, but no one listened.

The clicking was getting louder. Glancing up, he saw things moving in the darkness. They were large shapes that clung to the ceiling, moving about faster and faster, as if they were getting agitated.

And then one of them opened its eight bright-red eyes. Then another, and another, and another.

"Everyone . . . look up." Watcher pointed with his bow. "Spiders."

Planter skidded to a stop and stared at the ceiling. The darkness was now filled with red dots. When they spotted the intruders, spiders clicked their mandibles faster, then descended from their lofty perch. The fuzzy monsters climbed down the wooden columns, some of them descending on the finest strand of spider's web. As they moved into the light, Watcher gasped.

"Are those . . ." Mapper didn't finish the sentence.

Blaster nodded his head. "Yep . . . they're spider jockeys."

Riding on the backs of the spiders were skeletons, some armored in chain mail and iron while others wore nothing but their pale bones.

"We need to get into the treasury room before—" Cutter started to say, just as a dozen spider jockeys scurried out of the treasury room, cutting off their escape. "—before that happens."

"These must be the Royal Guards that Sweeper warned us about." Mapper put a splash potion of healing in each hand, then handed one to Er-Lan.

"Everyone, get back to back," Watcher said.

The spiders and their skeleton riders slowly approached, the bony monsters drawing back their arrows, but withholding their fire.

Planter moved next to Watcher, Needle in her right hand, the enchanted shield from the watchtower in her right. She looked at him, a fearful expression on her face.

"Don't worry . . . it's gonna be all right." Watcher knew his face betrayed the lie.

One of the spiders scuttled forward and glared at the villagers, then screeched in a high-pitched voice. "Royal Guardssss . . . ATTACK!"

CHAPTER 31

The spiders scurried across the stone floor, the claws at the end of each leg making a scratching sound as they went. They moved forward cautiously, trying to get close enough so the skeletons could release their deadly projectiles.

The bony monsters drew their arrows and notched them to their strings. They pulled back their shafts in unison, aiming at the invaders.

"Er-Lan . . . you ready?" Mapper asked.

The zombie gave off a soft moan.

"Mapper, what are you doing?" Watcher glanced at the old NPC.

"NOW!"

At the same instant, Mapper threw splash potions of healing at the monsters on one side while Er-Lan did the same on the other. The sparkling liquid coated the skeletons and instantly tore into their HP. Many of the bony creatures fell off their mounts, writhing on the ground in pain. Their emaciated bodies flashed red as the healing potion, normally helpful to living creatures, poisoned the undead skeletons.

They threw another volley, and another and another, spreading the glass vials all throughout the chamber.

The skeletons screamed in pain, the monsters flashing red over and over, then disappearing with their health became exhausted.

"Mapper . . . what's happening? I thought only zombies were hurt by the healing potion." Watcher drew back an arrow and fired it at the closest skeleton still riding a spider.

"Skeletons are part of the undead, just like zombies." The old man threw another bottle as Er-Lan launched one to the back of the horde.

The last of the skeletons finally perished, leaving a mass of angry spiders glaring at them with angry red eyes.

"Planter, protect Mapper and Er-Lan with your shield." Watcher turned and fired an arrow at a spider climbing down one of the chests. "Everyone . . . ATTACK!"

Watcher charged forward, his bowstring singing. He fired three arrows into a spider before it even had a chance to move. Cutter, with his enchanted armor and diamond blade, crashed into the fuzzy monsters like a storm from the heavens. He slashed and kicked the monsters, tearing HP from the dark creatures. Watcher fired on the monsters that tried to attack his flank, his deadly missiles keeping the monsters from sneaking up from the rear.

Behind him, Blaster was jumping from spider to spider, leaping off their backs as he raked them with his curved blades. The monsters tried to reach up and slash at him with their wicked, curved claws, but the boy was just too fast.

Watcher glanced over his shoulder to check on Planter. She'd left Mapper and Er-Lan to join the fray. Needle flashed through the air like an enchanted bolt of lightning. She hit one spider after another, all the while blocking the monsters' attack with her green shield. She was a force to be reckoned with, and the spiders knew it.

Watcher moved to Cutter's side, his bow humming. He fired at spiders as they approached, his shafts making the monsters think twice before coming too close. Notching two arrows at a time, he fired them at monsters one or two blocks away. The monsters screeched in pain, then veered off, only to be caught by Cutter's blade.

Loading three arrows into the bow, he fired them into monster after monster. The trio of projectiles silenced many of the monsters before they could get close enough for Cutter's blade.

Charging into the spider horde, Cutter focused his rage on the largest beast. She was the spider who had signaled the attack, and likely their leader. The monster slashed at the big warrior with her claws. He blocked an advancing claw, but missed one from the other side. Her razor-sharp claw cut across his enchanted iron armor, leaving a deep gouge. Watcher moved forward and fired on the closest monsters. Meanwhile, some of them were trying to sneak up behind Cutter's back, but Watcher wasn't going to allow that.

Cutter glanced over his shoulder briefly, a look at worry on his face.

"Don't worry . . . I got your back." Watcher fired at another spider with a trio of arrows, driving the monster back. "Just take care of their leader."

Blaster appeared at Watcher's side, a huge grin on his square face. He kicked one spider away, then slashed at another with his twin, curved knives. Planter joined them on his other side, her blade tearing into fuzzy bodies. They drove the monsters back, allowing Cutter to face off against the leader.

"Come on, spider. Let's finish this." Cutter charged, swinging his blade with all his might.

At the same time, the spider jumped high, hoping to land on top of the warrior. As the huge monster soared through the air, Watcher put two arrows into her, making the massive creature flash red, taking damage. When the creature hit the ground, it was Cutter that was in the air. The NPC landed on the monsters back, swinging his blade faster than ever. The spider flashed red again and again until she finally disappeared with a pop, her HP exhausted.

Watcher turned to the other spiders and fired, the *Infinity* enchantment giving him endless arrows. The monsters, seeing that their leader had been destroyed, turned and fled amidst the hail of pointed shafts. They ran to the stacked chests and scurried up the wooden columns, disappearing into the darkness that hugged the ceiling, their bright red eyes peering down at them from the shadows.

"We did it!" Blaster exclaimed.

"Not yet," Watcher warned and he checked to make sure everyone was okay. "We still have a wither king to deal with."

 "First, we need to take care of the gold." Cutter stepped through the field of bones, some of them crunching under his boots. Moving into the next room, he found a huge pile of gold blocks, each crafted from nine gold ingots. "There must be a thousand blocks of gold in this pile."

The flickering light from the torches danced across the reflective blocks, casting a yellow glow on the white walls and ceiling.

"We gotta get this done before the spiders bring back reinforcements." Watcher turned and faced Blaster. "You have any ideas about how we can get rid of all this gold?"

Pulling a block of TNT from his inventory, the boy nodded and smiled. "I know exactly what to do, and all of you are gonna help me."

Blaster quickly handed out the TNT and redstone dust, then sprinted into the chamber. The six companions crawled across the pile of gold, placing the TNT, then ran a line of the red powder down to the ground. In a few minutes, blocks of TNT covered the mound of precious metal, the redstone starting from each block and leading to the ground where they joined into a single line, repeaters distributed throughout.

When they were finished, Blaster ran throughout the chamber, checking their work. It had to be right or the gold would not be destroyed. Watcher and Cutter moved to the treasury entrance and watched for more spiders as Blaster finished his inspection.

"It looks good . . . everyone ready?" He took off his black leather cap and scratched his head. His curly black hair was matted to his scalp, tiny, square beads of sweat dripping down his face. "Everyone get back. When we set this off, I guarantee you the wither king will know we're here . . . if he doesn't already."

The rest of the party moved into the next room, making sure they were far from the pile of gold. Blaster ran the redstone all the way out of the quartz chamber, then pulled out a redstone torch.

"This is my favorite part." Blaster smiled, then placed the torch to the ground.

Instantly, the redstone powder grew bright, the signal flowing through the crimson lines. Where it hit a repeater, the dimming signal was amplified again, flowing away from the device stronger and brighter.

The blocks that lined the perimeter of the pile ignited first. This threw the next layer of already blinking cubes toward the center. They detonated, focusing the blast inward, tearing into the pyramid of gold, just as Blaster had planned. More blocks flashed white, then exploded, tearing into the mass of gold. Finally the rest of the blocks erupted. The ground shook as the blast echoed off the walls, nearly deafening the companions, the force of the explosion knocking all but Cutter to the ground. A huge cloud of smoke filled the room as blocks of quartz flew in all directions.

Watcher coughed as he stood back up, his legs feeling shaky. A ringing filled his ears, but it slowly dissipated. He moved forward and stood at Blaster's side in the entrance to the treasury. Where the huge pile of gold had stood, now there was only a crater, a handful of quartz blocks floating at the bottom.

Through the walls of the chamber, a shriek cut through the air like a knife through flesh. It was an enraged, bloodthirsty kind of wail, like a wounded animal. But they all knew what it was . . . Kaza, the King of the Withers. That monster knew what they'd done, and he was enraged.

"I don't like the sound of that." Planter rubbed her arms, trying to get rid of the goosebumps . . . it didn't work.

"Kaza knows what has been done," Er-Lan said.

"You think?" Blaster gave the zombie a smile.

"Yes, Er-Lan thinks."

"Look, there's a hidden passage." Mapper pointed to the far side of the chamber. A dark passage led into the rock of the island, the steps clearly carved into the stone. "I can only think of one person that would want a secret entrance to the treasure."

"Kaza," Watcher said.

Mapper nodded his head. "I say we go up there and give that monster a little surprise."

"The wither king is very dangerous . . . very dangerous." The zombie glanced at his comrades. "Er-Lan does not want new friends to get hurt. All must run away."

"We can't do that." Watcher stood next to the zombie and put a reassuring hand on his armored shoulder. "If we leave now, we can save our friends and family, but that monster up there will just capture more villagers and make them suffer. He'll force more into slavery to mine his gold. We can't let that monster awaken an army of withers . . . they'd be unstoppable."

"What you're talking about is incredibly dangerous," Cutter said.

Watcher nodded his head. "We can't just leave." He glanced at Cutter and could see the strength and courage in the big warrior; it was something to be admired. He was jealous. "Sometimes, you have to just stand and fight, and all the thinking in the world won't help."

Now it was Cutter who was nodding.

"Then I think we need to get this done," the big warrior said.

Just then, another screeching shriek resonated through the Capitol. The sound drove any newly gained courage deep into the recesses of his mind. Watcher shook slightly, then took a nervous swallow. Trying to stand tall, the young boy walked to the secret passage and started climbing the stone steps, knowing full well the most dangerous monster in Minecraft awaited them . . . and wanted revenge.

CHAPTER 32

The stairway was as dark as a tomb. Watcher led the group, placing torches every six paces which spilled light onto the steps and walls but did not reach the ceiling. Glancing up, Watcher probed the darkness with his keen eyes. He could barely make out the top of the passage. It was likely twenty blocks high, if not more.

"Why would the builders of the Capitol want the ceiling to be that high?" Planter's voice echoed off the cold stone walls.

"I don't think this passage was built in the ancient times," Watcher replied. "It doesn't have that ageless feel to it. I think this passage was dug recently, maybe after the wither king took over."

"We need to hurry." Cutter's voice boomed through the stairwell. "There don't seem to be any holes, trip-wires, or pressure plates on the steps, so start running."

Watcher nodded, then sprinted up the stairway, continuing to place torches as he went. They moved in single-file, none of them speaking, the sound of their boots filling the air. Finally, the stairs ended at a set of iron doors, a huge space over the top of them left open.

"I think this is it," Watcher whispered.

He moved to the pressure plates that sat before the doors, looking for any hidden dispensers or trap doors. It all seemed innocuous. Watcher glanced at his companions and nodded.

"We go in fast. Planter, you go with me to the right, Blaster and Cutter to the left." He notched an arrow to his bowstring. "Mapper and Er-Lan, it's probably best you two stay back. If we don't survive, then try to find the mines and help the prisoners to escape the island."

Mapper nodded, but Er-Lan had a sad expression on his scarred face.

"Er-Lan can help." The zombie stood a little taller. "Er-Lan *will* help."

"I don't want you to get hurt, and I don't think your claws will help in this battle." Watcher placed a hand in the center of his chest plate, as if he were feeling his heart. "I know you are brave, but you need not die to prove it. Just stay here and be safe."

A pained look spread across the zombie's green face.

Watcher felt guilty, as if he'd just done something to hurt the little monster, but he knew this was not the time for Er-Lan to prove his courage.

"Everyone ready?" He waited for a nod from everyone. "Then here we go."

 Watcher stepped on the pressure plate. Instantly, the door swung open, revealing a huge chamber with a ceiling at least thirty blocks above them. He dashed into the room, scanning the chamber for the dark monster. Torches lit the walls, revealing bookshelves that lined the wall. High overhead, wooden rafters crisscrossed each other, the beams stretching from one wall the next. They were at various levels, extending all the way to the ceiling. It looked like a crazy parkour course.

"I see I have visitors." The voice boomed throughout the building, coming from somewhere high overhead. "Perhaps I should introduce myself before I destroy you all." A scratchy laugh floated down, but it seemed different from the first voice. "I am Kaza, King of the Withers, and you are trespassing, the punishment for this transgression is, of course, death."

"This is the Capitol and . . . and it belongs to all NPCs." Watcher tried to keep his voice strong and confident, but it cracked with fear.

"Ha ha ha . . . the boy is already afraid," the monster said. "He hasn't even seen us yet."

"Wait until we are face-to-face," a different voice, more lyrical, added. "Then you will know real fear."

Watcher glanced at his companions, and gestured for them to hide in the shadow of a large bookcase.

"Then come down and show yourself, unless you are afraid." Watcher put his bow back into his inventory. "I've put away my little bow and arrow. You have nothing to fear. I am just here to talk."

"Talk . . . I like talking," the scratchy, violent voice said.

A shadowy figure slowly descended from high overhead. It drifted around the rafters, moving silently through the air. Dark ribs stuck out from a long, curving spine, the bones blackened as if charred. It reminded Watcher of the wither skeletons he'd seen once in the Nether, but this creature was bigger . . . much bigger. As it neared, the monster's three heads became visible, the center one wearing a golden crown with tiny black skulls embedded in the rim.

Each head glared at Watcher, their pale eyes emanating such vile hatred, it almost hurt to return their gaze.

"I can only assume it was you that destroyed my gold," the center head said, his voice booming throughout the chamber.

Watcher nodded and tried to smile . . . but he was too afraid.

The head on the left laughed, but Center cast him a warning glance, then turned his attention back to Watcher.

"You have delayed our plans," Center said, "and that makes us very angry."

"*Very* angry!" Left added.

"Left, be quiet." The right head shushed the left one.

"Your punishment for this destruction will not be death, and it will not be slavery." Center leaned forward a little. "I think we will torture you in front of all the other villagers, so they might learn the cost of treachery."

"I don't think so." Watcher took a few steps back. Fear washed over him like a tidal wave, every fiber in his being telling him to run. But he knew he had to get the monster closer. "I'm not going to allow that. It's time you were punished for your crimes, wither, and I'm here to carry out your sentence."

All three heads laughed and moved closer. Watcher backed up a little more.

"And what are you going to do, boy, insult us to death?" Kaza drifted closer, his stubby spine dragging slightly across the wooden floor.

Watcher moved back another step, then bumped into the wall; he had nowhere to run.

Kaza moved closer. "Maybe instead of torturing you, we'll just destroy you. Left, what do you think?"

"Destroy . . . destroy," Left cackled.

"This time, I agree with Left," the right skull added.

"Then it's unanimous." The center head glared at Watcher. "Prepare to meet your doom."

Watcher glanced at the shadowy recession between the bookshelves. Kaza's right head turned in that direction, but it was too late. Cutter and Blaster charged out of the darkness, their blades crashing into the dark creature.

"It's a trap!" Kaza screeched.

The monster started to float upward, trying to flee. Er-Lan bolted out of the doorway and dove through the air. He grabbed the stubby end of the monster's exposed spine, pulling it back to the ground. Blaster and Cutter attacked again, this time with Planter adding the sharp point of Needle.

Kaza screamed in pain as he flashed red. The monster tried to move upward, but the weight of the zombie was too much. Bending his heads down, Kaza fired a flaming skull. The projectile, wreathed in black flames, exploded into the ground, throwing the attackers through the air and causing Er-Lan to lose his grip.

Watcher drew back an arrow and fired, then drew and fired again and again, his arrows causing the monster to scream in agony. Kaza drifted higher and higher into the air, far from the reach of any blade. Now, Watcher's weapon was the only one that could reach the creature.

He drew an arrow back and aimed slightly over the monster's head. He was just about to release when he was knocked to the side by Mapper. At the same time, a flaming skull hit the ground where he had just been standing, the explosion barely missing him.

"You cannot hurt me. I am of the undead, and will regenerate." Kaza laughed from behind one of the rafters.

"Did he say undead?" Watcher glanced at Mapper as they stood.

The old man nodded. "Undead . . . I didn't even think about it." He pulled out a potion of healing and held it in his wrinkled hand.

Watcher reached into his own inventory and withdrew one of the healing arrows, the shaft shimmering with red sparks. He glanced at the bookcases, then instantly identified the proper course.

"Cutter . . . to the rafters." Watcher kept his voice low. "Planter, extinguish the torches. We don't want Kaza to know where we are." He turned to Mapper. "You have any more night vision potions?"

The old man nodded, then threw a splash potion on him. Instantly, colored spirals floated about Watcher's head. The old man threw potions on the others, giving each the ability to pierce the darkness with their eyes.

"Follow me," Watcher said.

He took off running. When he reached a low book-case, he jumped into the air, then leapt onto the next shelf and the next until he reached the first set of raf-ters. Drawing his bow back, he fired the healing arrow at the wither. Before the shaft hit, Watcher sprinted across the narrow beam to the other side. He kicked at torches that were within reach, extinguishing them.

Kaza groaned when the sparkling projectile hit him, the healing effect like poison to the terrifying monster.

Watcher drew and fired again, then jumped to a small ledge, climbing higher into the huge chamber. When he reached the second level of rafters, a flaming skull streaked toward him, hitting the young boy in the chest. The blast pushed him against the wall, tearing at his HP. Pain erupted throughout his body, causing every nerve to scream out in agony. Quickly, he dragged him-self to another ledge and climbed higher along the wall, trying to get away as another skull headed toward him. Pulling out another healing arrow, Watcher gripped the shaft and stabbed the sharp point into his leg. Pain shot through his thigh, but at the same time, a soothing cool-ness drifted across his body; his HP was regenerating.

Cutter jumped onto the next ledge.

"You okay?" the warrior asked.

Watcher nodded.

"Stay here, I'll drive him down to you." Cutter bolted away, jumping from ledge to ledge, then crossing the next rafter and climbing even higher.

"Be careful, a fall from this height would be fatal," Watcher said, but Cutter was already too far away.

He stood and hugged the wall, watching the big war-rior's progress. Blaster shot past him and climbed the opposite side of the chamber, both NPCs trying to close in on the wither king.

A splashing sound drifted up from the ground. *That's strange,* Watcher thought.

Notching two healing arrows, Watcher stood and climbed the wall, wanting to get closer. He knew shooting multiple arrows was only useful if the target was close. Reaching into his inventory, he pulled out a third arrow and notched it to his bowstring; he would have to be really close now.

The sound of battle erupted from high overhead. Cutter shouted as he swung his sword. Blaster laughed as he added his knives to the attack. Glancing upward, Watcher could see the two NPCs standing on a beam above the wither. Their blades crashed into the monster's skulls, making him flash red, taking damage. Suddenly, a sparkling blue sheet of energy enveloped the wither, causing the swords to do less damage. At the same time, the wither sank downward, which always happened when the monster's shimmering shield was present.

"It's rejuvenating," Mapper shouted from the ground. More splashes sounded from below.

Kaza drew closer. Pressing his back to the wall, Watcher tried to merge with the shadows, waiting for the monster to draw close enough. He passed right by him, but the blue-white shield was still present. Watcher knew his arrows would have no effect until the rejuvenation was complete.

Leaping from ledge to ledge, Watcher descended with the monster, waiting patiently for his opportunity. He moved to the next set of rafters and ran across while Kaza drifted even lower, the energetic shield lighting the darkness that now covered the floor.

Leaping down the ledges to the lowest rafter, Watcher sprinted across, hoping to get close enough to attack. But the monster was too far away; he had to get onto the ground. Watcher leapt from the beam to a bookshelf, then followed it to the floor. Scanning the chamber, he spotted the monster and sprinted toward him.

A sparkling iridescent circle of light appeared against one wall. Watcher could see it was Planter, her enchanted shield in one hand and Needle in the other. The wither turned toward the light.

Oh no. A feeling of dread enveloped Watcher.

The sparkling shield faded from Kaza. The monster laughed as his rejuvenated health gave the creature renewed confidence.

"I see a little creature hiding in the darkness." Kaza's voice boomed through the chamber.

Watcher sprinted as fast as he could, but water now covered much of the floor, making him move too slowly. He still wasn't close enough to shoot.

"I think it's time to show the might of Kaza, the king of the withers."

The left head laughed a harsh, scratching laugh as the right head smiled. The center head nodded, then each skull leaned forward and fired flaming skulls at Planter, the barrage impossible to survive.

CHAPTER 33

Planter brought her shield up, but Watcher could see it would be too late. Dropping two of the healing arrows, he drew a single arrow back and fired it at his friend. Once it left his string, he picked up another and fired, then launched the third shaft directly at Planter.

The arrows struck her at the same time as the flaming skulls. The blast of the explosion pushed her against the wall, landing right where Watcher expected. His second and third arrows stuck just after the last two flaming skulls. She flashed red with damage, but the healing arrows helped keep her alive.

Watcher pushed his way through the layer of water covering much of the floor, drawing more of the healing arrows from his inventory. Loading his bow with two more shafts, he fired them at Kaza, then pulled out more. The arrows struck the monster, splashing the healing potion across his ashen body, the liquid dripping from rib to exposed rib.

Kaza screamed in pain, then turned and fired a skull at the archer. Watcher leapt to the side, submerging himself in a block of water, as the terrifying projectile flew just overhead. When he rose from the water, he fired again, launching more of the shafts. The sparkling arrows hit the monster in the chest and shoulder, making him flash red again. Seeking safety, the monster started to rise into the air. But this time, there were threats overhead as well.

Blaster slashed at the monster as it rose, his curved knives tearing into his charred bones. Once it had moved past, the young boy dashed for the walls of the chamber and started climbing in pursuit.

Watcher dashed to Planter's side. She was slumped against the wall, her shield falling to the ground.

"Planter, are you okay?"

She opened her eyes and looked up at him, then nodded. "I know you saved me . . . thank you."

Planter reached out and grabbed his hand. It was trembling . . . but so was his. Her normally bright green eyes looked up at him, but now they were dulled with pain and fear.

"Don't worry, Planter. We'll take care of the monster that did this to you."

"Just be careful. I couldn't bear it if you got hurt."

"No problem. I'll be careful . . . I'm always careful."

Suddenly, a flask shattered against Watcher's chain mail. A potion of healing coated them both, restoring Planter's health. He looked up and found Mapper smiling at the pair.

"Watcher, the wither is going back up into the rafters." The old man had emerged from behind a bookcase with Er-Lan at his side. "You can't let that monster rest. If you stop doing damage, the regeneration shield will appear and revive its HP. You have to keep hitting Kaza with damage or we'll never survive this contest. But I don't know if your arrows will be enough alone. You'll need Blaster's and Cutter's blades at the end."

"Got it." Watcher stood and looked up toward the ceiling. "Blaster and Cutter are up there waiting for him."

"You must to get up there with your bow," the old man said. "Keep the pressure on Kaza and take out his HP as fast as you can."

Watcher stood and pushed his way across the soggy floor. When he reached the lowest bookcase, Watcher shouted at the top of his voice, trying to draw the wither's attention to him and away from the others. The monster fired a volley of flaming skulls down in his direction. Climbing the shelves, he moved out of the blast zone, the flaming skull exploding harmlessly below. Dashing across the rafters, he charged at the wither and firing healing arrows as fast as he could draw and release. The sparkling shafts struck him in the ribs and spine, making Kaza flash red as one of the heads howled in pain. The monster glared down at Watcher as it floated higher up into the air.

"You'll have to do better than that, fool," the left head said.

The monster spat another barrage of skulls at him.

Watcher smiled, knowing Blaster and Cutter were taking advantage of the distraction and closing in.

He knelt and grabbed the beam, swinging his body over the side and dangling in the air as the dark projectiles streaked past, barely missing him. Watcher climbed back up and quickly fired another round of arrows, then sprinted to the end of the beam, hiding against the wall.

The first arrow flew upward and hit the monster, making him flash red. The *Punch* enchantment on the bow pushed him backward, right toward Blaster. The young boy reached out with his dual knives and began to slash. Instantly, a sparkling shield formed around the dark creature, protecting it from Watcher's arrows and rejuvenating Kaza's health, but it was not strong enough to protect him from Blaster's curved knives. He cut at the monster again, then sprinted across the wooden beam that stretched across the chamber. The wither fired at the boy, but Blaster was too fast, sprinting across the rafter, leaping effortlessly from one beam to another to avoid the flaming skulls.

Then the wither's sparkling shield disappeared,

leaving his dark body vulnerable. Watcher fired another three arrows in quick succession, hitting the monster with the health-infused shafts, the poison spreading across the ashen bones. The *Punch* enchantment pushed the monster backward, right toward Cutter who was waiting on a higher beam. As soon as the monster was within arm's reach, Cutter swung his diamond sword. The sparkling shield went up, but it was not strong enough to deflect the warrior's blade. Cutter tore into the monster's HP, swinging his weapon as fast as he could.

The right head screamed in fear as the monster was hit again and again. The left head shouted in an angry rage while the center head just surveyed the chamber. Ignoring Watcher's arrows, the center head turned toward Cutter and fired a blue, flaming skull. It struck the warrior in the chest and knocked him off the beam, causing the big NPC to fall. Cutter let go of his diamond blade as he fell, reaching out to hopefully avoid the lethal fall to the ground. His weapon clattered to the floor far below. He grabbed a lower beam and held on with one hand as he dangled in the air, helpless.

The center head on the wither laughed an evil, maniacal laugh, then slowly descended, ready to finish Cutter off. Watcher reacted without thought. He leapt to the ground and sprinted across the chamber, scooping up the diamond blade. Without slowing, the boy charged up the book shelves as if they were stairs. He reached the first wooden beam and ran across it. Stuffing the sword into his inventory, he fired arrows as fast as he could draw and release. The fourth arrow left his bow just as the first one struck home. A great scream echoed through the chamber as the healing arrow pierced the monster's flesh, followed by another and another.

As soon as he saw the shield materialize around the monster like a sparkling skin, Watcher sprinted across the beam, then leapt up to get to a higher one. He had to reach Cutter before he fell.

Blaster snuck behind the monster as the three heads tracked Watcher's progress, waiting for a clear shot at the NPC. The young boy saw his friend skulking along the edge of the chamber and smiled.

"Come on, Kaza," Watcher shouted. "Let's see if you're as cowardly as I've heard."

A screech like that of a wounded animal echoed off the walls of the chamber. It was a terrible sound, filled with such venomous rage that it hurt his ears. Glancing out of the corner of his eye, Watcher saw the left head screaming uncontrollably, firing flaming skulls in all directions.

Watcher ducked just as one of the projectiles streaked over his head. He jumped up to the next rafter, then fired more arrows back. The creature was hit by the *Punch* enchantment, moving right into Blaster's waiting blades. The villager, in his black leather armor, struck out from the shadows. He tore into the monster's flesh, making Kaza scream in pain again.

With the monster distracted, Watcher ran across the rafter and knelt, grabbing Cutter's hand just as he lost his grip. Watcher held onto the villager, then pulled with all his strength, every muscle straining. Sweat trickled down his forehead and dropped onto his arm. If the beads of sweat made it to his hand, he'd likely slip and Cutter would fall to his death.

"Cutter, reach up here . . . fast," Watcher said.

"Leave me, I can't do it," Cutter said. "I can't tell how much health I have, I must be almost dead."

"Don't be an idiot," Watcher growled. "That's just the wither effect . . . don't you know anything. Just get up here and help me. Don't you dare give up."

He glared down at the warrior, determination in his blue eyes. Cutter looked back at Watcher, then nodded and reached up to the beam. He grabbed it with one hand, then swung his legs up over the edge. Slowly, Cutter made it to the beam and stood. Watcher drew a healing arrow from his inventory and poked it into the warrior's arm. Color flowed back into Cutter's skin as his HP returned. And then, without warning, Watcher shoved Cutter onto his back to avoid a trio of flaming skulls that buzzed just over the top of them.

"What's the big idea?" Cutter complained.

"Yell at me later," Watcher said.

He stood, then helped the big warrior to his feet. Reaching into his inventory, Watcher pulled out the diamond sword and handed it to Cutter. "Let's finish this."

Cutter smiled, then turned and ran to the opposite end of the beam. He climbed up to the next wooden support and crouched, waiting. Watcher nodded, then moved to the other end and took aim with his bow.

Blaster was running across a lower rafter, Kaza's flaming skulls in hot pursuit, but the little boy was just too fast for the monster. Suddenly, the smell of apples wafted into Watcher's nose. Planter! She had an enchanted shield out and took up a position in front of her friend.

"Shoot that thing," she growled, then patted him on the shoulder.

Her touch was like electricity all through his body. Drawing an arrow, he fired at the monster as it moved to the center of the chamber. The arrow struck Kaza and pushed him back. He shot again and again, each healing arrow taking more of the creature's health. Instead of using his shield, the monster fired flaming skulls at his attacker. Planter braced herself and held the enchanted shield up high, blocking the projectiles. Her shield started to crack, but she held it firm while Watcher fired over her shoulder. They were the perfect team; Planter lowering her shield for Watcher to shoot, then raising it to block the wither's attack.

Kaza screamed in rage, then moved closer. He didn't see Cutter's attack from behind. The warrior slashed at the creature, tearing into his HP with reckless abandon. Watcher could see the right head slump to the side as the monster's HP was nearly consumed. Cutter slashed again and again. The left head closed its hate-filled white eyes and lulled to the side; the monster was almost dead. But then the wither turned quickly and fired a devastating shot into Cutter's chest. It knocked him off the beam. The warrior reached out for a beam to catch his fall, but his fingers just grazed it, grabbing only air as he fell.

"No!" Watcher yelled as Cutter plummeted the impossible distance to the floor.

He heard a scratching sound over his left shoulder, but didn't bother to look. The grief over Cutter was too great. The scratching sound moved up the wall, getting higher and higher.

"Cutter . . . I couldn't save you." Watcher wanted to weep, but he knew the big warrior wouldn't want that. Instead, his sorrow morphed into anger, then exploded into rage, pure uncontrolled rage.

"Take this and finish that monster off. I'll hold the shield." Planter handed Needle and her shield to him.

When he touched the handle of the enchanted blade, it felt as if a bolt of lightning had just flowed into him, energizing every fiber. He stared down at the sword in wonder, then shoved it and the shield into his inventory. Moving by Planter, he sprinted across the beam, firing arrows as he dodged flaming black skulls. His pointed shafts struck the wither king again and again, causing the monster to flash red as it took more damage. Kaza screamed in rage, then floated higher up into the chamber, maneuvering around rafter and wooden beams.

Lost in a rage, Watcher followed the monster, using the narrow ledges that lined each window as a parkour track, moving up the walls, then jumping onto the next set of beams. He fired again, but the monster activated his sparkling shield. The arrows bounced harmlessly off the wither, but still pushed Kaza backward from the *Punch* enchantment on the bow. Watcher sprinted across the wooden beam, then followed the steps up the walls to the next rafter. The wither king seemed to know what Watcher was doing and drifted all the way to the roof, beyond any of the beams that spanned the tower. Watcher fired again, hitting it with two healing arrows. The monster screamed in pain, then fired a pair of flaming skulls at him. Quickly he brought up his shield and blocked the two shots, but after the second impact, the shield shattered into a million pieces.

Kaza laughed as he floated higher, out of reach of any swords. "Your arrows will not be enough to finish me off, fool."

The center head glared down at Watcher while the left and right heads both closed their eyes and went limp. The monster's HP was now dangerously low but it would take a sword strike to finish the creature off. All it had to do was stay up there, near the roof, hiding behind support beams that Watcher could never reach, and wait for its health to regenerate. The center head gave the boy a smile, then rose higher, far out of reach.

"I can't reach it up there," he said to no one. "I can't even shoot at it that high."

Then, something Mapper said emerge in the back of his mind. *"Sometimes, a clever idea can be stronger than the sharpest sword."*

He looked at his bow, then reached into his inventory and pulled out Needle, the blade sparkling in the flickering light of the torches that dotted the walls. As he did, he remembered something Cutter had said a few days earlier.

"Of course," Watcher said with a smile. "I'll use both, but I have to get Kaza to come closer to me . . . how?"

Suddenly, a green blur shot up the wall and out into the air. It landed the back of Kaza, causing the monster to screech in surprise. Er-Lan had somehow climbed the structure using his claws to grip the stone wall, and now clung to the back of the wither king. His green arms wrapped around the monster's head, holding on for dear life. The extra weight forced the monster downward.

Watcher knelt on the beam and slowed his breathing. He'd get only one shot. If he missed, then likely they all were going to die. Dropping the arrows from his hand, he held Needle before his eyes, the narrow blade sparkling with energy. Carefully, he placed the jeweled hilt against the string and drew it back.

Kaza yelled and screamed, trying to shoot at the zombie assailant, but Er-Lan held onto the monster, his claws digging into the dark bones.

Watcher held his breath, then tried to slow his heart beat. Fear and uncertainty pulsed through his nerves, but he pushed the feelings aside. He had to get this shot right, for Cleric and Winger, for Blaster and Cutter, for Mapper and Er-Lan . . . and for Planter. Everything depended on it.

The monster floated closer and closer, turning his center head toward Watcher, his eyes growing wide with alarm.

He released the bowstring.

Needle streaked through the air like a steel missile. The enchanted blade struck the wither king in the chest, the *Punch* enchantment pushing the monster backward to the wall, causing the zombie to fall off and land on a rafter with a thud. Kaza grunted in pain, then looked down at the thin sword protruding from his chest.

"It's not possible . . . you aren't . . . a swordsman," Kaza said, struggling to speak. He flashed red again and again.

"You're right, I'm not a swordsman. I'm just a kid with some clever ideas. I'm also the protector of my village." Watcher stood and pointed at the monster with his enchanted bow. The wither flashed again. "We don't want you around anymore." He took a calming breath. "I think it's time you were going!"

With the last of his HP, Kaza fired one last flaming skull at Watcher. The dark blue skull, wreathed in black flames, streaked toward the boy, hitting the beam under his feet. When it exploded, it sent Watcher flying helplessly into the air. Midair, the boy saw the wither king disappear, leaving behind the golden Crown of Skulls, as well as Needle. He watched the crown tumble through the air, then disappear in a cloud of purple mist, as if teleported to another location. Then Watcher was left to fall to his death.

CHAPTER 34

Watcher closed his eyes as he fell from the disastrous height. He knew his likely fate, but he didn't really mind. Planter was safe, as were the others, except for Cutter. He'd already met the same fate that Watcher was about to. *I wonder if this is gonna hurt?*

He thought he heard Planter's voice shout out. Her words were barely audible, the rush of the wind past his ears like a hurricane.

"I'll miss you, Planter," he said in a loud voice.

He wanted to say more, but knew he didn't have time. Any instant, he would be . . .

Suddenly, Watcher was drenched in water, the cold liquid soaking his clothes. Unconsciously, the boy held his breath. Glancing around, he realized he wasn't under water, just sitting in a shallow pool.

"I'm alive?" Watcher was confused. He must have fallen from a height of thirty blocks, maybe forty. "I'm alive!"

"That's right," a deep voice said. "You're alive!"

A pair of strong hands lifted him to his feet, then spun him around. Watcher found himself staring into a pair of steel-gray eyes, a huge smile beaming back.

"Cutter . . . *you're* alive too?"

"It seems we're both alive." The big warrior pointed to Mapper. "Apparently, our wise friend was smart enough to spread water across the floor of the chamber. It cushioned our fall."

Mapper did a graceful bow, then slipped and fell in the water.

Watcher and Cutter laughed, then moved to help the old man to his feet.

"Planter and Blaster are still up there." Watcher moved to the bookcase, getting ready to climb.

"Wait." Cutter put a hand on Watcher's shoulder. "Here they come."

Glancing up, Watcher saw Planter and Blaster moving across a beam, walking carefully so as to avoid falling. They reached the wall and climbed across the bookcases, slowly moving to the floor.

The old man pulled out a torch, then placed it on the wall. A flickering circle of light illuminated the floor, causing the beams overhead to cast long shadows on the chamber's walls. Watcher pulled out a torch and waded through the water until he reached the wall, then planted it atop a bookshelf. It illuminated the shelves Planter and Blaster were using to get to the floor.

Watcher ran to Planter and wrapped his arms around her. "You're okay?"

She nodded. "I was so afraid when I saw you fall. I thought you wouldn't survive, but here you are. What happened?"

The young boy pointed to Mapper, then gestured to the water. The old man smiled.

"The water kept us from taking any damage when we hit." Watcher released the hug. "Cutter and I are both all right."

"And I'm okay, too, in case you're interested." Blaster gave him a smile. "But I am a little upset you didn't give me a big hug." He laughed as Watcher blushed.

"You dropped this." Cutter extended Needle to Planter. She took it into her hand but immediately let it go.

"It bit me!" She stared down at the weapon, afraid to reach out and pick it up.

Watcher bent over and retrieved the weapon, holding it gently in his hand. "Here."

Rubbing the palm of her hand, she shook her head. "I don't think it wants me anymore. Needle is yours now."

Watcher thought for a second, then remembered the sensation the sword had given him in the middle of battle. *Maybe Planter was right*, he thought, then put the blade into his inventory. There would be more time to think about all that later.

"Where's Er-Lan?" Mapper asked.

"Oh no . . . Er-Lan." Watcher glanced at his friends. "He saved us all. That little zombie jumped on Kaza and forced him down so I could shoot him with Needle. I have to go check on him."

Not waiting for a reply, Watcher took off up the bookcases. He leapt up the walls, across the beams, and headed even higher into the chamber. Placing torches as he went, the archer filled the chamber with light as he ascended through the parkour course. Finally, he reached the level where the zombie sat on a rafter, leaning against the wall.

"Er-Lan, here, eat this apple." Watcher handed the zombie the fruit.

The little monster took the fruit and looked down at it, then glanced up at Watcher. "What happens to Er-Lan now?"

"What do you mean?"

"Villagers no longer need Er-Lan. Will Er-Lan be exiled and sent away?"

"Of course not. You're our comrade, you're our friend. You are part of our family now, whether you like it or not." He helped the little zombie to his feet. "Villagers don't cast others aside just because it is convenient. We stick by our friends when it's easy and also when it's hard." Watcher smiled. "You're stuck with us."

Er-Lan's eyes grew wide with disbelief. A toothy smile slowly spread across his face. From any other zombie, it would likely have been a terrifying expression to behold close up, but from Er-Lan, it was a simple expression of joy.

The zombie stuffed the apple into his mouth and chewed, the smile now permanently etched onto his square face.

"Come on, let's go down." Watcher led the zombie back down to the ground. He knew he could have jumped, but he didn't relish the thought of experiencing that fall intentionally.

When they reached the ground, they found a huge group of villagers in the chamber. Hundreds of NPCs were pouring into the building with even more choking the hallways. Instantly, Watcher spotted one with a white smock, a gray stripe running down the center . . . it was Cleric, his father.

Watcher ran to him, but was intercepted by his sister, Winger.

"Watcher . . . you're here?"

"Yep, we defeated the wither king and freed all of you." The boy smiled as his father approached.

"*You* did that?" Cleric asked.

"We stopped that evil wither king." Watcher stood proud.

Just then a big hand settled on his shoulder. Glancing back, he saw Cutter.

"This boy of yours saved us all," Cutter said to Cleric. "He did a trick with a bow and a sword that I wouldn't have thought possible."

"Well . . . it was really your idea." Watcher looked up at the warrior. "I said that I fight from afar, and you asked if I was going to throw a sword at the enemy . . . remember?"

Cutter looked sheepishly at the ground and nodded.

"Your words popped into my head at the right moment and I suddenly knew what to do. I fired Needle like an arrow at Kaza. I knew he wouldn't be able to survive that."

The big warrior raised his head, an expression of admiration on his square face. "I was wrong about you, Watcher. You are clever and patient and careful and wise . . . all of the things that I lack. But there is one thing in which we are the same."

"What's that?" Watcher shifted nervously from one foot to the other, unsure of what he would say next.

Cutter held out a hand and clasped it around Watcher's, his strong fingers squeezing gently. "You are a warrior for the Far Lands, that is certain, and never let anyone convince you otherwise."

Watcher beamed.

Cutter stood tall, his voice booming for all to hear. "There isn't anyone I'd rather have at my side in battle than the great destroyer of withers . . . Watcher!"

The villagers cheered.

Planter moved to Watcher's side and gave him a hug . . . he felt electrified.

"You really did all this?" Cleric asked, a look of pride on his aged face.

Watcher nodded. "Well . . . *we* did it." Watcher pointed to his friends, then moved into a dark corner and put his arm around Er-Lan. "Come on, I want you to meet someone."

Watcher guided the zombie into the light. Many of the villagers screamed in fright when they saw the monster, some shouting threats of violence. Suddenly, Cutter was at the zombie's side, his diamond sword in his hand. And then Blaster stepped up, joined by Planter and Mapper as well. The companions walked out with their green friend beside them and stopped before the crowd.

"Cleric, Winger, this is Er-Lan. He's our companion, and is not the enemy." Watcher gazed at his father and sister, waiting for them to challenge him.

"He saved our lives more than once," Planter added.

"And he helped us to destroy both the zombie warlord and the wither king." Cutter glared at the villagers. "He's my friend and is under my protection. If anyone has a problem with this zombie, then you better speak up right now. I won't tolerate him being mistreated."

"But those zombies did terrible things to us," one of the villagers shouted.

"That may be true." Mapper stepped forward, his aged voice filled with wisdom. "The zombies, under the orders of the zombie warlord, did do terrible things. But Er-Lan harmed no one. You cannot judge all zombies by the actions of one. All must be judged on the quality of their character, and I'll put Er-Lan up against any of you. He is kind and thoughtful and loyal, which I know is not true for every villager in this room."

"But . . ." one NPC started to object, but Watcher stepped forward and raised a hand.

"The time for fighting is over. It is the time for peace, and that peace starts with Er-Lan. If we cannot accept him as he is, then there will never be peace between villagers and zombies, and I cannot accept that."

The NPCs grumbled comments under their breath, many of them glaring at the little zombie. But when Cleric stepped forward, all grew silent. He moved directly in front of the monster and gazed into his eyes.

"If my son says you are a friend to him, then you are a friend to me."

"And me, too," Winger added.

Cleric moved next to the monster and put his arm around the creature's armored shoulders.

"From this day forward, Er-Lan is now a part of my family. This will be an example of peace between villagers and zombies that will hopefully stop more violence in the future."

The little zombie looked up at Cleric, then glanced at Watcher, then did something for the first time in his life . . . Er-Lan wept tears of joy. Planter wrapped her arms around him and squeezed as she too wept.

Many of the villagers cheered again while some grumbled complaints under their breath, but none openly objected. The matter was closed.

"I think maybe we should vacate the premises," Mapper said as he placed blocks of dirt on the ground to absorb all the water. "The wither king might be gone, but there are still Royal Guards down in the Treasury. I think it's best if we got out of here while we can."

"I agree." Cleric released his grip on Er-Lan and faced his son. "Watcher, we need a warrior to lead us out of here. You think you can do that?"

Watcher smiled. "I think I can do that. Everyone follow me. It's time to go home."

AVAILABLE NOW FROM MARK CHEVERTON AND SKY PONY PRESS

THE GAMEKNIGHT999 SERIES
The world of Minecraft comes to life in this thrilling adventure!

Gameknight999 loved Minecraft, and above all else, he loved to grief—to intentionally ruin the gaming experience for other users.

But when one of his father's inventions teleports him into the game, Gameknight is forced to live out a real-life adventure inside a digital world. What will happen if he's killed? Will he respawn? Die in real life? Stuck in the game, Gameknight discovers Minecraft's best-kept secret, something not even the game's programmers realize: the creatures within the game are alive! He will have to stay one step ahead of the sharp claws of zombies and pointed fangs of spiders, but he'll also have to learn to make friends and work as a team if he has any chance of surviving the Minecraft war his arrival has started.

With deadly Endermen, ghasts, and dragons, this action-packed trilogy introduces the heroic Gameknight999 and has proven to be a runaway publishing smash, showing that the Gameknight999 series is the perfect companion for Minecraft fans of all ages.

Invasion of the Overworld (Book One):
$9.99 paperback • 978-1-63220-711-1

Battle for the Nether (Book Two):
$9.99 paperback • 978-1-63220-712-8

Confronting the Dragon (Book Three):
$9.99 paperback • 978-1-63450-046-3

AVAILABLE NOW FROM MARK CHEVERTON AND SKY PONY PRESS

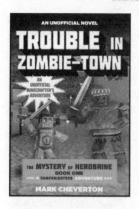  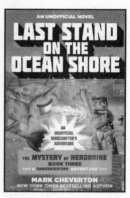

THE MYSTERY OF HEROBRINE SERIES
Gameknight999 must save his friends from an evil virus intent on destroying all of Minecraft!

Gameknight999 was sucked into the world of Minecraft when one of his father's inventions went haywire. Trapped inside the game, the former griefer learned the error of his ways, transforming into a heroic warrior and defeating powerful Endermen, ghasts, and dragons to save the world of Minecraft and his NPC friends who live in it.

Gameknight swore he'd never go inside Minecraft again. But that was before Herobrine, a malicious virus infecting the very fabric of the game, threatened to destroy the entire Overworld and escape into the real world. To outsmart an enemy much more powerful than any he's ever faced, the User-that-is-not-a-user will need to go back into the game, where real danger lies around every corner. From zombie villages and jungle temples to a secret hidden at the bottom of a deep ocean, the action-packed adventures of Gameknight999 and his friends (and, now, family) continue in this thrilling follow-up series for Minecraft fans of all ages.

Trouble in Zombie-town (Book One):
$9.99 paperback • 978-1-63450-094-4

The Jungle Temple Oracle (Book Two):
$9.99 paperback • 978-1-63450-096-8

Last Stand on the Ocean Shore (Book Three):
$9.99 paperback • 978-1-63450-098-2

AVAILABLE NOW FROM MARK CHEVERTON AND SKY PONY PRESS

HEROBRINE'S REVENGE SERIES
From beyond the digital grave, Herobrine has crafted some evil games for Gameknight999 to play!

Gameknight999, a former Minecraft griefer, got a big dose of virtual reality when his father's invention teleported him into the game. Living out a dangerous adventure inside a digital world, he trekked all over Minecraft, with the help of some villager friends, in order to finally defeat a terrible virus, Herobrine, who was trying to escape into the real world.

Gameknight thought that Herobrine was gone for good. But as one last precaution before his death, the heinous villain laid traps for the User-that-is-not-a-user that would threaten all of the Overworld, even if the virus was no longer alive. Now Gameknight is racing the clock, trying to stop Herobrine from having one last diabolical laugh.

AVAILABLE NOW FROM MARK CHEVERTON AND SKY PONY PRESS

 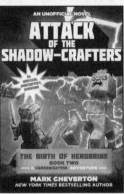 

THE BIRTH OF HEROBRINE SERIES
Can Gameknight999 survive a journey one hundred years into Minecraft's past?

A freak thunderstorm strikes just as Gameknight999 is activating his father's Digitizer to reenter Minecraft. Sparks flash across his vision as he is sucked into the game . . . and when the smoke clears he's arrived safely. But it doesn't take long to realize that things in the Overworld are very different.

The User-that-is-not-a-user realizes he's been accidentally sent a hundred years into the past, back to the time of the historic Great Zombie Invasion. None of his friends have even been born yet. But that might be the least of Gameknight999's worries, because traveling back in time also means that the evil virus Herobrine, the scourge of Minecraft, is still alive . . .

The Great Zombie Invasion (Book One):
$9.99 paperback • 978-1-5107-0994-2

Attack of the Shadow-crafters (Book Two):
$9.99 paperback • 978-1-5107-0995-9

Herobrine's War (Book Three):
$9.99 paperback • 978-1-5107-0996-7

AVAILABLE NOW FROM MARK CHEVERTON AND SKY PONY PRESS

THE MYSTERY OF ENTITY303 SERIES
Minecraft mods are covering the tracks of a mysterious new villain!

Gameknight999 reenters Minecraft to find it completely changed, and his old friends acting differently. The changes are not for the better.

Outside of Crafter's village, a strange user named Entity303 is spotted with Weaver, a young NPC Gameknight knows from Minecraft's past. He realizes that Weaver has somehow been kidnapped, and returning him to the correct time is the only way to fix things.

What's worse: Entity303 has created a strange and bizarre modded version of Minecraft, full of unusual creatures and biomes. Racing through the Twilight Forest and MystCraft, and finally into the far reaches of outer space, Gameknight will face his toughest challenge yet in a Minecraft both alien and dangerous.

Terrors of the Forest (Book One):
$9.99 paperback • 978-1-5107-1886-9

Monsters in the Mist (Book Two):
$9.99 paperback • 978-1-5107-1887-6

Mission to the Moon (Book Three):
$9.99 paperback • 978-1-5107-1888-3

EXCERPT FROM
THE BONES OF DOOM
A BRAND NEW FAR LANDS ADVENTURE

The villagers all ran toward the jungle, everyone anxious to get out of the sweltering dry heat of the desert. Though not as hot, the jungle was incredibly humid, making it feel just as uncomfortable as the previous biome.

Watcher continued heading to the east, using the compass his father had given him long ago. Blocks of leaves and thick shrubs blocked their progress, and at times it was necessary to use axes to cut through the undergrowth. Glancing around, he saw the villagers were scattering, the difficult terrain forcing many to choose alternate paths around the frequent obstacles.

"This is not good," Watcher said, searching for Cutter. He found the big NPC chopping through blocks of thick leaves, creating a path for the wounded. Motioning with his bow, he gestured for him to come near. "We need to keep everyone together. I suspect this is called the Creeper's Jungle for a reason."

"I know," the big warrior said. "I'm trying to—"

BOOM!

An explosion rocked the jungle. The ground shook and so many leaves fell from the towering trees that it was difficult to see for a moment. Cutter stared down at Watcher with fear in his eyes.

He's deathly afraid of creepers, Watcher thought. *But he doesn't want anyone to know.*

"Archers, form a perimeter around me!" Watcher yelled as loud as he could. "Everyone, come to the sound of my voice." He glanced up at Cutter. "Bang your sword on that armor of yours . . . make some noise."

The villagers glanced around at the green blocks that surrounded them, his head moving from place to place in a panic. Watcher drew Needle from his inventory, then smacked Cutter across the chest with the flat of the blade. The warrior turned and glared down at the boy, his hand reaching for his own sword.

"Bang on your armor and get everyone's attention. We need the army together, in one place." Watcher smacked his chest again, lightly. "Do it!"

Cutter shook his head, as if trying to dislodge his fear, then pulled out his huge diamond sword and another piece of iron armor. He banged on the metal plating as if it were a gong, the clanking noise drifting out into the jungle.

"Everyone come to that sound!" Watcher shouted. "Come together . . . here, with me and Cutter."

Villagers moved toward them, their eyes darting about, eyeing the green surroundings with suspicion. As soon as Watcher had enough archers, they fanned out into a large circle. Next, he sent the woodcutters to clear out some of the brush so they could see each other without having to look around shrubs or large clusters of leaves.

Psssss . . . BOOM!

Another creeper detonated, but this time, the explosion was punctuated by a terrified scream that was suddenly cut off.

I hope my friends are okay, he thought. Just then, a terrible image came to Watcher's mind.

"Where's Planter?" Watcher searched frantically for his friend.

"I'm here." Her voice was like the ringing of a perfect bell to Watcher. He took a breath and allowed the stress that had built up slowly seep away.

The villagers were beginning to set up defenses, placing blocks of dirt on the ground to make it difficult for creepers to approach. Swordsmen pulled out shields and blades, ready for any monster attack.

"I think we have everyone together now," Blaster said, his green leather armor merging with the background. "I'm going to the treetops with some other scouts. We'll try to find the creepers. When we do, we'll let you know where they're at."

"How will you let us know where the monsters are hiding?" Winger asked.

"Don't worry . . . you'll know." The boy smiled.

"Wait . . . take these." Winger handed him four pair of Elytra wings. "They might make it easier for you to get back to the ground."

Blaster took the shimmering gray wings, then ran to the largest junglewood tree with three other villagers following close behind. Using blocks of dirt, he built a set of stairs that spiraled around the trunk of the looming tree until they disappeared into the foliage high overhead.

A hissing sounded off to the right.

"Creeper!" one of the archers yelled.

The twangs of bowstrings filled the air as a group of warriors fired on the creature. In seconds, a cheer rang out, signaling the monster had been destroyed.

"Watcher," a voice said from high overhead. "Keep moving to the east. There's a large group of creepers sneaking up from behind. Get moving!"

Cutter turned and looked behind the group, but the only thing visible was the thick jungle foliage. He put his diamond sword back into his inventory, then pulled out an axe.

"That's a good idea." Watcher smiled up at the big warrior. "Swordsmen, take out axes. We're cutting through the jungle as we head for the ocean. Archers, keep your eyes open for creepers. Use your ears . . . their hissing will give them away." He glanced around at the army of NPCs. They were scared; he could see it in their eyes. But now, his friends and neighbors were looking for him to lead them to safety.

Maybe I can *do this.* Watcher found Planter and gave her a smile, then pulled out his enchanted bow and notched an arrow to the string.

"Everyone forward!"

The army moved through the jungle to the sound of chopping. The soldiers tore into the leaves and shrubs as if they were cutting through an army of monsters. As they attacked the jungle with their axes, the archers stood guard on the perimeter, ready to silence any creeper that might be foolish enough to approach.

An explosion detonated high in the treetops, far to the north.

"That must be the signal from Blaster," Cleric said. "There's creepers to the north."

Another explosion then rocked the jungle to the south.

"More creepers," Cutter said, his voice lacking it's normally confident and booming edge to it.

"Come on, everyone . . . we need to move faster!" Watcher put away his bow and pulled his own axe out, lending the iron tool to the effort.

The army of NPCs moved through the jungle, but it was slow going. The growth of shrubs, trees, and vines were thick, and almost seemed to be getting denser as they delved deeper into the biome. Sweat rained down from Watcher's forehead as he hacked at the blocks of leaves before him. He could just imagine the mottled green creatures sneaking up on them from the three sides, the strange, four-footed monsters wanting to end their lives by destroying as many of his friends as possible. It made him shudder with dread.

Just then an explosion punched through the sounds of the jungle high in the treetops. Then more blocks of TNT went off behind and to the left and right . . . the creepers were closing in from all sides.

"We're surrounded," Cutter said, his voice shaking.

Watcher put away his axe and glanced around at the members of their army. Everyone had stopped and were just staring at him, terrified expressions on their faces . . . all except Er-Lan. The zombie seemed to be looking off into the distance, listening to the animals around them. The faint growls and howls of wild ocelots could be heard through the foliage, the spotted cats illusive and difficult to tame.

"What I wouldn't give for a clowder of cats right now," Watcher muttered.

"Clowder of cats?" Er-Lan asked.

"Yeah, clowder means group of cats. Creepers are afraid of cats." Watcher turned in a circle and surveyed their surroundings. He glanced at Cutter and could tell the big NPC was paralyzed with fear. "Here's what we're gonna do. Everyone pull out blocks of dirt or stone or whatever you have. We're building our own little castle right here in the jungle." He took out his enchanted bow. "We aren't gonna let any creepers get close to us without paying a price."

A few villagers cheered . . . but only a few.

"I know you're all scared, but we can get through this if we work together." Watcher held his bow high over his head. "This is not the end . . . it's only the beginning of our defense against the monsters of the Far Lands."

A whistling sound filled the air. Behind him, Er-Lan had two fingers in the corner of his mouth and was making a piercing sound that cut through the noises of the jungle. Instantly, parrots descended upon the circle of villagers. A rainbow of color beyond anything Watcher could imagine descended on their clearing, all of the birds flying toward the zombie.

The decaying creature held his arms out, allowing many of the creatures to land. They bobbed their heads up and down, squawking and squeaking. Er-Lan said something quietly to those closest to him, then flung his arms upward, sending the parrots back into the air. The feathery creatures squawked to each other and dispersed out in all directions.

"What was that?" Watcher asked.

Er-Lan smiled. "Clowder means a group of cats." His grin grew larger.

"I think the zombie is losing it," Cutter said.

Watcher spun around and saw his friend approaching. "You okay?"

"Yeah . . . sorry. Creepers are not my favorite monster."

"I know, I'm afraid of them too."

"Who said anything about being afraid?" Cutter snapped.

"Ahh . . . well, I . . . umm." Watcher looked for something to say, but found no words that would help.

"And who put *you* in charge?" The big NPC glared at Watcher. "*I'm* leading this army, not you. You're just leading the archers, but everyone does what I say. You got that?!"

Watcher nodded and took a step back. The angry edge to Cutter's voice was a little frightening.

What did I do? I was just trying to help, the boy thought.

Notching an arrow to his bow string, Watcher moved to the perimeter and watched for the green monsters. Villagers all around him were building barricades of dirt and stone. Swordsmen were clearing away shrubs beyond the impromptu barricade, making it easier for the archers to find their targets. Archers built tiny towers of dirt, then attached wide platforms on top able to hold four defenders, allowing them to shoot over the walls at any approaching monsters.

The defenses came together quickly, but Watcher knew they would not be enough. He knew if only one creeper made it to their wall it would detonate, tearing open their defenses. The rest of the monsters could then pour into the clearing. Their explosive lives would then destroy every last member of their army.

I've led everyone into a trap, and their deaths will be my fault, Watcher thought. *I can only hope I don't survive; I don't think I could bear this guilt.*

"They're coming!" a voice said from high above him.

Four figures jumped out of the trees overhead, then leaned forward, causing their Elytra wings to snap open, and allowing the villagers to fly in a wide circle around the perimeter of their formation, slowly floating to the ground. They landed gracefully, then removed their wings and replaced them with armor.

"Thanks for the wings," Blaster said to Winger. "They got us down so we wouldn't miss the fun."

"What do you mean?" Winger asked.

Blaster sighed. He removed his leather armor, and replaced it with thick iron.

"You can't run very fast or hide in that," Watcher said.

"I don't think we're going to do much running or hiding." A sad expression came across the boy's face.

He reached out a hand to Watcher, the archer doing the same. They clasped each other's wrists, a sign of both greeting and parting. This time, Watcher knew it was meant for the latter.

"Here they come," an archer shouted from his perch. "Oh no . . ."

"What?" Watcher stared up at the villager. The archer looked down with a resigned expression on his face and just shook his head.

Pulling blocks of dirt out of his inventory, Watcher jumped into the air and placed the block under his feet.

He repeated this six times, then slowly turned. Emerging from the jungle were countless creepers, their dark eyes filled with hatred. Some of the monsters sparkled as electric sheets of energy hugged their bodies; these were the charged creepers . . . and they were very dangerous.

He tried to count the monsters, but there were just too many. The creepers were packed together, shoulder to shoulder, with more and more pushing through the underbrush. They probably outnumbered the villagers ten to one . . . it was impossible to imagine defeating them all.

Watcher gazed down at his companions.

"Well?" Planter stared up at him.

Her green eyes and long blond hair had never looked so beautiful to Watcher. *I should have told her how I feel . . . Now I'll never get the chance.*

"What do you see?" she asked.

What should I say . . . that I see everyone's death? It's hopeless.

He said nothing, just stared down at Planter, trying to burn her image into the back of his mind so it would be there to comfort him in his final moments.

"Here they come!" another villager shouted.

Watcher turned toward the treeline as hundreds of creepers charged toward them. It was the end.

COMING SOON:
THE BONES OF DOOM:
THE RISE OF THE WARLORDS BOOK TWO